The Art of Loving Lacy

Sweet with Heat: Weston Bradens

Addison Cole

ISBN-13: 978-1-948868-11-2
ISBN-10: 1-948868-11-3

THE ART OF LOVING LACY

Cover Design: Elizabeth Mackey Designs
Cover Photography: Regina Wamba

WORLD LITERARY PRESS
PRINTED IN THE UNITED STATES OF AMERICA

A Note to Readers

Dane and Lacy are one of my favorite couples. They both needed to dig deep within themselves to figure out how far they were willing to go for love. I hope you enjoy their love story as much as I do. If this is your first Sweet with Heat book, each love story is written to be read as a stand-alone novel or as part of the larger series, so dive right in and enjoy the ride.

Remember to sign up for my Sweet with Heat newsletter to be notified of the next release:
www.AddisonCole.com/Newsletter

Sweet with Heat titles are the sweet editions of *New York Times* bestselling author Melissa Foster's steamy romance collection, Love in Bloom, and are written under her sweet-romance pen name. Within the Sweet with Heat series you'll find fiercely loyal heroes and smart, empowered women on their search for true love. They're flawed, funny, and easy to relate to. These emotional romances portray all the passion two people in love convey without any graphic love scenes and little or no harsh language (with the exception of an occasional "damn" or "hell"). Characters from each series appear in future Sweet with Heat books.

For more information on Sweet with Heat titles visit
www.AddisonCole.com

If you prefer more explicit love stories, please pick up the steamy edition of this book, *Sea of Love*, by Melissa Foster.

Chapter One

LACY SNOW SAT between Kaylie Crew and Danica Carter, literally surrounded by her half sisters. In the year and a half since she'd met them, they'd become her closest friends, her coconspirators, and the women she most looked up to. She'd known they existed her whole life, but as the child of their father's mistress of more than twenty years, she couldn't exactly knock on their front door and introduce herself.

Kaylie reached for her hand and squeezed, flashing a sisterly smile. She and Lacy shared the same robin's-egg-blue eyes and buttery blond hair, though Kaylie's was shiny with a natural wave and Lacy's was a mass of spiral curls, like Danica's, save for the color. Danica took after their father with dark hair and olive skin.

"Wow, this place is gorgeous," Kaylie said.

"It was built in a similar fashion to the original Chequesset Inn, which perished during an ice storm in the 1930s," Lacy said.

Max and Treat had fallen in love in Wellfleet, Massachusetts, and it was only fitting that they wed at the Wellfleet Inn. The two-story inn overlooked the bay. Treat owned resorts all over the world, so it came as no surprise when he purchased the inn and added it to his collection.

"Sheesh, Lacy," Kaylie whispered. "You're such a fact girl." She looked at the altar. "Excited?"

Nervous, Lacy mouthed. She'd met Dane Braden, Treat's younger brother, at her sisters' double wedding, and she'd waited all this time to see him in-person again. More than a year of sharing texts, emails, intimate phone calls, sexy video chats, and too many unfulfilled fantasies to count. Months of working twelve-hour days seven days a week, vying for a promotion at her job, and long nights spent dreaming of Dane. She reached for Danica's hand and—deep in conversation with her husband, Blake—Danica took Lacy's hand like it was the most natural thing in the world. She'd met Danica and Kaylie just before their double wedding, in a Nassau resort owned by Treat Braden, the six-foot-six, darkly handsome man now standing at the altar, gazing into their friend Max Armstrong's eyes. Max's dark hair fell in gentle waves over the spaghetti straps and soft lines of the beachy wedding gown that Riley Banks, Treat's brother Josh's fiancée, designed for her. Weddings had a way of making the beautiful even more glamorous. Max and Treat were a striking couple, and they should have held Lacy's attention as Treat held Max's hand and looked lovingly into her eyes, promising her a lifetime of adoration, but Lacy's gaze shifted to his right. To the line of Treat's four striking brothers, proudly standing as his groomsmen, each one more handsome than the next. Each brother's dark eyes were trained on their eldest brother as he vowed to love, honor, and cherish his soon-to-be wife—each one except Dane. Dane's smoldering dark eyes stared hungrily at Lacy, sending a shock of heat right through her. Lacy couldn't blink. She couldn't look away. She couldn't even breathe.

"Careful," Kaylie whispered, "you'll drool on that pretty dress of yours."

Lacy felt her face flush, but she still couldn't tear her gaze away. Each of the Braden brothers had thick dark hair, and while Treat and Josh wore their hair short and Rex wore his cowboy-long, covering his collar, Dane's hair fell somewhere in between, as if he'd missed his last trim; it brushed the tops of his ears, with sides that looked like he'd just run his hands through them. *No.* Lacy narrowed her eyes. *That's not it at all.* As she watched Dane's lips lift into a smile, she bit her lower lip and thought, *He looks like he could have just come from the bedroom—or, like he's ready for it.*

He winked, and Lacy caught her breath.

"Behave," Kaylie warned.

"Oh my goodness," Lacy whispered, drawing her eyes to her lap. "He's so…"

"Sexy? Gorgeous? Hot?" Kaylie offered, arching a brow.

"Shh." Danica shot a harsh stare at them.

Lacy and Kaylie drew their blond heads together with a silent giggle. Danica shook her head, and though Lacy couldn't see her face, she knew that her eldest sister was rolling her eyes at them with her lips pinched in a tight line.

"Ladies and gentlemen, I give you, Mr. and Mrs. Treat Braden."

The announcement sent a shiver of nervous energy through her stomach. Everyone stood as Max and Treat walked down the aisle hand in hand. Max's smile lit up her eyes, and Treat walked with his shoulders back, his eyes on Max, beaming with pride. Kaylie's blond hair tumbled down her back as she reached her sinewy arms around her husband Chaz's neck and kissed him. Lacy watched Danica smile lovingly at Blake; then he took her chin in his hand and kissed her. Lacy turned away, thinking about Dane.

As Treat and Max approached, Lacy and her sisters tossed rose petals.

"Congratulations!" Lacy shouted, but her eyes had already left Treat and Max and had settled on Dane once again. She hadn't remembered how broad his chest was, and the wanton look in his eyes hadn't seemed quite as strong over Skype and FaceTime. Her pulse ratcheted up a notch.

"You're so beautiful!" Danica said to Max.

The groomsmen made their way down the aisle next, and Kaylie squeezed Lacy's hand so hard that Lacy winced.

"There he is," Kaylie said.

"Stop," Lacy said under her breath. "I'm nervous enough."

Dane walked toward her, his perfect pearly white teeth visible through his wide smile. His broad shoulders swayed slightly, and those dark eyes of his never wavered from hers. Her legs turned to Jell-O, and she gripped the back of the chair for stability. The man in the aisle in front of hers reached for Dane.

"Hey, buddy. I haven't seen you in months. Good to see you," the older man said.

Dane embraced the tall, thin man, his eyes still pinning Lacy in place. "You too, Smitty. We'll catch up at the reception." Dane took a step closer to Lacy's row. He embraced his cousin. "Blake, great to see you." Then he pulled Danica into a soft hug and kissed her cheek. "You look as gorgeous as ever," he said. He reached for Kaylie next.

Lacy's heart slammed against her chest as Blake and Danica moved into the aisle, following the rest of the guests into the reception room. She had forgotten how tall he felt when he was near, and as she watched him wrap his arms around Kaylie, she realized that she'd also forgotten how large his hands were. *Big hands, big—Stop it!*

"We need to call our sitter before the reception. Good to see you," Kaylie said. She gave Dane a quick hug and pulled Chaz behind her, leaving Lacy alone with Dane.

IT HAD BEEN far too long since Dane had seen Lacy in person. He reached for her hands and then drew her close, placing one soft kiss on each cheek and inhaling the sweet smell that he remembered: a combination of citrus and floral with an underlying hint of musk. To anyone else, it was Chanel Coco Noir. To Dane, it was the smell of Lacy that he remembered from the day they'd met, and their only afternoon together, the day before her sisters' double wedding in Nassau. The smell he'd dreamed of, which had carried him through those long afternoons out at sea when they were tagging sharks miles from shore.

"Lacy."

Her slim fingers trembled against his palms. A shy smile lifted her supple lips and sent Dane's pulse into overdrive.

"Hi," she said softly.

Her blond curls fell in thick spiral ropes across her tanned, lean shoulders. She wore a royal-blue halter dress that fell to the middle of her thighs, revealing her long, toned legs. It just barely covered the edge of the scar Dane knew held the worst of her fears. Dane lowered his lips to one of her slender hands and pressed a soft kiss to it. All those months of texts, phone calls, and video chats came rushing back. They had never been enough, but his demanding travel schedule as founder of the

Brave Foundation made it almost impossible to steal away for a weekend, and Lacy was working day and night in hopes of obtaining a promotion, so even if he had found the time, she probably wouldn't have been able to break away. Brave's mission was to use education and innovative advocacy programs to protect sharks, and in a broader sense, the world's oceans. Dane's passion for saving and educating had begun right after college and had only grown since. He'd created a life around doing what he loved, and now he lived on a boat off the coast of Florida, where Brave's headquarters were located. He had a small administrative staff and was well connected enough to have temporary staff and volunteers in the areas where he worked. When he wasn't in the water, he could be found running the foundation, which required heavy travel, a busy social calendar, and a boatload of butt-kissing. Unfortunately, over those months, his and Lacy's schedules hadn't come together.

"Are you going to introduce me, or just block the aisle?" Dane's younger brother Rex pushed in between them.

Dane shook his head to clear his thoughts. Rex was a year and a half younger than him and had worked their family ranch for years, which was apparent in his brawny cowboy build. Dane turned to face his brother with a joking sneer.

"Isn't Jade around here somewhere?" Dane asked.

A year earlier, Rex had fallen in love with Jade Johnson, and their love had brought a long-standing family feud to a head—and then to a long-overdue end. Dane had never seen his brother so happy. Rex and Jade had bought the property in between the two families' ranches in Weston, Colorado, and had recently built a house there.

As he stared into Rex's dark eyes, he had a momentary flash

of unease. His height matched Rex's six-foot-three inches, but his brother's arms were as thick as tree trunks, and the way his tux stretched tightly over his massive chest would turn on any woman. He knew his brother's ever-present five-o'clock shadow and longish hair gave him a bad-boy quality that had sent even the strongest women into a state of rapture. But Dane also knew that there was no need for a silent warning, or even a hint of possessiveness where Lacy was concerned. Rex had eyes only for Jade, and he was all too aware that Lacy wasn't his to possess.

"Step aside." Rex pushed his massive forearm across Dane's chest and held out a hand to Lacy. "I'm Rex, Dane's brother. You must be Lacy."

Lacy blushed. "Yes, hi," she said. Her eyes darted to Dane, and the surprise in them was blatant. "He's mentioned me?"

Rex laughed. "Oh, he might have mentioned you once or twice." He cracked a crooked smile at Dane. "Pleasure to meet you, Lacy. No wonder Dane was so distracted during the ceremony. Well"—he let out a dramatic sigh—"you two kids have fun. If you'll excuse me, I need to find my girlfriend."

"Jerk," Dane whispered as Rex passed with a sly grin and gave Dane a playful shove. The room emptied quickly as the guests moved toward the reception hall. Dane turned his attention back to Lacy.

"I'm glad you're here."

"Me too." Lacy smiled. "Your brother seems nice."

"Yeah, he is," Dane said. The image of Lacy wearing the tiny bikini she'd worn in Nassau came rushing back to him. He swallowed hard to repress the memory before it could excite him the way it had over recent nights, when he knew he'd be seeing her again.

"Save me a dance?" He'd felt the anticipation of seeing Lacy mounting for weeks, but he hadn't expected his nerves to be strewn so tight, or the desire to kiss her to be so strong. He stood so close to her that all it would take was the slightest dip of his head to settle his lips over hers, to tangle his hands in her hair and pull her against him.

"Sure," she answered, and he'd almost forgotten that he'd asked her a question.

"Dane."

His father's deep voice pulled him from his thoughts.

Hal Braden took a couple steps toward them. He stood a few inches taller than Dane. His skin was a deep bronze, rivaling Dane's rich tan. Fine lines snaked out from his father's eyes and mouth, and a deep vee hunkered between his thick brows. "Excuse me. I'm sorry for interrupting." He held his hand out to Lacy. "Hal Braden, Dane's father."

Lacy shook his hand. "I'm Lacy."

"Dad, this is Lacy Snow." Dane watched his father's dark eyes change from serious to warm.

"Lacy Snow. Related to Blake's wife, Danica?" he asked.

"Yes, I'm her half...her youngest sister." She flushed again.

Dane had an urge to put his arm around her and comfort the nerves he heard in her voice.

Hal nodded. "Well, any sister of Danica's is a friend of ours. It's a pleasure to meet you. They're taking pictures, Dane. Don't be too long."

"I'll be right in, Dad," Dane said. He watched his father walk away and felt pride swell in his heart. He'd always had a good relationship with his father, and now, at thirty-six years old, he found himself seeing his father in a different way. Dane's mother had passed away when he was only nine years old, and his father had raised him, his four brothers, and their sister. And to this day, when he spoke of their mother, the love he exuded hadn't dimmed. Dane hadn't thought of marriage very often, but lately he wondered—no, he hoped—that one day he'd find whatever it was that his parents had found together. He wanted to experience that love.

"You'd better go in," Lacy said. She blinked her long lashes several times and fidgeted with her hands.

Man, you are cute when you're nervous. Dane wondered if she could tell that he was just as nervous as she was. The last thing he wanted to do was leave her side, but the sooner he got those pictures over with, the sooner he could be with her again. "Yeah. I'd better. Remember our dance, okay?"

"I look forward to it."

Chapter Two

"SPILL, WOMAN," KAYLIE said to Lacy. She and Danica flanked Lacy, while Chaz and Blake were off retrieving drinks from the bar. The photographer had just finished taking photographs, and Dane and his family were filing back into the room.

"Yeah, what's the deal?" Danica asked. "You said you two hadn't even seen each other, but from the looks of it, I'd swear you two were picking up where a hot date might have left off."

"Don't be silly," Lacy said. "We haven't seen each other since your wedding. I always tell you the truth. Well, unless you include Skype or FaceTime."

Kaylie took a sip of her drink. "Uh-huh. Virtual sex counts, sis."

"Kaylie!" Lacy said in a harsh whisper.

"Sisters, remember? We want details," Kaylie pushed.

"Not one single time," Lacy lied. Some things were too private. Even for sisters. "Between his schedule and mine, we never connected." She looked across the dance floor at Dane, standing with his younger brothers, Josh and Hugh. "Can you believe they're all that good-looking?"

"Josh looks like he belongs on a runway," Kaylie said.

"He's a clothing designer, not a model," Lacy said.

"Yeah, well, look at Hugh. He's the racecar driver, right? Look at the way he's eyeing all the women." Kaylie nodded toward him. She looked at Max smiling at the head table, the sole object of Treat's attention. He whispered something into her ear, and Max blushed. "Look at Max. Can you imagine how good-looking their children will be?"

"You go from topic to topic," Danica teased. "Yes, they're all cute, but no cuter than Blake and Chaz, right, Lace?"

When she didn't answer, Danica elbowed her. "Right?"

"Oh, yeah, right." Dane had locked eyes with her again, and she swore the temperature in the room increased ten degrees.

"Here comes your virtual honey," Kaylie teased.

Dane crossed the dance floor. Each determined step caused the butterflies in Lacy's stomach to flutter.

When he reached their table, he held out a hand. "I believe you promised me a dance," he said in a seductively low tone. He drew her to her feet and placed his hand on the small of her back as he led her to the dance floor.

A shiver ran up her spine. She felt so feminine beside him. Lacy glanced over her shoulder at her sisters. Danica had one hand over her heart and a dreamy look in her eyes. She smiled at Lacy.

Dane wrapped his arms around Lacy's waist. She placed her hands behind his neck and felt heat resonating between them. Lacy couldn't remember ever feeling so drawn to a man. The soft lines of his cheeks were so different from the sharp edges of his brother Rex's chiseled jaw or the refined angles of Treat's nose and chin.

Dane leaned his forehead against Lacy's and said, "I've missed you."

She could get lost in Dane's eyes, the way he looked at her like she was the only girl in the room.

"I missed you, too." She rocked her hips to the slow beat of the music, and he moved in perfect rhythm.

"Why did we wait so long to see each other again?" he asked.

Lacy had been wondering the same thing. "Schedules," was all she could manage. She'd been up for a promotion at World Geographic, where she worked as an account executive, creating and managing marketing strategies for nonprofit organizations. After five years of working her way up the corporate ladder, she finally had a shot at a senior-level position, and with the other account executives nipping at her heels, she hadn't been able to afford to take time off.

He leaned closer, and Lacy held her breath, thinking he might kiss her right there in the middle of the dance floor.

"Stupid schedules," he whispered next to her ear.

His breath was warm on her skin.

"You smell so nice," he said, nuzzling into her neck.

Every nerve in her body tightened, including the ones down low—the ones she'd been trying so hard to ignore for the last few months, which called out for Dane and only Dane. Lacy had gone on a few dates when she and Dane first began their long-distance relationship. If she could call it that. She wasn't sure how to define what had developed between them, but she knew that she couldn't go to sleep without hearing his voice, and even now, so many months later, when she saw his name on her caller ID, her heartbeat quickened. She'd had opportunities to sleep with the men she'd dated, but every time a date turned intimate, she pulled away. It was Dane she wanted to be close to. It was him she craved. *How on earth did that happen after one afternoon together?* The answer was not far behind. More than a year of sharing secrets without the pressures of sex had allowed them to develop a closeness that included sharing their hopes, their dreams, and their fears.

Dane said something, but Lacy was too lost in her own thoughts to comprehend it.

"I'm sorry, what?" *Get a grip.*

"The song is over," he said.

Lacy looked around and cringed. She and Dane were the only couple left on the dance floor, moving against each other in a sensual rhythm…with no music.

"Oh my gosh. I'm sorry." She pulled away.

Dane kept hold of her hand. "Come with me," he said. He pulled her through French doors that led out to the terrace. The cool night air sent goose bumps racing up her arms as she hurried beside him to the waist-high wrought-iron railing overlooking a carpet of grass below. She could hear the crashing of waves in the distance.

The stars speckled the blue-black sky like hundreds of eyes gazing down on them. The moon cast a romantic haze into the night. Music filtered out from the reception and disappeared into the breeze. Lacy gripped the edge of the railing, hoping Dane wouldn't notice how nervous she was.

"I know we spoke earlier when you were on your way into town, but how are you?" he asked.

Nervous. Horny. Embarrassed. "I'm well." *I'm well? I might as well have said that I'm a loser.* "The wedding was beautiful, wasn't it?" she asked, trying to find something to talk about that would take her mind off of how much she wanted him.

"Treat knows how to put on a wedding." He moved closer to her, his shoulder rubbing against hers. "Lacy, talk to me."

She turned to face him, and all those nights flashed in her mind like a silent movie: the way Dane had been overcome with sadness when he spoke of his mother's death and how he'd stayed up all night with her on Skype when she'd had the stomach flu, just to make sure she wasn't alone. She'd be lying to herself if she didn't admit that in all those nights of sexual innuendos and—oh, my goodness, virtual sex—as the months pressed on, she wondered why they hadn't found a way to be together.

He reached over and ran his finger down her cheek, then lifted her chin so her eyes met his.

"Why didn't we see each other?" she asked, then immediately regretted it. Dane probably had a zillion women at the ready. Why would he take time away from his schedule just to see her?

He put one strong hand on each of her arms and looked into her eyes. He shook his head. "Stupidity?"

Lacy laughed, but her heart secretly cracked. She'd been engrossed in chasing her promotion and was working every second, too, but if he had mentioned the chance of a visit, she would have tossed that aside and found a way to be with him.

"Really, Lace. I should have made it happen, and when I couldn't, I made sure we spoke almost every night. I feel like I've known you all my life, and I was sure we'd see each other again after Nassau. But then I had to go to Maui, then Belize, then California."

"You were in Florida, too," she reminded him.

"Right. But I was never in Massachusetts, and that was very bad planning." He stepped closer, his eyes darkening until they were almost black; the hunger in them made her shiver. "I'm so sorry. I thought of you every second."

She swallowed hard. Being this close to Dane, feeling the

heat between them, Lacy wondered if making the promotion a priority over Dane had been the stupidest decision she'd ever made. *I could have been with you.* She knew that was a pipe dream. Dane's schedule was even crazier than hers had been.

"Lacy," he whispered. "I'm sorry."

She opened her mouth to speak, but no words came. She was flustered by the hunger in his dark eyes and the way it quelled her heart and revved her desire. He pulled her closer, and she flattened her hands against his chest, feeling his heartbeat beneath her palms.

"Lacy, I have to kiss you," he said, piercing her with an intense stare.

She gripped his lapel to stabilize her rubbery legs as he lowered his mouth to hers, gentle at first, then taking her in a greedy, passionate kiss. Every stroke of his tongue sent her stomach aflutter. He slid his large hands down her slim waist and clenched her hips, pulling her against him.

When they finally drew apart, Lacy felt intoxicated. The sweet taste of alcohol and lust lingered on her tongue as Dane gripped the railing on either side of her, trapping her in between. He leaned forward. His breath was warm on her neck, his body a living, breathing furnace against her.

"What are we going to do with my months of fantasies about you? They've stolen any chance I have at rational thought," he whispered.

Lacy hoped that when she opened her mouth to speak, her voice would find its way past her pounding heart. "Who needs rational thought?" *Kiss me again. Please kiss me again.*

Dane's eyes flashed hot. Lacy held his stare. He didn't say a word. He didn't need to. She'd go anywhere he wanted, whenever he was ready.

The door to the reception room swung open, and Max and Treat stood behind them. "We were looking for you," Treat said.

Dane took Lacy's hand and turned around. Her pulse raced and her mind ran in circles. How could she possibly wait until the end of the reception to kiss him again? He squeezed her hand. Lacy bit the inside of her mouth to keep from saying something stupid out of sheer nervousness.

Treat ran his eyes between them. "Lacy, what a pleasure to see you again." He leaned forward and kissed her cheek, never letting go of Max's hand.

"It was a beautiful wedding," she said, relieved that her voice didn't shake. She'd thought it might. "Max, you look stunning. I am so happy for both of you." Max worked for Chaz, and she and Lacy had become fast friends after meeting at her sisters' wedding.

"Do you mind if I catch up with Lacy for a few minutes?" Max asked Treat.

"Of course not, Mrs. Braden. I've got you for the rest of our lives." With one strong arm, he swept her against him and kissed her. When they parted, Max's cheeks were flaming red.

Max took Lacy's hand and pulled her away from Dane, but he held on tight, their arms stretched between them.

"Dane, really?" Max said with a sigh.

"Okay, but bring her back," he teased.

Lacy glanced at him over her shoulder as Max led her back into the reception hall and toward Kaylie and Danica's table. Part of her wished she hadn't been swept away.

"You have that recently bedded look," Max said.

"Max!" Lacy could tell from her serious eyes and wide smile that she was only half joking. She saw Dane and Treat enter the room.

"Your cheeks are flushed, and your eyelids are dreamily heavy. Seriously, if you don't want your sisters to know, you'd better pull it together."

Lacy shot a look at Danica and Kaylie. Kaylie had one hand cupped around her mouth as she spoke into Danica's ear. Their eyes were locked on Lacy. She took a deep breath and flopped into a chair, throwing *pulling it together* out the window.

"Well?" Kaylie and Danica asked in unison.

"We kissed. Oh my gosh, did we kiss," she said breathlessly.

Kaylie put her hand out toward Danica. "I believe you owe me five bucks."

Danica reached for her purse. "Really, Lacy? You couldn't have waited just two hours after the wedding? That's not asking for a lot. A few lousy hours." She smiled as she handed a five to Kaylie.

"You bet on when I'd kiss him?" Lacy said sharply, trying to appear upset while holding back a smile. She secretly loved the sisterly banter she'd missed out on for so many years. "And really, Danica? Could you wait two hours when that was waiting for you?" She lifted her chin toward Dane, who was watching her from across the room. *I want you* was written in his eyes.

Max leaned over the table. "I'll pay you later," she whispered.

"Max! You too?" Lacy said with a *tsk*.

Max pretended to inspect her newly manicured fingernails.

Lacy slapped her hand. "I can't believe you guys. Is this why you dragged me away from Dane?" *When I could be kissing those luscious lips of his again?* She shivered just thinking about it.

"Oh, please. Of course it is." Kaylie rolled her eyes. She

pushed her hair over her shoulder. "You didn't expect us not to talk about you and Dane, did you? He's all you've thought about since Nassau."

"He is not." Lacy had been thinking and talking about Dane nonstop for months. She had no idea why she was denying it. "Okay, fine. Geez, what am I going to do? I can't look at him without feeling all those months of wanting him coming forward, but then it kind of hurts that he never actually came to see me."

"We've talked about this for more than a year. You said it was a scheduling thing. Do you think it was something else? Do you think he's a player?" Danica asked.

Do I? "No, but you have to admit that it's a really long time."

"It is, and you've known that. You said you talked about it with him. And now you want to know why you are having such a hard time, right?" Danica asked. She didn't give Lacy a chance to answer. "It's because you're here and ready to take the past several months of fantasies to the next level. Intimacy can be a huge step."

"You're still such a therapist," Kaylie said. Danica had given up her therapy practice when she'd fallen in love with her client—Blake.

Lacy sighed. "I feel like there's so much more than just lust between us."

"Does he know about your fear of sharks?" Kaylie asked.

Lacy bristled. "Sort of." She'd been trying to ignore that worry for weeks as the wedding had neared.

"You're afraid of sharks?" Max asked. "But you went in the water in Nassau."

"It's weird. I *think* I'm afraid of sharks. There was an incident when I was younger. I don't really want to talk about it, and I haven't really tested the theory that I'm afraid of them. I just have a feeling that when I step out of my controlled environment, the fear might take over."

"You do know he's a shark tagger, right?" Max asked.

"Of course. Can we change the subject?" Lacy asked. "I just need to know that I'm not making a mistake. You guys don't see any glaring red flags do you?" *Please say no and let me get back to kissing him.*

"No, Lace," Danica answered.

"What's the worst that happens? Let's say you sleep with him and then decide you made a mistake," Kaylie said. "You only live once. You'd survive."

Max patted Lacy's shoulder. "Dane's a great guy, Lacy. He and Treat are really close, and Treat's said only good things about him. Well, except for that one thing, but…you know."

"What thing?" Danica asked.

Lacy didn't miss Max's quick head shake.

"It's okay, Max. Go ahead." *We've shared everything.*

"Okay, but…" Max looked at Lacy, and Lacy waved her hand in approval. "Dane slept with one of Treat's girlfriends in college."

"Really?" Kaylie and Danica said in unison.

"I know all about that. Dane told me. I told you guys we talked about everything." She remembered the conversation well. They'd been on Skype, and never once during the whole uncomfortable conversation did he look away or try to evade her questions. She'd known then that he was a man she could trust. "It was ages ago, but he wasn't *just* being a jerk. He told Treat last year that he'd felt guilty about it forever. He always felt like he was in Treat's shadow, and just for once, he wanted to be the front-runner."

"I'd say that given what we saw in Nassau, he's a front-runner all right," Kaylie said with a grin.

"Kaylie," Lacy chided, but she'd known that one of them would make a joke about how well endowed Dane was. It had been a difficult attribute to miss when he'd been in swim trunks in the Bahamas, and overhearing Treat make a comment about *ten inches* had sent a lingering wonder through her mind.

"What? You saw it," Kaylie said.

Lacy shook her head.

"Remember, these are guys who lost their mother when they were little boys," Danica said thoughtfully, "and although they had their dad, from what I hear, they really depended a lot on one another. And you know they had to carry a lot of anger and unrealized grief for years. Lacy, if he shared something like that with you, I don't think you have much to worry about."

Lacy's eyes were drawn to Dane again. Treat's arm was slung comfortably around his shoulder, and they both wore wide smiles. They didn't look like two brothers who had experienced such a painful time. *Does anyone ever wear the pain of their past for everyone to see?* She glanced at Danica and Kaylie, the sisters she felt she'd known all her life, and yet Kaylie wouldn't even speak to her when they'd first met. *Fences can mend, even broken-down, worn-out, splintered fences.*

Chapter Three

DANE STOOD WITH Treat by the bar watching Lacy with her sisters and Max, deep in conversation. Even from across the room, he recognized the nervous smile on her lips, and he wondered what they were discussing—and if she was thinking about their kiss as much as he was.

"Listen, Dane, Lacy is Danica's sister, which makes her Blake's sister-in-law. If you're just having fun, please let her know up front." Treat spoke in a hushed tone, his dark eyes filled with compassion and his mouth close enough to Dane's ear that Dane was sure no one else overheard his suggestion.

As much as Dane didn't want or need advice from his eldest brother, he had been thinking the same thing. The last thing he wanted to do was to put Lacy in an uncomfortable position. Before the wedding, he'd decided that he would take things slowly with Lacy, but when he saw her sitting a few rows back, with those big baby blues drinking him in, he'd been unable to turn away. He'd spent the majority of the last year and a half walking across a tenuous tightrope; on one side was Lacy, and on the other, the career-driven, commitment-phobic man he'd always been—the part of himself he was trying to leave behind. If he were to look down from the tightrope, he'd see the man he'd always been, the man who never thought of a woman beyond a few dates and a few good times. The man who did, indeed, have an incredibly beautiful woman—or two—in every port, women who never pushed for more than he was willing to give, whom he'd forget the minute his boat was put to sea until the next time he arrived.

From the moment he met Lacy, he'd been drawn to her for more than her seductive body and the sweet, innocent facade that he was dying to peel away. He'd shared more with Lacy over the past several months than he'd shared with any of his brothers, or even his best friend and employee, Rob Mann.

Dane had yet to meet a woman who could handle his crazy travel schedule, or the dangerous work he did for a living, and he hadn't given it much thought...until Lacy. He'd tried guarding their conversations, testing the waters. It hadn't taken long before he knew he wanted to dive in headfirst. But fear held him at bay. Once he allowed himself to fall, there'd be no turning back—and if their sensuous kiss was any indication of what was yet to come, he knew he'd have a hard time keeping his emotions in check. What if he allowed himself to fall for her and she didn't want the travel and the sharks, the fundraising events and the busy lifestyle? He knew he couldn't do what Treat had done for Max and change his way of life for her—then again, if he'd been asked two years ago if he'd ever want a monogamous relationship, he would have said, *no freaking way*. But that was before Lacy.

Savannah, his younger sister, joined them before Dane could respond to Treat.

"Three brothers down; now just two more brothers to go," Savannah teased. Her auburn hair flowed in natural waves past her shoulders. A thick lock fell forward, covering one of her mischievous green eyes.

Josh sidled up to her. "You're kidding, right? Hugh and Dane? They think we're the anomalies." He winked at Treat. Though Josh was as tall as Dane and Rex, and every bit as masculine, as an upscale fashion designer, he kept his body strong and lean while his brothers' physiques bulged with muscles from their more physically demanding lifestyles. Josh's clothing hung handsomely from his broad chest and slim hips, and with his close-cropped hair, he looked like he'd walked out of *Esquire* magazine.

"How about you, Savannah?" Josh asked. His fiancée, Riley Banks, appeared by his side.

"You'd make a beautiful bride," she said to Savannah.

No one had taken the Braden siblings by surprise more than Josh when he fell in love with Riley. He hadn't ever so much as brought a woman home or talked about a serious relationship, and suddenly his and Riley's friendship turned into a love affair, and overnight Josh went from one of America's most eligible bachelors to being engaged and having a new business partner.

"What's happening with Connor Dean, anyway?" Treat asked. The last time they'd all been together, Savannah had just broken up with her client-slash-boyfriend, actor Connor Dean. Her job as his entertainment attorney had turned into something more intimate, the details of which she hadn't shared with any of her brothers.

Dane half listened to their banter. He was still weighing Treat's comment. *If you're just having fun...* Lacy was so much more than fun.

Savannah rolled her eyes. "I told you, it's complicated. Besides, now Josh and Riley have to design her wedding gown. That should keep them busy for a while."

Josh wasn't one to be waylaid. "Word on the streets is that your newest client is something of a ladies' man." Josh and Savannah both lived and worked in New York City, and although Josh generally kept out of Savannah's professional life, he still kept an ear to the ground when it came to his older sister.

"Dylan Ross? Yeah, he's kind of a ladies' man, but wouldn't you be if you were the hottest country singer around?" Savannah brushed a piece of lint from her rose-colored, strapless bridesmaid dress. "Anyway, I don't want to talk about work. This is Treat's night. I finally have a new sister-in-law, and I'm thrilled about it. There's enough testosterone in our family for twelve football teams. It's time for a little feminine influence."

"I'm liking the direction of this conversation," Jade, Rex's live-in girlfriend, said as she joined them. Her jet-black hair hung almost down to her waist, and the cream-colored dress she wore contrasted sharply with her olive skin. She reached a hand out to Rex and blinked her long eyelashes flirtatiously. "What do you think, Rexy?"

Rex groaned, then leaned down and kissed her. "I think you know I'd do just about anything you want when you look at me like that." He lifted his chin to Dane. "But maybe you should ask Dane about the lip-locking he was doing out on the terrace. I think he's got more female influence headed our way."

Jade put her hand on Rex's chest and narrowed her eyes. "Don't embarrass him."

"No embarrassment here," Dane said, throwing his shoulders back. "I was with Danica's sister Lacy." *Lacy. Sweet, delicious Lacy.*

"And?" Savannah pushed.

"And it's none of your business." Dane kissed Savannah on

her cheek and stepped away, knowing he was leaving his siblings with as many unanswered questions as he had reeling around in his head.

Two steps later Treat's hand landed on his shoulder. "Just tell me that I don't have to be in damage control mode tomorrow for the family gathering. That's all I want to know."

Dane turned a harsh glare at Treat, then softened when he saw the empathy in Treat's eyes. "Truth?"

"Always," Treat said.

"I don't know what this is." Dane looked across the room at Lacy, and his heart skipped a beat. "All I can tell you is that I've thought about her nearly every minute since Nassau, and I plan on getting to know her better this weekend."

Treat followed Dane's eyes to the table, where Max and Lacy sat with Danica and Kaylie. A smile spread across his lips. Dane recognized the love in Treat's eyes that hadn't been there two years before. That love was wholly meant for, and because of, Max. He was contemplating that look when Treat interrupted his thoughts.

"And Lacy?" Treat finally asked.

Dane shook his head. "She's receptive. Interested. We've been so close, just not physically close." He looked at his brother and was thrown right back into his teenage years—hoping his older brother, who seemed to hold all the answers to life, would share his knowledge and help him find his way.

"Get to know her," Treat said quietly as Max approached. "Then you'll know exactly what she wants and if it's what you want. Things will become clear."

"Thanks, bro." Dane smiled at Max. "Don't you two have to leave before any of us can?"

"Darn right they do." Their father's deep voice boomed

between them.

"Are you kicking us out of our own wedding?" Treat asked.

"You bet I am. I'm an old man, and I need my sleep. Now, take that pretty little wife of yours and get to your suite so I can go to bed." He looked at Dane and patted his cheek. "Let this other son of mine move along with his evening plans."

Dane shook his head.

Hugh tapped his spoon against his glass. Soon, the whole room was doing the same, and Treat beamed at Max as he swooped her into his arms. He towered a foot above Max. Dane didn't think he'd ever seen Max look so beautiful, or so in love, as she did at that very moment: staring at Treat with adoration in her eyes, her lips slightly parted, her cheeks flushed. Treat bent down, his lips moving silently. *I love you.* Then he dipped her in his arms and kissed her until the entire room cheered.

A moment later, they were laughing, holding hands as they ran across the floor toward the exit, Max's dress trailing behind them.

The second they were out the door, Dane headed toward Lacy.

Chapter Four

LACY GRIPPED THE edge of the chair. Her heart slammed against her chest as she watched Dane walking toward her. *This is it.* This was the night she'd been fantasizing about. His eyes were trained on her, and with each of his determined steps came a new worry: *What if my expectations are too high? What if in person we're not compatible sexually?*

"Lace, look at me, sweetie," Danica urged as she took her hand. "*Now*, Lacy, before he gets here."

Lacy turned her eyes to Danica's serious face. "You are a beautiful, confident woman. Don't be so nervous or too eager. You do not have to do anything you don't want to do."

Over the last year and a half, she'd come to appreciate Danica's advice, even if it sometimes bordered on motherly.

"What if I want to do all sorts of things that I've never wanted to do before?" Lacy's voice was a thin, shaky thread. She squeezed Danica's hand. "Dan, should I be worried about...you know...that ten-inch comment that Treat made in Nassau?" *Did I really ask that?*

Danica leaned in close. "All guys exaggerate. Ten is probably more like eight. Besides, we pop out babies; we're made for big things." She hugged her tight and whispered, "This is your night. Whatever you want to happen will happen. If you don't want anything to happen, then it won't. You're in control, so enjoy it. Promise me?" Danica pulled back and searched Lacy's eyes.

Lacy felt a little better. *How did I ever get along without you?* "I promise."

Kaylie leaned over Lacy's shoulder and whispered between them, "Don't forget, we want all the juicy details tomorrow. Breakfast?"

"Okay." Lacy realized with a start that she might still be with Dane in the morning. She had no plan. *Do I need a plan?* "Um, let's play it by ear. Text me in the morning."

"I am so going to win my bet on this one," Kaylie teased. She kissed Lacy's cheek. "Hi, Dane, we were just leaving."

"You can stay," Dane said, pulling out a chair.

"I'm beat, and Chaz has been hanging out by the doors for the last twenty minutes. I think he's ready to go, too." She put a hand on Lacy's shoulder. "G'night, sis."

"This was such a beautiful wedding," Danica said as she rose to leave.

"I'm glad you enjoyed it. Will we see you tomorrow afternoon?" Dane asked with an easy smile.

"Oh yes, we'll be there, and maybe we'll see you for breakfast tomorrow, Lacy," Danica answered before leaving them alone.

Dane leaned in close and whispered, "Did our time apart feel like a lifetime to you, too?"

His breath was warm against her cheek, and when he drew back, there was no mistaking the hunger in his eyes. "More than that," she said.

"Would you like to take a walk?" Dane reached for Lacy's

hand.

"That would be really nice." Every nerve in her body pulled tight as they walked out to the terrace and down the steps to the lawn.

The wind swept through the chimes hanging in the trees, creating a faint tinkling against the natural melody of the leaves in the breeze.

The balmy night air carried the scent of salt water and Dane's cologne: a sweet, manly smell that Lacy knew she'd never forget. Like the first time they'd met, the way the air felt electrically charged when they'd first locked eyes, it was etched in her memory.

The grass gave way to sand beneath their feet, and Lacy stopped to take off her heels. "Do you mind if I leave my heels here?" Lacy leaned down and pulled off one shoe, then reached for the other and lost her balance.

Dane caught her before she landed in the sand. "Whoa."

She bit her lower lip and smiled. "Thanks. I'm not very graceful."

He took a step closer to her and ran the knuckle of his index finger down her cheek. "Graceful is boring."

He stared at her so long and with such yearning that Lacy thought she might stop breathing.

"I should leave my shoes, too." The way he said it, he might as well have been saying, *I want to take your clothes off and ravish you*. He sat on the edge of the grass and removed his shoes and socks.

"Aren't you worried about your tux?" Lacy asked just to keep her mind from thinking of him ravishing her.

"Nah, that's what dry cleaners are for." He rolled up his pant legs and reached a hand up to her.

It took a second before Lacy realized he was asking for help to his feet, like they'd been there for each other their whole lives. She took his hand and, with his help, pulled him up, just inches away from her. Her pulse soared. His breath filled the space between them. *Kiss me. I should kiss you. I'm so nervous.*

Dane licked his lips, and Lacy swallowed hard, bracing herself for a kiss.

"Let's...go down to the water," Dane said.

Water? Oh, wow. I totally misread you.

Their feet sank into the deep sand as they headed toward the water. Dane's hand was like a warm glove around hers, but it did nothing to lessen her embarrassment over misreading his intentions. After the kiss on the balcony, she was sure he'd kiss her the next chance he got—and she worried about why he hadn't.

The sound of the waves crashing became louder, and Lacy was surprised to find that the longer they walked, the more her nerves calmed. When the sand beneath their feet became firm and wet, they followed it along the water's edge.

"Are you as nervous as I am?" Dane asked.

Lacy let out a breath she hadn't realized she was holding. "Oh my gosh, yes. I thought it was only me."

"I just can't believe you're finally right here by my side. It's been tough, all this time apart. Sometimes days went by quickly, but others moved treacherously slow, and the distance between us always seemed too vast." Dane paused to pick up a shell. "I can't tell you how many times I wanted to just forget about work and get on a plane to see you. I was so nervous about today, tonight. We've gotten so close that part of me worried what might happen when we finally came together."

Me too. Me too. Me too.

DANE LOVED THE feel of Lacy's feminine hand in his own and the way her slender fingers curved over his knuckles. Every time he looked at her, his gut tightened. Even when they'd been texting and video chatting, it had taken all of his focus not to let his nerves get the better of him.

"I'm thirty-six years old, Lacy, and I can't remember the last time I was nervous around a woman." Dane saw the tension in Lacy's shoulders ease. "I don't know how I can feel comfortable and nervous around you at the same time. It's very weird."

"I know. I feel it, too."

"Yeah? Good. Then we can be nervous together." He squeezed her hand and thought about Treat's warning. "My brother warned me to be careful with you," he admitted.

"Your brother? Why?" Her voice escalated in surprise.

"It was Treat. He's very protective of family, and you're Danica's sister." He shrugged. "He wants to make sure I'm not going to hurt you." He searched her eyes for a response and wondered what she'd think of his honesty. Dane was nothing if not honest, in all aspects of his life. He'd learned a harsh lesson about breaking trust with those he loved when he'd slept with Treat's girlfriend, and it had cost him years of his brother's trust. He'd never make such a mistake again.

"Well, are you going to? Hurt me, I mean." Her eyes grew wide like two blue moons. Lacy drew her eyebrows together and bit her lower lip again.

You look adorable when you do that. Dane shook his head. "It's not my intent to hurt you." Her bare shoulders glistened in the moonlight. He ran his finger from the arc of her shoulder down to her elbow.

"Lacy…" He lowered his voice to nearly a whisper. "I don't know what this is, or what it will end up being. All I can say is that I've thought of no woman but you for more than a year." Treat's words came back to him. *Get to know her.* "Maybe it's because I thought we'd have more time together in Nassau and then I was called away, or maybe it's because the attraction was so intense my stomach was tied in knots for the first time in forever. I don't know, but I know that when we kissed earlier this evening, it was like no kiss I'd ever experienced before."

Lacy lowered her eyes, and even in the dim moonlight, he could see her cheeks flush. He brushed a strand of hair from her cheek.

"Did you feel it, too?" *I have to know.*

She nodded, looking at him from beneath those glorious blond curls. He stifled the urge to pull her to him. Treat was right. He needed to be careful with Lacy, but not because she was Danica's sister. It was the tenderness he saw in her eyes that made him want to protect her. She wasn't a girl he was interested in just for fun, and he had to make sure she knew that.

"I'm a big girl, Dane. I make my own decisions and my own mistakes, so tell Treat that he doesn't have to worry about me."

She looked so sexy that for a moment Dane forgot he need- ed to hold back; then the warmth of her touch on his hand reminded him.

"I guess I don't know what this is either, but I want to find out." She held his gaze for a beat too long, translating her desire loud and clear. "When do you leave again?"

"I'm here for the next week or two, depending on the suc- cess of our tagging. They've had a number of great white sightings this summer on the Cape, and they've asked Brave to tag and track them." Dane loved traveling, and every tagging mission renewed his focus and drive. He'd been tagging sharks for thirteen years, and he never stayed in one place very long. Normally, he looked forward to the next mission, the next state or country. Tonight, he wished he had a month, or a year, before heading out again. He wanted more time with Lacy.

"Is Rob here, too?" Lacy asked. Dane had spoken highly of Rob over the past year. She knew they were very close.

"He arrives Sunday. When do you go back home?" he asked.

Lacy lived just outside of Boston, two hours from the Cape. "Sunday. I have to be at work on Monday. I heard about the sharks around Chatham. Is that where you're working?"

"I don't want to talk about work, Lace. We have forty-eight hours, and I don't want to waste a second of it."

"What did you have in mind?" Lacy asked.

"I have no idea, but I know I want to kiss you again." He leaned in close, then hesitated, until he was sure the darkening of Lacy's eyes was a sign of acceptance. She tightened her fingers around his and closed her eyes. The moment his lips met hers, every muscle constricted. She wrapped her arms around his waist and kissed him deeper. Adrenaline pumped through his veins, and he felt a familiar tightening in his groin. He swept her mouth with his tongue, drew one hand up to the back of her neck, kissing her deeper, then, fighting every force of nature that was driving him forward, forced himself to draw away.

"Lacy, I could make love to you right here."

"Here," she whispered.

Dane was unsure if it was a question or a statement. What was he doing? He might not be certain of what was between them, but he knew Lacy wasn't a girl he wanted to forget—or could forget. He needed a distraction to keep his lust in check.

"We need to walk," he said with a wavering voice. He took her hand and walked down the beach. "I'm sorry. I know I'm hot and cold, and I'm not usually like this."

"Is it me?"

He heard the worry in her voice and stopped abruptly, looking her in the eye. "Yes. It's you, Lacy, but not in a bad way. Believe me. I want to make love to you here and now, but I told myself we'd take it slow. It's just…" He rubbed his forehead, wondering how he could possibly explain what he didn't even understand. "Lacy, I've got months of fantasies racing through my mind. Images of what I wanted to do with you, thoughts of touching you. I can practically feel you beneath me." He pulled her closer. "All those intimate thoughts and pictures are chased by my wanting to slow down and get to know you better." He searched her eyes again, looking for a clear indication of what she felt. What he saw was something he didn't expect—surprise.

Lacy let out a long breath. "Dane, that's exactly how I feel, like there's all this pressure to make those thoughts come through, but then there's the other side of wanting to get to know you, so it doesn't feel so…I don't know…dirty."

"You're anything but dirty." He kissed the tip of her nose, and she smiled. "Although, we could be dirty if you wanted to." He raised his eyebrows in quick succession.

Lacy's jaw slacked and her eyes opened wide in an exaggerated fashion.

"I'm kidding," he said quickly.

"I know. So was I. Didn't you get my over-the-top gawk?" she teased.

He pulled her to him and kissed her again.

"You surprise me so much." He touched the soft skin of her

jaw and kissed her again. "So, we should take it slow?" he asked when they parted. "Get to know each other?"

"I think we should just let nature take its course." She leaned in and kissed him.

All it took was that one kiss to send his desires careening out of control. He took her hand and, while still kissing, they stumbled up the beach to the dunes, where the grass grew in tall tufts. He pulled his lips away long enough to find a path up the sandy hill.

He threw his jacket on the sand, and before he could reach for her, Lacy was in his arms, kissing him again. Her tongue probed his mouth with urgency, as she pulled the tail of his shirt from his pants, then slipped her warm hands underneath. He heard himself groan and winced, not wanting to seem too eager, but she met his groan with a moan, and it spurred him on and kicked his steely resolve to go slow out with the tide. He untied the halter of her dress with trembling hands—he'd waited so long to be with her that his breath caught in his throat. He kissed the tender spot at the base of her neck, reveling in the taste of her, and trailed kisses across her breastbone as her dress dropped to the sand. His gaze swept over her sexy curves, remembering every word they'd spoken over the previous months, every secret they'd shared, every intimate desire they'd whispered in the dark.

"You're beautiful, Lace." In all the months he'd dreamed about seeing Lacy again, he couldn't have come close to the way his heart seemed to swell within his chest at the sight of her and how his body ached for more as he tasted her sweet flesh.

THE SHOCK OF the brisk air against Lacy's bare skin sent goose bumps up her arms. Dane wrapped her in his arms, held her against his chest, and kissed her until she could barely think. Months of restrained desire fueled her need to feel his skin against hers. She drew back, nimbly freeing him from the buttons on his shirt. Her fingers traveled over the rough hairs on his chest. She'd waited so long to touch him and knew she should go slowly, but his skin was hot beneath her palms and she couldn't help herself. Her hands moved down his body, feeling the ripples of his rock-hard abs, and quickly unbuttoning his slacks.

He stripped off his clothes, and gathered her close. Their bare chests came together, every breath rushed and needy. His mouth found hers again, and he kissed her with a force so strong it took on a blaze of its own. They lowered themselves to the sand—missing his jacket altogether.

"Lacy..." he said breathlessly. His eyes were pitch-black as he stared into hers.

Lacy trembled beside him. His hand slid over the crest of her thigh, and Lacy froze when his fingers grazed the scar that covered her upper thigh.

"What's wrong?"

She didn't answer as she moved his hand and he kissed her again, touching her sensually. Thoughts of her scar fell away. The sand scratched her back and shoulders, reminding her of where they were. She had a fleeting worry of being caught on the beach, and pulled herself from her reverie long enough to look around.

"What is it? Did I hurt you?" he asked.

"No." *Why is my voice trembling?* "I just don't want to be caught...you know."

Even in the darkness she could see Dane's adorably sexy smile and realized she didn't really care if they were caught. She was not going to stop what they'd started.

"We're pretty deep in the dunes." He kissed her softly. "And we're far from the building. I don't think anyone will see us, but I don't want to do anything that you're not comfortable with. Want to go back to the hotel?"

Heck no! Lacy reined in her desire long enough to settle her voice. "No. It's okay."

Dane wrapped his hand around the back of her neck and drew her into another deep kiss, then licked her lower lip as they separated.

"Still nervous?" His voice was warm and comforting.

"A little," she admitted.

"Lie back," he said, gently guiding her down to her back. He lay beside her, and they stared up at the stars. In the darkness, he reached for her hand.

Lacy closed her eyes and took a deep breath, then blew it out slowly. What was wrong with her? Why on earth was she so nervous? She was with the man she'd been dreaming about for months. She wanted him so badly she couldn't think straight, and there she was, trembling like a scared child. She tried to clear the wanton thoughts from her mind long enough to form coherent ones and weave her way through her nervousness.

"Remember the afternoon we first met?" he asked.

"Yeah."

He leaned on one elbow and traced her ribs with his finger. "My whole life I'd been looking down, down into the water when I'm looking for sharks, down at the computer when I'm researching funding sources, and even down when I'm just going through my daily life. Think about it. How often do you really look up?"

Lacy couldn't remember the last time she'd looked up at the stars.

"The night we met, I looked into the sky and thought about you, and when we started talking on the phone and texting, I found myself looking for the stars. Even on the rainy nights, I was searching for the stars. And somewhere along the way, I realized that I wasn't really looking at stars, Lace. I was looking for you. And now I wonder if you had been there all the time, just waiting for me. *The Lacy Star*," he said with a smile.

Lacy snuggled against him. Her head rested in the crook of his arm, her hand on his stomach. The dune grass swished beside them. Dane put his arms around Lacy and held her close. He tilted her chin up and looked into her eyes.

"Lacy, I'd wait for you forever."

She saw the truth of his words in his serious gaze.

"We don't have to do anything tonight. We can get dressed and walk some more, or go back to the hotel. Whatever you want. The night is yours. I just want to be with you."

Could you be any more perfect? Lacy wanted nothing more than to push through her nerves and be closer to Dane. His tender words tugged at her heart, and his gorgeous body tugged at all the intimate parts of her that she'd been trying to ignore. She gathered her courage and remembered Danica's words. *Whatever you want to happen will happen.*

She leaned over and kissed him, and when they came apart and he opened his mouth to speak, she settled her mouth over his again, kissing him deeper and leaving no room for misinterpretation. She ran her hand down his muscular body and she felt him smile against her lips. He reached down and touched her hand, stopping her from going lower.

"Lacy."

There was such a serious note to his voice, and she was so nervous, she started laughing. *Laughing!* His brows drew together, and it made her laugh harder. In the space of a second, he flipped her on her back and stared down at her with a curious, amused grin.

"You're not very good for my ego," he teased.

"I can't help it." She was pinned beneath him, naked. Her gaze slithered down his body, giving her a clear view of his arousal. *Treat hadn't exaggerated.* That thought caused her to laugh even harder. She turned her face away from him, trying to quell her laughter. What was wrong with her?

"I'll give you something to laugh about," he said, tickling her so hard she curled her legs up and tried to turn onto her side, but he was too heavy, and his arousal knocked against her ribs, sending her into more fits of laughter.

"Get that *weapon* away from me," she said between laughs.

"It's been called a lot of things, but a weapon was never one of them," he said, trying to contain his laughter, which only made her crack up more.

Tears of laughter streamed down her cheeks.

DANE HAD ALWAYS wondered what women *really* thought when they finally saw the size of him. He was usually met with wide eyes and gracious hunger. Lacy's laughter, he realized, was probably the most honest reaction he'd ever encountered. When he was a younger man, he'd tried to hide his enormity. He had enough brothers to know he was more than well endowed—he had a python in his pants. When he was in college, he'd finally embraced his gift. It had given him courage and a cocky air, which had roped in many women. But after meeting Lacy, he'd come to loathe his revolving bedroom door. And watching the relationships between his brothers and their girlfriends made him crave more than a good lay.

He started to move to Lacy's side, and she grabbed his arm.

"Don't go," she said, shifting so she was lying beneath him again. "I'm sorry I laughed." She touched his face and kissed him. "I want you, Dane. I'm just nervous."

He brushed his lips over hers and said, "Then we'll go slow."

And they did.

He wanted her so badly he could barely breathe, but he worried about how quickly they'd come together. He didn't want her to get the impression that sex was all he was after. They kissed and touched for a long time beneath the starry sky, and before their bodies became one, he gazed into her beautiful blue eyes and said, "Are you sure, Lace?"

A sweet smile appeared on her lips as she said, "More than sure."

As their bodies became one, Lacy gasped, pinning his heart to hers with the desire in her eyes.

Afterward, their bodies were slick with sweat despite the cool air. Rough grains of sand dug into his knees and stung his toes, but he didn't care. He was finally with the only woman he wanted. He and Lacy lay spent, panting with pleasure. Then he kissed her again, long, slow, and tender.

He thought again of why he hadn't gone to see her for all those months. He knew now that he'd been right to worry that once he was with Lacy he'd never be able to turn away. Like Treat had done for Max, Dane would do whatever it took to be with Lacy.

Chapter Five

A BREEZE WHISPERED across Lacy's bare body. Every nerve tingled, and her fatigued muscles were unable to respond to the chill on her skin. From where she lay next to Dane in their hidden nest on the dune, she saw a halo around the moon. In her mind, words danced in quick succession—*Wow. Amazing. So hot.* The feel of Dane moving closer beside her—their arms touching, his thigh flush with hers—sent a chill through her.

"Lace," Dane whispered.

"Yeah?" *I love your voice.*

"I didn't plan for that to happen."

The sincerity in his voice tugged at her heart. She turned her head, his features slowly coming into focus against the darkness. "I know."

He touched her thigh with his hand, and she froze.

"You don't need to flinch when I touch you." He squeezed his warm palm against her scarred thigh.

Lacy almost never thought about her scar—or the incident that had caused it. The *incident*, that's what she and her sisters called it. She'd been only seven when the shark had grazed her leg. She closed her eyes and willed the thoughts away as she'd done so many times before. Usually, men who happened to notice her scar and ask about it were eager for a quick answer and a change of subject. Dane wanted more. He wanted to know the truth, but she wasn't ready to share it with him. She took his hand in hers, raising it off of the patchy, rough skin that covered the upper part of her right thigh. She'd told him that she thought she might be afraid of sharks, but she hadn't shared why, and as he touched her thigh, the admission hung on her tongue, but fear swallowed it down. She wanted a relationship with Dane, and if she could keep her fear at bay, she just might have a chance.

He came up on one elbow and kissed her softly. Lacy closed her eyes as he touched her cheek with one hand and released her hand with the other, resting it on her scar once again.

"Dane." Her heartbeat quickened. She reached for his wrist, but he held firm.

"Shh. You're beautiful," he whispered. Then he kissed his way down her side to her thigh. He ran his finger along the long, thin grooves that marred her thigh. Slowly, he followed each pattern, which swam fast and deep in some places and rode the surface in others.

As he traced the deeper grooves, Lacy closed her eyes, losing sensation for a few seconds as Dane's fingers traveled the paths she'd worked so hard to forget. When his warm lips touched her thigh, she held her breath and squeezed her eyes shut, disappearing into the quiet, dark place she'd learned to escape to when the memories came rushing back. She concentrated on the sounds of the waves, the salty sea air, anything but the feel of Dane touching, exploring, and caressing her scar.

"Wanna tell me about it?" he asked. Moving away from her scar, he laid his head on her belly.

"I'm getting a little cold," she lied, warmed by the heat of his body against her. He lifted his head and returned her gaze. Lacy held her breath again, expecting him to push her for answers—answers she didn't want to think about. She was too happy. She'd waited months to be with Dane, and as she looked into his eyes, silently hoping he'd let it go, she didn't know how she'd make it through a day, a week, or a year without seeing him again.

He pulled her close and rubbed his hand thoughtfully along her back. "Let's get you back inside."

She let out a relieved sigh and reached for her dress. Dane stopped her from pulling it over her head and first gently brushed the sand from her legs, her butt, and her back. He ran his fingers through her hair, shaking free the sand crystals, and warmed the back of her neck with tender kisses. Then he took her dress and slipped it over her head and tied the halter.

"Here," he said, placing his jacket around her shoulders. Then he stepped into his pants and put on his shirt, leaving the top buttons open, his curly dark chest hair peeking out.

He's too handsome. Too kind. He must have some fault she was missing.

He held out his hand. "Shall we?"

They walked through the cool sand toward the lights of the inn. Worries sailed through Lacy's mind: What now? Would he act like nothing had happened when they were with his family? Should she?

As if he'd read her mind, he asked, "Will you still be my date tomorrow?"

When he smiled, Lacy's pulse ratcheted up a notch again. "Are you sure?"

Dane stopped walking and touched her cheek. "I've never been more sure of anything in my whole life."

He stepped closer, and the memory of his kiss brought a smile to her lips.

"Lace, I'm happier than I have been in a very long time," Dane said.

Her heart soared. "Me too." *Me too? What is wrong with me?*

"Then, it's a date."

They stopped to retrieve their shoes. Dane slipped his fingers into the straps of her heels, then picked up his dress shoes and carried them in one hand, never letting go of her hand with the other.

Once inside, the lights of the inn were too bright, the hardwood floors smooth beneath her bare feet. Lacy held tight to Dane's hand, not wanting the night to end. The middle-aged woman behind the counter smiled as they passed, and Lacy wondered if she could tell what they'd just done. She reached up to touch her hair, startled when she felt the mass of frizz that her corkscrew curls had morphed into. *What was I thinking?* She cringed at the thought of what she must look like. They took the stairs up to the second floor, passing a mirror that hung on the wall. She turned away, embarrassed, and made a mental note to be sure she looked great tomorrow.

Standing before the door to her room, she felt her nerves tighten again. Should she invite him in? Would he want to come in? She dug through her purse for her room key.

"I had a really nice time tonight," Dane said.

Lacy bit the inside of her mouth, afraid to lift her eyes and meet his. She wanted to kiss him again so badly that she didn't trust herself. "Mm-hmm."

"You're meeting your sisters in the morning, right?"

She'd already forgotten. She grabbed her key card and fumbled with inserting it into the slot. "Yeah."

He nodded, and Lacy saw a question in the narrowing of his eyes and the nod of his head. He took the key card from her hand and unlocked the door.

"After you meet Danica and Kaylie, since we don't have to meet everyone until around four o'clock, maybe we can go for a sail," Dane suggested.

"On the boat you're staying on?" Dane had borrowed one of Treat's sailboats to live on while he was on the Cape. He'd lived on boats for so many years, he'd told Lacy that he missed the feel of the water beneath him when he was on dry land.

"No. That one is in Chatham already. He has two other beauties. I'm staying at the inn tonight."

Here? Please don't go.

Dane pushed open the door and stepped closer to Lacy.

"I want nothing more than to come inside and hold you in my arms until we both fall asleep, but I'm worried I'll smother you," he said.

She reached for his waist. "Smother me, please."

Chapter Six

"I CAN'T SEE how you'd expect anything else." Kaylie wore a peach tank top and white shorts. Her blond hair cascaded in waves over her shoulders, one side tucked behind her ear. She lowered her big brown sunglasses and spoke to Lacy while looking over the rim of the frames. "I mean, you guys lusted after each other for more than a year. It's only natural for you to end up doing the dirty on the beach."

Lacy and her sisters sat around a small wooden table on the patio of the Bookstore Restaurant, sipping coffee and nibbling on croissants.

"I feel a little like I don't know where we go next," Lacy admitted.

Danica set down her coffee mug and adjusted her sunglasses against the bright morning glare. "Lacy, you've had one-night stands before. Does this feel like that?"

Lacy sighed. "No, definitely not. To be honest, afterward it felt kind of natural, like we'd been dating forever, but you know how that goes. I'm still in that afterglow stage. The *holy cow, he's too good to be true* haze." She looked toward the beach, thinking of their incredible night together and how they'd made love into the wee hours of the morning. His every touch had been filled with a heated combination of tenderness and sheer, masculine sexuality. She felt a flush warm her cheeks and tucked the memory away.

"The real question is, what do you want from this? Women always let the guys decide, and really, it's just as much up to us." Danica nodded toward the beach across the street. "Weren't you worried about being seen?" Her dark curls were secured with an elastic band at the base of her neck, and as she turned toward Lacy, a few sprang free just behind her ear.

"We were up on the dunes. I worried, but only for a second." Lacy thought about how quickly she'd fallen into Dane's arms and how badly she'd wanted him. She had to tamp down her desire if she was ever going to be able to evaluate what their relationship was—or could be. She was used to sizing up clients, figuring out what they wanted, where they needed to be, and then getting them there. Relationships weren't that different from clients. The problem was, with clients she had a data sheet, a starting place. She knew their goals before they'd even met. With Dane, the data sheet was only partially complete and the goals were muddled with desire.

"He's so nice, and a gentleman, and great at...you know...but what can really come of us when he travels all the time?" Lacy had been thinking about Dane all night. He hadn't promised her the world or even hinted at anything more than what she knew they were—two people who were attracted to each other—but who knew where that might go. "He touched my scar," Lacy said quietly.

"Oh, gosh. I totally forgot about that." Danica leaned across the table and touched Lacy's hand. "I never put two and two together on that front."

"Wait. You went snorkeling in Nassau, so how afraid of

sharks can you really be, and why should your scar matter?" Kaylie finished her coffee and sat back in her chair.

"But snorkeling was in shallow water, and you guys were all around me. To be honest, I've thought about it all night, and I realized that I've pretty much kept things within my comfort zone when it comes to open water." Lacy touched her thigh. "I think I realize why my mom used to keep me so busy with day trips during the summers. We were always running to museums and going to the pool. We lived two hours from here. You'd think we'd have come to the beach at some point, but we never did. Even when she brought me here for an occasional weekend, we never went to the ocean."

Danica squeezed her hand. "Lacy, whatever your mom did, she did because she loves you, and if she felt you needed to be away from the ocean, then maybe you really were afraid of sharks after the incident. It makes sense, but you've never tested it as an adult. Maybe you're not really afraid of them, but you've been taught to think you are."

Lacy squinted in the direction of the beach. *Am I afraid of sharks?* "I have these memories of being petrified after the incident, but I can't remember even thinking about it much in the years since. It was so long ago."

Danica looked at Kaylie. Kaylie slipped off her sunglasses and said softly, "Lacy, if there's one thing I learned from Danica, it's that sometimes we hide our fears even from ourselves."

"I don't even know what that means." Lacy rubbed her temples. "Really, this is all kind of silly. We're seeing each other today, but he hasn't even said anything about after that." *And I can't stop thinking about it.*

"So…what? Then you go back to texting and an occasional

video sex call?" Kaylie ran her hand through her hair and shook her head. "I don't know how you put up with that stuff. I'd figure out what you want this weekend, and if it's Dane, then let him know in no uncertain terms."

"Kay, give her a break. She's just seen him for the first time in more than a year." Danica turned a serious gaze toward Lacy. "Lace, ignore the ultimatum advice; it rarely works. Just enjoy yourself and let things happen naturally. But if you think about things and you realize that sharks are a bigger issue—which given your history, they very well could be—then he deserves to know now rather than later."

"Speak of the devil," Kaylie said with a smile.

Lacy turned around and spotted Dane and Hugh at the gate of the patio. Her heart rate hastened when Dane's eyes locked on hers—the memory of their night together translated in his heated stare.

"Hey, ladies." Hugh waved as he pulled a chair from a neighboring table and straddled it backward. "How's the coffee?"

Dane squeezed Lacy's shoulder, and she thought her heart might leap from her chest. He leaned down and kissed her cheek.

"Hi, beautiful," he whispered. "I missed you over the past hour."

Lacy felt her cheeks flush. Now that she knew what was beneath Dane's white shorts and tan Brave Foundation T-shirt, her fingers itched to touch him. She wrapped her hands around her mug to keep them from acting on their own.

"You guys sleep okay? I slept like a rock." Hugh's light yellow polo shirt stretched tight across his muscular chest. His hair looked as though it had dried in the wind, with thick waves pulled back from his handsome face, in contrast to Dane's finger-brushed hair, the front of which hung thickly above his eyes. "Savannah, Josh, and I had a few drinks in Savannah's room, and by the time I fell into bed, I was zonked. You should have joined us," he said to Danica and Kaylie. "I told Blake and Chaz what we were doing."

Danica looked down, and the blush on her cheeks told Lacy what her sister was doing the evening before.

"Chaz was so tired," Kaylie explained. "But maybe we can catch up with you guys tonight."

"Maybe so," Hugh said. "I have to be in California Tuesday for a charity race. I can't drink a lot, but we can go have some fun." Hugh flagged down a waitress and ordered coffee. "Anyone else want a cup?"

"No, thanks," Dane said. "Lace, Treat said we could take out his Talaria. It's not a sailboat, but she's a beauty. I thought we'd take a whirl around the bay." He raised his eyebrows toward the others.

Lacy struggled to tame her excitement at spending an afternoon with Dane, and in the next moment, she worried he might want to swim in the deep sea. *That* was definitely out of her comfort zone. She touched her scar. "Sounds great. Will we be swimming?"

"Not if I can help it," Dane said with a wink. "Any other takers?"

Lacy knew how close Dane was to his family, and she wasn't surprised when he invited the others along, though she was a little disappointed at the idea of not having him all to herself.

"Savannah and I were going to hang out at the beach this morning. We'll come along, if you don't mind," Hugh said.

"We're going into Chatham today with Kaylie and Chaz,

but thanks anyway," Danica said.

"Sounds great," Dane said to Hugh. He squeezed Lacy's shoulder. "Great." Dane looked at his watch. "Why don't I go get things ready, and I'll meet you guys at the dock in half an hour."

"I'll help." Hugh sucked down his coffee in two quick gulps and jumped from his chair. "Nice to see you guys. We'll see you this afternoon."

Dane kissed Lacy's cheek, and as she watched him walk away, she felt the heat of her sisters' stares.

"Looks like you're going to a boat party," Kaylie said.

Danica leaned in close to Lacy and asked, "Did Dane say he missed you *the last hour*? I guess you had company overnight?"

Lacy felt heat rush up her cheeks again. "Okay, yes, he stayed in my room." She sighed. "I was going to tell you guys, but…"

"Good for you, Lace," Kaylie said.

"I'm happy for you," Danica said. "But you should be honest with him about your scar before you guys get any closer. Hiding things just causes trouble later."

Any closer? I'm already waist deep.

Chapter Seven

DANE THOUGHT IT had taken all of his restraint to walk away from Lacy's room this morning when he really wanted to keep her in bed for another two hours. He'd been wrong. It took even more control to keep from swooping her into his arms at the Bookstore Restaurant, when she was with her sisters. Now, as he watched her walk down the dock toward the boat, he knew he should play it cool, pretend that his heart wasn't thundering in his chest and every nerve in his body wasn't calling out for her. If he let loose that bundle of emotions, he might never let her go again.

As she approached with a trusting smile and those gleaming blue eyes that slayed his heart, his body had a mind of its own. He jumped from the boat to the dock and hurried toward her. *The heck with making a good impression.* He took Lacy in a deep, passionate kiss, lifting her feet off the dock, his chest pressed against hers, her heart hammering in perfect timing to his. And when he drew back, he was relieved to see a wide grin on her lips.

He set her feet back down on the dock just as Hugh and Savannah came up behind them.

"What is this, the *Love Boat*?" Savannah teased. "Hi, Lacy," she said with a wave. Savannah's brown bikini showed through her white cover-up. She stood next to Hugh, who was wearing swim trunks and a tank top. Both looked at Dane and Lacy with approving smiles. Savannah arched a brow. "Is this going to be a make-out trip? Do Hugh and I need to find dates?"

Lacy blushed, and Dane pulled her against his side. "We have a lot of time to make up for, but I promise we'll behave." He winked at Lacy.

Lacy wore the same blue bikini she'd worn in Nassau—the one Dane had pictured her in until last night, when his visions of her no longer required clothing.

Dane and Hugh climbed aboard the forest-green Talaria, a forty-eight-foot Hinckley yacht. Dane helped Lacy aboard, and for a moment they stood gazing into each other's eyes.

"Come on, lovebirds," Savannah said as she grabbed Lacy's hand and dragged her toward the bow.

Lacy looked back over her shoulder with a wide smile, and Dane felt a tug in his heart. What was it about her that was so different from the dozens of other women he'd been with over the years?

"Dude, are we going to pilot this boat or stare?" Hugh teased. Hugh was six and a half years younger than Dane, and as the youngest of the Braden siblings, he'd picked up on all of the ribbing from his older brothers and sister, and over the years, he'd learned how to dish it out as well as take it.

Dane gave him a playful shove, and they went to work untying the ropes that tethered them to the slip. Dane piloted the boat, watching Lacy standing at the bow; her curly blond hair whipped around her, and the cover-up she wore flapped in the wind. He couldn't wait to get farther out to sea, so he could spend some time beside her. He felt most at home on the water, and he'd imagined what it would be like to go boating with Lacy every time he'd been at sea. Now he knew that being anywhere with Lacy would make it sweeter.

Lacy took off her cover-up, and she and Savannah turned and waved at them.

"Man, bro. She's hot," Hugh said.

Hugh's tone was a little too hungry for Dane's liking. He was used to his brother making comments about women—all women, with no regard for if they were taken or single. Because of his high-profile career, Hugh had more supermodels chasing him than Josh ever did, and Josh designed the clothes they would do anything for.

He knew Hugh was harmless when it came to Lacy, but that didn't tame his urge to stake his claim.

"Watch it," he warned.

"Dude, really? She looks at you like you're the main course. I wouldn't even try."

The main course? Really? Dane smiled, casting another glance at Lacy, who was now passing by portside on her way to the seats in the rear of the boat. She waved, and Dane blew a kiss in her direction. Savannah was right behind her. She pretended to catch the kiss he blew and stuck her tongue out at him. Dane shook his head. Savannah could make anyone smile.

The sun shone brightly, and a nice breeze kicked off the water. He cut the engine.

"Ready to catch some rays?" Dane asked.

Hugh flashed a knowing smile. "That's not all you'll be catching."

"Do you ever think of anything other than sex?" Dane pulled off his shirt and grabbed a towel.

Hugh shrugged. "I try not to." He followed Dane out of the

cockpit and down into the cabin. They came back on deck with four wineglasses and a bottle of Didier Dagueneau Silex.

Hugh poured four glasses of the white wine, handed each person one, and raised his glass. "To a perfect afternoon."

"Nice." Savannah picked up the bottle and squinted. "Isn't this the wine that mountain man made?"

"Yeah," Dane said. "Didier Dagueneau was a wine maker in the Loire Valley. He had a huge cult following for his sauvignon blanc wines. He did look like a mountain man with his big bushy hair and massive beard. Poor bastard died when his plane crashed. I believe his son took over the business."

"That's horrible," Lacy said.

"That's why I'll never pilot a plane." Dane winked at Lacy.

"No, you'll just swim with the deadliest animals around." Savannah rolled her eyes.

"I thought that was your job," Dane teased.

"Like I haven't heard that a hundred times," Savannah said. "I wish someone would start a rumor that attorneys are kind, generous, beautiful people."

"Vanny, you are all those things." Dane lifted his glass. "To a perfect afternoon with beautiful company." He clinked glasses with Lacy.

"Lacy was telling me that she lives near Boston," Savannah said.

Dane had wondered when Savannah would begin to pry into their personal life.

Dane settled in beside Lacy and swung an arm around her sun-warmed shoulder. He felt her stiffen for a beat, then relax against him.

"How long are you staying on the Cape?" Savannah asked Lacy.

"Just till tomorrow. I work Monday, so…" Lacy took a sip of her wine.

"Dane's going to be here for a week or two, right, Dane?" Savannah pushed.

"I think what Savannah is getting at is that you and I should try to see each other since we'll be only two hours apart." Dane wrapped his other arm across Lacy's chest and kissed the back of her head. "Don't worry, Savannah. Lacy and I will be making the most of our time together."

Dane whispered in her ear, "Savannah's a little pushy."

Lacy smiled. "I want to spend time with you."

"Good." He'd been thinking about how to ask her to stay for another day, but he didn't want to be presumptuous, and he definitely didn't want to put her on the spot in front of his siblings. "We'll figure it out."

"Just go with him on his tagging mission. You'll love it. Dane's all slick and sexy in his wet suit, being all macho and alpha." Hugh grinned, his eyes bouncing from Lacy to Dane and back again.

"Nothing like putting them both on the spot." Savannah gave Hugh a shove.

"What?" Hugh protested.

"I have a meeting Monday morning. I really couldn't stay, even if I wanted to," Lacy said. "I'm up for a promotion in a few weeks, and I've been working really hard to get it. I don't want to jeopardize that."

"We'll figure it out," Dane assured her. So much for asking her to stay.

"What's that scar from?" Savannah asked, pointing to Lacy's thigh.

Dane felt her flinch against him and instinctively knew she

needed to be rescued from the line of questioning Savannah was putting her through. He rose to his feet and headed for the cabin.

"Lacy, wanna help me get lunch together? I'll show you the rest of the boat."

"Sure." Lacy followed him down the stairs.

Out of earshot of his siblings, he reached for her hands. "I'm sorry about that. They're a little aggressive, but they mean well."

"It's okay. I like them a lot. They're really nice."

Dane touched her cheek, and all the yearning he'd been holding back came tumbling forward. He kissed her. The sweetness of the wine mixed with the heat of their bodies, and he felt Lacy respond as she sank into him, kissing him deeper, thrusting her tongue against his, then running it over his teeth, sending a pulse of need through his groin.

He pulled back, his body already raring to go. "Lace," he whispered.

She grabbed his cheeks and pulled him into another kiss, then pushed back quickly. "I'm sorry. I don't know what's come over me." She kissed him again. "But I can't help making out with you."

He took her hand and led her to the bedroom, closing the door quietly behind him.

"Dane, we can't," she said. "Not with them up there."

"What kind of guy do you think I am?" He led her to the bed and sat next to her. "All I want to do is kiss you, nothing more." He pulled her down next to him and kissed her again. His body screamed for more. She reached for his hand and brought it to her bikini top.

He drew his mouth from hers long enough to say, "That's

hardly fair."

"Shut up and touch me," she said.

"Lace, I'm only human," he whispered.

Before the words had left his lips, she was locking the door, and sauntering toward him with a seductive sway and a hungry look in her eyes.

"So am I," she said. "I changed my mind. I don't know what happens to me when I'm around you, but I swear I can't control myself. It's like I'm addicted to your touch." She ran her finger down the center of his chest.

Dane groaned, unable to think about how wrong it was that his siblings were right outside that door while he was in heaven with Lacy. He kissed her passionately, surrendering to the heat between them and loving her until nothing else existed.

Only afterward did he worry. He wanted to cherish Lacy, to explore everything about her, and not just once, but twice, he'd taken her in less-than-appropriate places.

"I'm sorry, Lace," he said.

"Why?"

Her eyes were so big and round, so innocent, that Dane knew she really had no idea why he was apologizing. He took her in his arms and said, "Because I like you too much for these quickies."

"That's good to know," she said sweetly. "But after waiting all this time, I'm not sorry."

AFTER RINSING OFF, being careful to keep their hair from getting wet, they carried lunch up to the deck. Dane was sure his siblings had heard the shower, but he knew they'd never embarrass Lacy by saying as much.

"Did you have to bake the bread?" Savannah asked with a wink.

"Yes, as a matter of fact, we did. Did you miss us?" Dane asked.

"I did, but only because I'm starved," Hugh said.

Dane set the tray of sandwiches down on the table. Lacy smiled at Hugh as she sat beside him.

"Racing must be really exciting. How did you get into that type of career?" she asked.

Dane slid in beside her. He'd heard Hugh explain his career path more times than he could count. He watched a glimmer of excitement widen Hugh's eyes as he leaned forward, resting his elbows on his knees.

"It was my dad, actually," Hugh answered.

What? Dane narrowed his eyes, wondering what Hugh was up to now. Hugh was a self-proclaimed thrill junkie, and that had nothing to do with their father.

Hugh continued. "I watched my brothers each make these great careers for themselves—all from nothing more than an idea, or a passion. When I was in my second year of college, I was talking to my father about what I wanted to do when I graduated. I majored in business, so I figured I'd end up behind a desk somewhere."

"Under a desk, maybe. On top of a desk, definitely, but behind a desk?" Savannah shook her head. "No way."

"Anyway," Hugh said, shaking his head at Savannah's comment. "I was home for spring break, and my father asked me what business I wanted to go into. I had no idea. None. So I told him so, and he asked me one question: Was there anything in life that brought me happiness no matter when I did it." He shrugged. "That was it. I told him driving fast, and he said, *Then do it.*"

"That's the same thing Dad asked me," Savannah said.

"Me too," Dane added. "Hugh, why haven't I heard this version of the story before?"

Lacy whipped her head around. "The thing in your life that made you the happiest was swimming with sharks?"

Hugh laughed. "No, it was convincing other people to forget their fears and save the animals they hated." He leaned back and clasped his hands behind his head, trapping his thick dark waves as they blew in the wind, and flashed a wide smile.

"You're kind of right," Dane said. He remembered the day his father had asked him what he wanted to do as clearly as if it were yesterday. They were in the living room, his father in his favorite leather recliner and Dane sitting on the sofa. "It was right after I graduated with my double major—biology and social science. The more I studied, the more I wanted to know. The summer before I entered my master's program, I completed a research internship, and something strange happened. My enthusiasm for knowledge and understanding became a passion for saving and educating. I think I told him something like, *I wanna know more about sharks than anyone else in the world.* I could see by the way he looked at me that he thought I was nuts, and honestly, I'm sure it sounded that way." He smiled at the memory. "But Dad being who he is, he said, *Then, by golly, make it happen.*"

Lacy put her hand on his leg. "Your dad sounds really supportive."

"Apparently, more so to the males in our family than to me," Savannah chimed in. "I told him I wanted to be an accountant."

"No way," Hugh said with a laugh.

"You were always great at math," Dane said.

"Yeah, and I like to figure things out, but he told me I was too smart to be a number pusher, and he asked me to think about it. The next day I told him that I didn't care what I did as long as I was the boss, and he said—"

"That's the Vanny I know," Dane and Hugh said in unison.

"I guess your dad says that a lot?" Lacy asked. She watched the three of them, enjoying the way they teased one another. She noticed the glance that Dane and Hugh shared when they called Savannah Vanny, like they knew all her secrets.

"Dad just knows how to guide us well, and sometimes Savannah goes down the wrong trail. He nudges her back onto her path," Dane explained. He lifted his glass toward Savannah and said, "You're an amazing attorney, and just look at all the perks."

Hugh said, "Connor Dean," disguised as a cough.

Savannah sipped her wine and rolled her eyes.

"You know Connor Dean? *The* Connor Dean?" Lacy asked.

"Yeah, we kinda date, on and off," Savannah answered. She gathered her long hair in her hand and twisted it, then laid it over one shoulder—it sprung free of the twist and covered that side of her chest.

Lacy's reaction to Connor sent jealousy slicing through Dane's gut. He put a possessive arm around Lacy and pulled her close.

Lacy put a hand over his arm and squeezed, then brought his hand to her mouth and kissed it before placing it back around her belly. "So how did you go from saying you wanted to be the boss to being an attorney?" Lacy asked.

"My father said that was the only profession where I could

use my manipulative skills for a good purpose." Savannah laughed. "He's so funny. Most people really don't like attorneys, but he said if I went into the entertainment business, maybe I could help clean it up. And now I can't imagine doing anything else."

"What about you, Lacy? What do you do?" Hugh asked.

"Nothing quite as exciting as you all do. I'm an advertising executive for World Geographic. I work mostly with nonprofits, building brands and bringing companies to the public's attention, engaging media outlets for features. I guess you could say that I pave the way for companies to make their mark."

"Do you like it?" Hugh asked.

Dane noticed that Hugh was stepping out of his typical self-absorbed bubble, and he wondered why. His brother held Lacy's eye contact, but he wasn't measuring her up or flirting. Dane shot a glance at Savannah, who appeared to be eyeing Hugh with the same curiosity.

"I do. I love my work, my boss, and my coworkers. I'm really lucky, actually, and the promotion I've been working so hard for could be really exciting. I've been there a few years now, and I can't imagine working anywhere else."

They ate the sandwiches and fruit Dane had brought from the inn.

Hugh lifted the bottle of wine. "Another glass?" He filled Lacy's and Savannah's glasses without waiting for an answer.

"Not me, thanks. I've got to get this beauty home safely." Dane winked at Lacy.

Savannah went to the railing. Her auburn hair blew across her face. She gathered her thick mane in one hand and drew it over one shoulder. "Dane, we're in the middle of the water. Can you conjure up some sharks?"

"Conjure them up?" Dane asked. "This isn't really a shark-seeking vessel. We have no chum, no equipment."

"We could throw Savannah in. She's chummy enough," Hugh teased.

Dane watched Lacy furrow her brow. Her eyes darted from Hugh to Dane.

"This is merely a pleasure cruise," he said easily.

"Oh, come on. Sharks are all over Monomoy Island because of the seals. Couldn't we just head over and see what we see?"

Lacy's face went sheet white.

LACY'S HANDS TREMBLED. She felt her breathing become shallow, and her body temperature dropped a notch. *What the heck is happening?*

"Lace?"

Dane? She felt everything around her fading away in the distance, like she was being sucked into a vacuum with no way to climb back out. She thought she opened her mouth but couldn't be sure.

"Maybe we'll get lucky and see a great white," Savannah said.

Great white? Lacy's throat tightened. She gripped the edge of the seat cushion so hard her knuckles turned white.

"Lacy?"

Dane. Focus. It's Dane. She heard his voice, but her mind was still struggling with the idea of a great white in the water around the boat.

"Lace?"

Dane knelt before her, his hands placed firmly on her shaking knees. Lacy tried to focus on his concerned eyes, but her mind tumbled back to the treacherously hot afternoon twenty years earlier—the afternoon she'd successfully pushed away for so many years. She knew it lingered in the recesses of her mind, but she'd never expected it to claw its way out, or to consume her when it did. The memory spiraled into her brain, seizing her concentration. The sun had beaten down on her family all afternoon as they trekked through the remote village of Bora Bora, finally taking a break at a restaurant built on pilings at the end of a long pier. The pilings looked as if they'd sprouted naturally from the water, and the entire pier seemed to sway with the movement of the water. She'd been seven then, and they'd been on an adventure. That's what her father had called it, *an adventure.* He said her mother had wanted to go all her life, so they went. She remembered complaining to him about the heat and feeling guilty because she knew she was ruining the afternoon for her mother. She'd complained so much that he'd finally said, "There's the water. You know how to swim." Lacy's body was sticky from sweat. She remembered how her curls had tightened and frizzed, like the Brillo her mother had used to clean dishes. The water looked so refreshing; she could almost feel the relief it would bring her. Her mother had told her that they'd be cool as soon as the sun set, and she'd laughed—like her father had been teasing about jumping in the water—but by then Lacy had already had her heart set on jumping in and cooling off. Even if she had to pretend to fall in so she didn't get in trouble.

"Lace. Look at me. Lacy."

Dane's voice wavered in her foggy state. Lacy felt the rough wood of the pier scratch the bottom of her toes as she pretended to fall off the edge. She felt the cold water against her skin as her toes broke through the surface and she slipped beneath, her eyes closed tight, as if she were seven years old again. She'd popped up above the surface quickly, kicking her feet wildly, excited and worried about fooling her parents. Something strong and cold—*a car, it had to be a car*—dragged its full length against her thigh—hard and painful. Spears of anguish seared through her. *A car. I've been hit by a car!* The water turned red around her, and it had taken a second before she realized it was blood. Her blood. *Wait. That can't be right. Cars don't go in the water. Daddy! Daddy!*

Dane's face blurred before her. Her heartbeat was drowned out by the sound of Dane's insistent voice.

"Lacy!"

Someone's hand touched her cheek. They were pulling her toward them. She was being carried, laid on her back. Lacy flailed, trying to get away from the water, but her arms were met with something firm. *A mattress. I'm on a bed.*

"Lace, you're okay."

Dane. I'm with Dane, on a boat. Reality crept back to Lacy as Savannah's voice came through her foggy mind.

"I'll get water," Savannah said.

"Panic attack. I've seen it a million times," Hugh said.

The right side of the bed sank beneath someone's weight. Then Dane's arms were around her, holding her tight, comforting her. She could smell him. *Dane. Dane.*

His breath was warm on her cheek. "It's okay, Lacy. I'm right here. You're safe."

Safe. I'm safe. Lacy blinked, trying to push away the memory. She was cold, so very cold. Even with Dane holding her, she still trembled. She held tight to him, her eyes finally coming into focus.

"I'm...I'm sorry," she whispered.

"It's okay," Dane assured her, kissing her forehead.

Savannah came rushing through the door—the door that just an hour earlier Lacy had locked so she and Dane could fool around.

"Is she okay?" Savannah handed a cup of water to Dane.

"She's going to be just fine." Dane sat up, and Lacy wrapped her arms around his waist and clung tightly to him. "Lace, drink some water." He helped Lacy take a sip, steadying her shaking hands.

Lacy nodded. "I'm okay," she said, avoiding Savannah's worried stare.

"What happened? One minute we were talking, and the next, Lacy looked like she'd seen a ghost," Savannah said.

Lacy covered her scar with her hand, and a shiver ran through her again. She moved closer to Dane, wishing she could crawl beneath the safety of his skin.

"I can take us back in," Hugh offered. "Why don't you stay with Lacy? Savannah, let's give them some privacy." Not only did Hugh race cars, but he'd also spent a few summers racing boats.

"You going to be okay? She's a big one," Dane asked.

His eyes never wavered from Lacy; his grip remained strong and secure. There was no doubt in Lacy's mind that he was not going to leave her side—even if it meant staying out on the boat all night.

"Sheesh. Piece of cake," Hugh said.

Hugh and Savannah left them alone, and the room became excruciatingly quiet, bringing Lacy's embarrassment to the forefront.

"Lace, talk to me," he urged.

"I'm so embarrassed." *What is wrong with me?* Lacy hadn't thought of her run-in with the shark in such detail for years. Why would it send her into such a tizzy after all that time? Why hadn't she seen some clue over the years that she was that scared? She grasped for answers, wishing Danica were there with her. She'd have the answer. She'd help her to understand what was going on in her crazy head.

"Don't be silly. The first time I went down in a shark cage, I freaked. Really freaked." He smiled. Dane reached up and tucked a wayward curl behind her ear. "Want to tell me about it?"

I'd rather be locked up with Jeffrey Dahmer. Lacy shook her head.

"Okay. I'm here if you want to."

Slowly, the tension in Lacy's body drained, the shaking subsided, and she realized that Danica had already given her the advice she needed. Her sister's voice ran through her mind. *He deserves to know.* She needed to tell Dane what she'd been through, even if she didn't understand the depth of her fears.

"You said you thought you were afraid of sharks, but I had no idea it ran so deep," Dane said.

Neither did I. He'd never want to see her after this nonsense. Heck, she didn't even want to be around herself, but if she'd learned one thing from her mother's affair with her father when he was still married to Danica and Kaylie's mother, it was that living honestly wasn't just the right thing to do—it was the only way to live. Filled with doubts over what might come next, she drew courage from his strength.

"I want to talk about it." *No, I don't, but I should.*

Dane didn't rush her, or push her to spill her guts. He simply folded her hand into his and stroked her back. He snuggled against her, and Lacy couldn't remember a time when she'd felt so loved, which she knew was completely ridiculous. He was being kind, comforting, nothing more. She had to remember that. He was doing what anyone else would do in that situation. *Was he?* Would any of the men she'd dated have done the same? She doubted it. She thought most of them wouldn't have known what to do. *How does he?*

Savannah appeared in the doorway. "Are you guys okay?" She walked into the room slowly and touched Dane's shoulder. "What can I do?"

Dane looked up at his sister. So much love and appreciation passed between the two of them in that instant that Lacy's question was answered without ever being asked. Of course he knew how to handle silent fears and unspoken emotions. As the second-eldest, he must have cared for his siblings in some fashion after his mother's death.

"We're okay," Dane said. "Thanks, Vanny."

Vanny. She loved the way they were there for one another and the way Savannah looked at her, with tenderness in her green eyes that matched Dane's concern—absent of judgment and filled with empathy.

"Okay. Hugh's got everything under control, so take your time." She came to the side of the bed and touched Lacy's shoulder. "The first time I had to meet with a celebrity, I had a panic attack. I was struck numb. It took me twenty minutes to remember my name." She smiled. "I think it's a show of strength in some ways." She shrugged when Lacy crinkled her nose in question. "Think about it. It's easy to be suave and cool, but it takes real courage to come back after falling flat in front of others." She bent down and whispered in Lacy's ear, as if she had read her mind, "Hang in there. He's worth it."

Lacy looked at her then and was surprised when Savannah squeezed her shoulder. She smiled again, feeling the warmth and generosity of another Braden. She watched Savannah leave the room and took a deep breath.

"She's so nice to me," she said.

"She likes you. I can tell." Dane placed his hand beneath her chin and lifted her face so she was looking into his eyes. "I like you."

She smiled and dropped her eyes. *I like you too—too much.* They sat quietly for the next few minutes, the boat moving swiftly, the gentle rocking soothing Lacy's worry.

"It was a shark," she said, touching her scar. "I was seven."

"I wondered," he said, and covered her hand with his.

"Why?"

"At first I wasn't sure. It could have been a rock-climbing accident, or maybe a viscous fight with sandpaper—that you lost. I work with sharks, Lacy. There isn't much I haven't seen."

"Right." *Of course you'd know.*

"It could have been a hundred things, but when I saw your reaction to Savannah's comments and the way you reached for your scar. You were kicking your feet, thrashing around like you were swimming, which is very different from running, I might add." He brought her hand to his lips and kissed it.

"We were in Bora Bora, at this restaurant, which was more like a hut on stilts. I jumped into the water next to the kitchen." Her eyes remained trained on her scar.

"And that's where they threw the excess and rotten fish and meat, which drew the sharks," he said.

"How did you know?" *How did my parents not know?*

"You're talking about twenty years ago, on a remote island. It's not like the United States, where everything is micromanaged. I've done a lot of research, Lacy. There's little that I haven't heard about or seen when it comes to sharks." He placed his hand on her scar, and when she tried to move it away, he held firm. "Sharks don't go looking for humans, Lace. You were in their chum bucket. I wish you would have told me."

So you could end it before we even got started? You can't get serious with someone who is afraid of sharks. "I didn't realize I was *that* afraid," she said honestly.

"You went into the water seamlessly in Nassau."

He held her gaze, and Lacy could see that he was waiting for an explanation of some sort. She sifted through her mind, reaching for something, anything that might explain why the fear returned at that moment—but she drew a blank and finally looked away. "I don't understand any of it." *But I know now that it's a problem—a big problem.*

"We're all afraid of something," he said.

Lacy inched away from the safety of his arms. It wasn't fair to allow him to be close to her. After what she'd just experienced, she was keenly aware that the fear was bigger than any emotion she could control. Or maybe even overcome. Dane deserved to be with someone he could share his life with, and his life meant his work, his travels—his career. *I can't let myself fall for you any more than I already have. We can't be together. I can't ruin your life. Heaven help me.*

Chapter Eight

IN THE SAFETY of her room at the inn, Lacy flopped across her bed facedown and buried her head under a pillow. Less than five minutes later, she was startled by several frantic knocks on the door. She groaned into the mattress.

"I know you're in there, Lacy. Open up."

Kaylie.

"Go away," Lacy yelled into the mattress. She didn't really want Kaylie to go away, but she didn't want to get up from the safety of her hiding place. If only she could hide there forever.

"Open up or I'll tell housekeeping that I'm afraid you're committing suicide and they'll open the door."

Lacy reluctantly climbed off the bed and threw the door open. "You are such a drama queen."

Kaylie rushed in, grabbed Lacy's hand, and pulled her over to the bed, where they sat side by side.

"How did you even know I was here?" Lacy asked, wanting to crawl beneath her covers and hide again.

Kaylie's skin had already turned golden brown from just one afternoon in the sun. She wore her hair in a high ponytail, which swung from side to side with each of her fast movements. "Savannah texted Josh and told him that Hugh was bringing the boat in and asked him to find me and Danica. She was worried about you."

Lacy groaned and fell backward on the bed, covering her face with her hands. "I'm mortified."

Kaylie got up to answer another knock at the door.

"Where is she?" Danica pushed past Kaylie and rushed to Lacy's side. "Are you okay? How are you feeling? What happened?"

"Give her time to breathe," Kaylie said with a sigh.

"I just want to go home." Lacy sat up and faced her sisters' concerned glares.

"You poor girl," Danica said. She sat down beside Lacy and wrapped her arm around her shoulder.

"She had a panic attack. She didn't break a leg," Kaylie said. She plopped down next to Lacy. "She's embarrassed, not hurt. She flipped out in front of Dane. Wouldn't you be embarrassed?"

"May I just remind you that I passed out on my wedding day?" Danica cast a harsh glare at Kaylie.

"Yeah, yeah. And I went into labor at my baby shower." Kaylie's twins, Lexi and Trevor, were now three years old.

"Can we focus on me for a minute?" Lacy said louder than she meant to. "Danica, what the heck happened to me? Savannah was talking about seeing sharks, and suddenly I was seven years old again. I don't get it. After twenty years? Why did it all come back like that?" Lacy shook her head and twisted out from between her sisters. She rose to her feet and crossed her arms over her chest, pacing in her cover-up and bathing suit. "What am I going to do now?"

"What do you mean? It's almost four o'clock. Shower, dress, and we'll go to the family function, have dinner, and move past it," Kaylie said. She walked to Lacy's closet. "Want me to help you get ready?"

"Geez, Kay. Give her a minute to figure this out." Danica rose and leaned against the dresser. "Lacy, it was a panic attack. That's not all that uncommon, and there's nothing to be embarrassed about."

"Oh, right. A guy like Dane doesn't need to deal with a girl who's afraid of the one thing he deals with every day. A guy like Dane doesn't need someone who freaks out without any warning. A guy like Dane—" Lacy swallowed past the growing lump in her throat. When had she begun to care so much?

Danica stood before her, stopping her from her frantic pacing. "A guy like Dane cared enough to ask me to check on you."

"A guy like Dane is lucky to date you, sis," Kaylie said. "I don't care if he's gorgeous and wealthy. You're stunning, smart, funny, and incredibly sexy." She winked, and Lacy couldn't help but smile.

"You're my sisters. You're supposed to make me feel better." She covered her face with her hands and groaned.

"Don't worry. I'm right here, and I'll stay with you all night if you need me to," Danica assured her.

"What if it wasn't a panic attack? What if it's something else? Something worse?" She gasped a breath. "What if—"

Danica grabbed her shoulders. "Breathe, honey, or you'll end up all anxious again. This all makes sense."

"Did he really ask you to check on me?" *Of course he did.* She thought of the concern she'd heard in his voice and the empathy she'd seen in his eyes when she'd regained her focus on the boat.

"He really did," Danica answered.

"He probably wanted to make sure that I wasn't an insurance liability," Lacy snapped. She didn't believe her own words, but she couldn't allow herself to continue to think about Dane as a prospective boyfriend and lover anymore. It would be a mistake to get any closer to him. She needed to forget how comfortable things were between them and the way he was so attentive to her. Lacy had to let him go. She couldn't be a noose around his neck, and the last thing she wanted was to be around sharks now that she knew how deeply the fear was seeded. She had to concentrate on getting home, where she could lose herself in her work and focus on things other than the feel of his lips on her skin or the strength of his arms as he held her. *Stop it!*

"Oh please. That man needs to worry about insurance like you need to worry about your hair being too straight," Kaylie teased.

Danica shook her head at Kaylie's lighthearted comment. "Lacy, panic attacks can be managed. I know this probably scared you, but you can learn to deal with your fears."

Lacy shook her head. She was too confused to deal with any of that right then. When she closed her eyes, she saw Dane. She smelled his cologne; she felt his touch. When she opened them, the overwhelming panic that consumed her on the boat came rushing back. She wished she could walk the fine line in the middle without teetering toward either side, but that was unrealistic, and Lacy saw that as clearly as she saw no way out of attending the family function in less than an hour.

"I don't know, Danica. I was totally blindsided by this. I realized today that all those trips my mom took me on in the summers, trips to the library, museums—everywhere but to the beach—they were probably guided by a well-defined plan to keep me from freaking out. I can't go with Dane tonight." Lacy clenched her teeth and reached for her phone.

Kaylie grabbed her arm, stopping her in her tracks. "Before you get too wrapped up in all of this, don't you think you should talk to Dane about it? I mean, the guy probably knows a zillion people who are afraid of sharks. He might not be put off by this at all."

Lacy stared into her older sister's eyes, which usually looked so much like her own, but at that moment, Kaylie's eyes held hope, while Lacy knew hers reflected a brick wall that she was unwilling to force her way through.

She pulled her arm free. "Kaylie, I've seen him *once* in more than a year. I'm nothing more than a blip on his radar screen— and a short blip at that." Lacy turned away before her sisters could see the tears in her eyes.

BY THE TIME her sisters left, they'd convinced her to go with Dane to the family function to say goodbye to Treat, Max, and the rest of their friends in person. She'd barely had time to shower and dress. She stood before the mirror in her gold cocktail dress thinking about the day she'd bought it. She'd thought it would be the perfect combination of formfitting sexy and classy coloring to hold Dane's attention, and now, as she surveyed herself in the mirror, sadness clung to her heart and hung in the dullness in her eyes.

Her cell phone rang, and she started at the sound, then remembered that it had rung twice when she was in the shower. She hurried to the bed and picked it up just as it stopped ringing. *Dane.* How was she going to handle being around him and remaining steadfast in her need to break away from him?

Already late, she put on her lipstick and finished applying her eyeliner; then she sat on the bed and returned Dane's call.

"Hi, Lace."

The happiness in his voice brought a rush of longing through her.

"Hi."

"Did you get my messages?" Dane asked. "I saw Danica on the way to your room this afternoon and figured you needed time with your sisters."

She pulled the phone from her ear and noticed that she had two messages. "I haven't listened to them yet, but Danica said you had asked about me. Thank you. It was a bit crazy around here." *I'm a bit crazy.*

"No worries. Are you about ready to go?" he asked.

"You still want to go with me? Even after everything that happened today?"

"Do you even have to ask?"

Lacy closed her eyes and let out a relieved sigh. In the next breath, she remembered her plan to pull away from him. He wasn't going to make this easy for her. She already felt her heart being torn to shreds.

"Lace?"

"Yeah?"

"I'm right here," he said. "Open your door."

Lacy crossed the small room and pulled the door open. Dane peered around an exquisite bouquet of white lilies. His eyes lit up when they met hers.

"Hi," Dane said.

He'd changed into a white button-down shirt and a pair of linen khaki pants that tied at the waist. Lacy stifled the urge to reach up and touch the exposed skin that peeked out of his open collar.

"Those are gorgeous." For a second she allowed herself not to think about what happened earlier. It had been only a few hours, but now she felt as if it had been days since she'd seen him. She wanted to fold herself in his arms and snuggle against his warmth. Desperation pulled at her heart—desperation for his comfort, desperation for Dane. *Maybe just one more night.*

"I thought these might make you feel a little better." He handed her the flowers.

"How did you know that I love Madonna Lilies?" She brought the blooms to her nose and breathed in their heavy floral, honeylike fragrance. He followed her into the room while she set them on the coffee table.

"You told me you loved lilies a long time ago, but I didn't know you loved Madonna Lilies in particular. I have a feeling there's a lot about you that I don't know yet."

It's probably better that way.

He reached for her hand. "But I intend to get to know everything there is to know about you."

One night. Just one more night; then I'll let him go, so he can find some woman who doesn't have shark issues. Lacy felt her resolve fading away with each beat of her racing heart.

"I'm sorry about before." *What am I doing? Stop liking him!*

"No need to be sorry. These things happen. I just want you to know that I'm here for you, Lace. If you want to talk about what happened today, or if you want to talk about anything else. I'm a really good listener."

Lacy's voice was stuck in her throat. *Please don't be so nice. I can't be your noose.*

Dane pulled her close, resting one hand on the small of her back and his cheek against hers; then he whispered, "You look amazing."

Lacy closed her eyes, memorizing the feel of his heart beating against hers. How could she let such a great guy get involved with her? How could she walk away from him?

"Thank you," she managed. She was so confused, and now, wrapped in the warmth of his arms, she had no idea what the right thing to do was. Whatever happened on that boat was bigger than she was, and Lacy had a feeling that even if Dane said he could deal with it, her fear might just be bigger than both of them.

Chapter Nine

THE PLUSH LAWN of the inn was bordered with thick New England gardens, bursting with colorful flowers, grasses that grew at different heights, and ground coverings that wound their way into every crevice in between. Tables covered with white tablecloths were arranged under gauzy white canopies and decorated with floral centerpieces. The afternoon heat faded as the sun began its descent, allowing the cooler air to come in off the sea. Dane had wanted to go back and see Lacy again after she'd said she wanted to lie down when they'd come in from the boat, but he thought time with her sisters would probably help her more than he could. Now he wondered if he'd made the wrong choice. Lacy seemed a little removed, like she was slipping away. *Maybe she's just embarrassed.*

Dane noticed Savannah heading toward him and Lacy seconds after they arrived. He held tight to Lacy's hand, anticipating his sister's bold nature.

"I'm so glad you guys made it. I was afraid Lacy might not be up to it." Savannah hugged Dane and then reached for Lacy. "Feeling better?"

"Yes, much. Thank you."

Dane felt her grip his hand tighter.

"I'm really sorry to have ruined the trip," Lacy said.

"Pfft." Savannah swatted the air. "Are you kidding? No need to apologize. I wouldn't know what to do if things always went as planned." She pointed at Max and Treat. "Look how happy they are. I wonder if this whole love thing is contagious." She lifted her eyebrows playfully.

Lacy blushed.

"I don't know," Dane said. "But I'm sick of seeing you without someone on your arm."

"Oh, please. When I do bring a man around, you guys surround him like vultures." Savannah rolled her eyes.

"It's a brother thing. You know you love it." Dane turned to Lacy. "Would you like a drink?"

"Sure. Whatever you're having is fine with me," she said.

"Ugh, it's starting already," Savannah teased.

"Excuse me?" Lacy said.

"The whole couple thing. You know, you drink the same things; then you start finishing each other's sentences."

Dane kissed the back of Lacy's hand before releasing it. "Ignore her. I'll be right back." He squinted at Savannah. "Think you can behave for five minutes?"

"Only if you bring me a Sea Breeze," Savannah answered.

Dane headed for the bar, worrying about Lacy. He ordered their drinks, then felt the familiar weight of his father's arm around his shoulder.

"I heard Lacy had a hard time today," his father said.

"Of course you did." He and his siblings were so close that when something happened to one of them, the rest were not far behind with open arms and a sympathetic ear.

"She okay?"

Dane nodded, though truthfully, he wasn't sure. She'd had

a pretty major panic attack, and from the brief conversation he'd had with Danica after she'd seen Lacy, Lacy really hadn't known her fear of sharks was so great. If there was one thing Dane knew, it was that when it came to a fear of sharks, the path to understanding and conquering the fear was not an easy one—but it was doable if the person was amenable to difficult, scary, and sometimes overwhelming steps.

His father looked across the room to where Lacy was talking with Savannah. "Savannah said it was a bad one."

"Yeah. Are there ever good panic attacks?" Dane sipped his drink. Lacy looked so pretty with her tanned skin against the light shade of her dress. It pained him to see the worry behind her eyes.

"I suppose not." His father crossed his arms and lowered his gaze, seemingly studying Lacy. "Your brother tells me that you haven't gone to see Lacy since you met her. That right?"

Dane looked away, sipped his drink, then ran his hand through his hair. His father knew him well, and he'd hoped to avoid this conversation. He still hoped to avoid it by remaining silent.

"What are you afraid of?" his father asked, turning an un-wavering gaze on him.

Dane broke the link and looked at Lacy. "I'm not afraid of anything, Dad. I was traveling." He felt his father scrutinizing his answer.

"Mm-hmm."

Dane shook his head.

"I know for a fact that you weren't traveling over Christmas."

"Dad."

"I'm not judging you." His father looked at Lacy. "Be careful, son. She seems like a nice girl, and from what Treat says, she's been through a lot." He sipped his drink. "She tell you about her father?"

Dane nodded. Lacy had told him that her mother had been her father's mistress, and she had gotten pregnant while her dad was married to Danica and Kaylie's mom. Lacy was the quintessential love child. She'd shared with him her excitement of finally meeting Kaylie and Danica and the anger that she'd never before felt toward her father, which mounted the weekend of her sisters' wedding. He'd wished he could have held her when she was pouring her heart out to him over Skype.

"She did," Dane said.

"You haven't seen her for more than a year. To some people, that might feel like a lifetime." The honesty in his father's voice was thick, the concern tangible. "Life's short, son. Figure out what your heart wants and follow it."

"That's easy for you to say, Dad. You had a stable life and lived in one state for your entire life. I travel all the time. I have a boat that feels more like a home than any house—besides yours—ever will. My life isn't an easy one alone. I'm not sure it would be any easier with someone by my side, relying on me for stability." Dane hadn't told anyone his concerns about his career, and now that the words were out in the open, they scared him.

"You chose that career. You'll figure out what's what. But see that woman over there?" He nodded toward Lacy just as Lacy looked over and smiled.

Dane held up a glass and blew her a kiss.

"Stringing her along isn't the right thing to do, and you know that. You're a good man, Dane. You'll figure it out."

Nothing like a little pressure. "I hope so."

LACY STOOD BESIDE Dane, trying to focus on the jovial conversation between Hugh and Savannah, but she felt like she was drowning. Each thought cried for oxygen, each breath twisted her thoughts back to the boat. Trying to gain understanding was like grasping at straws, and every time she looked at Dane, she envisioned a rope around his neck and knew she was the tightening factor. How could she live a normal life for so many years, go snorkeling, ride on boats, and never once realize that she had such an enormous fear of sharks hidden within her subconscious? *I'm really messed up.*

Dane squeezed her hand.

Lacy looked at him, hoping he hadn't asked her a question. If he had, she hadn't heard it. The pit of her stomach took a nosedive. A cool breeze wrapped itself around her shoulders and she shivered against him, wishing it would carry her away.

"Are you okay?" Savannah asked, looking at Lacy.

"Um, yeah, thanks. Just chilly," Lacy lied. *I wanna go home.*

Dane put his arm around her. "Actually, Lace and I are heading out for a bit."

"Where to?" Savannah asked.

"I want to show Lacy around," Dane said.

"I've been here before," Lacy said. "When I was young, we visited a cottage here a few times." She thought about those trips with her parents, a weekend here or there over the summers, and while it hadn't struck her as odd when she was younger, now she realized that they never took her anywhere to swim besides the local ponds. *Darn it.* Maybe if they had, she could have dealt with this mess instead of repressing it.

"Yeah?" Dane asked.

"It was a long time ago," Lacy said.

"Well, I bet I know of a few places you haven't seen," Dane said, holding her gaze.

"Oh." Savannah wiggled her eyebrows. "You two kids go have a romantic night."

THEY PARKED AT the Wellfleet Marina. Dane opened the door for Lacy and took her hand. She breathed a little easier, away from the worried eyes of Dane's family and her sisters.

Dane flashed a smile. "Come on. Let's get some ice cream." He pulled her toward Mac's Seafood and Ice Cream.

"I never turn down ice cream," she said. *One night. Just one night.*

"Then we have something else in common," Dane said.

They ordered chocolate cones and ate them as they walked along the pier. Lacy couldn't stop thinking about the panic attack, and as they neared the edge of the pier, she slowed her pace.

"You okay?" Dane asked.

She looked at the edge of the pier and felt her pulse speed up. *Come on! This is ridiculous.* "Yes," she managed. She looked back the way they came and spotted a store.

"Want to go look around?" Dane led her back away from the pier. "Come on. This place is really cool," he said.

The Frying Pan was an artist's studio, which also served as a store. Its floors were made of wide-planked wood, and the same wide-planked boards ran both horizontally and vertically along the walls. Lacy had never seen such interesting metal sculptures, some taller than she and Dane and some impossibly small and intricate, interspersed with paintings of fish, oysters, and other sea life.

"Every month, the artist features his newest piece on this wall." Dane pointed to a sculpture that looked alive. Two big metal fish chased a school of smaller fish, fanning out before them.

Lacy stood before it, mesmerized. She reached up and touched the shiny details of fins and scales, the hole of the eyes.

"It looks too real to be fake," she said.

"Funny how something so cold can look as if it lives and breathes," Dane said.

"It does. I can feel the heartbeats of each of those tiny fish, the fear as they swim for their lives." Her pulse kicked up again. *Oh no. Stop it. Don't think about fish or sharks.* "Dane, can we walk a bit?"

"Yeah, sure." He led her out the door, and they walked along the side of the road and past a tent, beneath which a small band was playing. "Over here," Dane said. They walked past the tent to a playground at the far end of the property, where Dane climbed up the colorful play equipment to a big square platform a few feet off the ground and patted the seat beside him.

Lacy smiled at his offer, then joined him on the playground equipment. "It's been years since I've been at a park."

"Me too. I spend most of my time on the water and as little as possible on dry land," he said.

Lacy's stomach twisted again. *What am I doing? I can't have just one more night.* One more night would secure his spot in her already swollen heart. He was too sweet to just break up with. She couldn't do it. *I have to do it.*

They listened to the band, and Lacy tried to imagine a future with Dane. Every time she thought of being on his boat, her throat tightened. She gripped the cold metal of the playground equipment. She had to end things and she had to do it now. She'd never be able to do it if she spent one more night in his arms. She looked at his profile, the smile that had first attracted her to him and those honest eyes that had stolen her heart over Skype and FaceTime. She hated herself for what she was about to do to him—and to them—but she knew he wouldn't let her go if she told him the truth, and then she'd feel guilty and his life would be ruined. She steeled herself to ask the question whose answer she didn't really care about.

"Dane, what was the real reason you never came to see me?" Lacy asked. "I don't want a pat answer. I'd really like the truth." *Stop. Stop. Stop.* She hated baiting him into a fight he couldn't win.

He looked at her then, his brown eyes warm and alluring. His hand moved to cover hers, and then he turned to look in the direction of the beach.

"Never mind. I...I get it." *What am I doing?* Anger tugged at her belly—anger at herself for having the stupid panic attack, anger at Dane for being so flipping perfect when he was with her. Fear wrapped around the hurt in her heart and squeezed tears from her eyes. She was throwing their relationship away, and it was killing her.

"I get it," she said more forcefully, pulling her hand from beneath his. "I don't know what I thought was happening between us or why I thought it was okay that you didn't see me because of your schedule or whatever, but..." *Stop it! I can't stop. I can't. I have to break it off, so why not lay it all on the line?*

"It's not what you think, Lace," he said.

She jumped off of the equipment. "Right." She turned away, then heard his feet land with a thump behind her and felt his hand on the small of her back.

"Lacy, I don't have a good answer," he said.

"That's what I thought." She twisted out of his reach. *Walk away. Just walk away.*

He grabbed her hand. "Lacy, wait. Please."

He looked into her eyes, and her tears momentarily blurred his image.

"Lace, when we talked, I wanted nothing more than to run to your front door and see you. To date you, take you in my arms and woo you like a queen, but…"

"But?" she huffed.

"But every time I started thinking of doing it, something held me back. I don't know if it was fear or what, but I knew that once I had you in my arms, I'd never want to let you go, and…" He shrugged.

It wasn't an I-don't-care shrug. It was an I-don't-understand-it shrug. Lacy sighed. Part of her wished he'd have told her something else, even if it were a lie. Something that would make it easier to walk away. Another, bigger part of her melted by the heat of the sincerity in his voice, the hopeful look in his eyes. She knew what he was trying to say, because as much as she wished he'd swooped in like a knight on a white horse, she'd been scared of what would happen if he had.

He reached for her hands, and this time the love she already felt blooming for Dane overrode the anger and confusion that tried to rip them apart, and she let him take her hands in his.

"I was right, Lace. I never want to let you go," he said.

The memory of the boat returned, bringing with it a searing tightness in her chest. "Neither do I, but…"

"But?" he asked.

"I have to leave in the morning." *I can do this.* "And I'm not sure we should continue talking after I leave." Tears sprang from her eyes.

"What? Lacy, why?" he asked.

"I'm not the right person for you, Dane. I have this…" She smacked her thigh, crying harder. "I don't know what I was thinking. I didn't even know I was so scared of sharks, but now I know, and you work with sharks." She laughed through her tears. "It's ridiculous."

"It's a setback," Dane said.

"Setback? Dane, you probably have a woman at every stop around the world, or two, or three, or whatever. The last thing you need is a setback." She swiped at the tears that burned her eyes.

"Is that what you think? That you're just another one of them?" He ran his hand over his face. "I knew we shouldn't have gotten close last night. You have no idea who I am."

"I know who you seemed to be over the phone, on Skype, and in all those sweet, romantic texts when you shared your days and told me how much you thought of me." She turned away and folded her arms across her stomach. "And how every time I heard your voice, you sounded genuinely happy to hear mine." She spun back around before he could respond, and when she spoke, all of the hurt at her own weakness and all of the pain of knowing she'd waited so long for a man that she now had to walk away from came rushing forward. "And I know that when I was in your arms, I never wanted you to let go, but now…I can't be your setback."

"You're not my setback. I was making a point. I don't want a woman at every port, Lacy." He touched her chin and drew her eyes to his. "I won't lie to you. I know women in the areas I work, but they're women I see once or twice a year. They're not women I even think about after I leave. I know how that makes me sound. I'm well aware of my relationship history, and, Lacy, that's another reason I was afraid to go see you. Come on, Lace, couldn't you tell when we were together that what we had was so much more than a fling?" He searched her eyes.

"I felt every blessed second of what I thought was so real and so magnificent, that it made me forget everything else, but I'm not a guy. I woke up and I remembered." Lacy thought she was only trying to pick a fight—but the reality of his answers now simmered beneath her feigned anger.

"What are you implying?" Dane asked.

Lacy gritted her teeth against the urge to run away or curl up in the fetal position and sob. She'd come this far. She had to finish. "While you were out sleeping with women across the world, I was waiting for you to show up at my front door," Lacy admitted. She hadn't realized how much those long months had upset her. The calls carried her through the next day, and the next, and weeks turned into months, and every time she'd start to get upset about not seeing him, he'd text or email and she'd remember that he was worth waiting for. *And darn it, you were worth waiting for. It's me who's messed up.* Before she knew it, she was coming to the wedding, and even then she'd panicked. She'd had a *long* time to build up expectations, and that was nerve racking. Once together, everything fell into place so seamlessly that she would have married him if he'd asked. But now that the pain of not seeing him for all those months combined with his admission of being with other women had broken through, she was powerless to stop it. She didn't recognize the voice that came from deep within her aching chest.

"I remembered how lonely I felt waiting to see you and how

I tried so hard to lose myself in my work just so I wouldn't think about you every minute of every day." She wiped her eyes and brought her voice under control. "I remembered the nights where I lay in bed, wondering if you were with someone else, and if you were, if you were thinking of me."

"Lace," he whispered.

She knew she was creating a fissure too deep to fill between them, but that was the point, wasn't it? The easier she made it for him to walk away, the easier it would be for her to do the same. She put the final nail in their relationship coffin with a whisper, a sole tear streaming from her eye.

"When I go back home, I don't want any more of those nights. I think we both know that between the panic attack and the reality check, this is one setback neither of us needs."

Chapter Ten

DANE AWOKE TO his alarm at five thirty Sunday morning. He hadn't spoken to Lacy since the night before. She wouldn't return his phone calls or texts, and he'd tried to reason with her, but how could he reason with someone who saw right through him?

He packed his bags, sent a text to his employee and friend, Rob, whom he was supposed to meet at the Chatham Marina. Disappointed that he still hadn't received a text from Lacy, he stuffed his phone in his pocket and headed downstairs. He was surprised to find Josh and Riley at the registration desk.

"You're heading out early," Dane said.

"Yeah. We're meeting with the attorney to finalize the partnership papers." Josh looked at Riley and smiled. When they'd gotten engaged, Josh had made Riley a full partner at his design company, JBD, which would now become JRB Designs. "After today, we'll be inseparable."

"Like we aren't now?" Riley teased. Her eyes swept over Dane. "You okay? You look really tired."

"Yeah, fine," he lied.

"Uh-oh. Trouble with Lacy?" Josh asked.

"You could say that." Dane set his bags down and dug his

hands into his shorts pockets.

"I'm sorry, Dane." Riley furrowed her brow and tucked a strand of her wavy brown hair behind her ear. She leaned against Josh and wrapped her arm in his. "She seems really sweet."

"She is," Dane said.

"What happened?" Riley asked.

"Let's just say that she sees me for who I am and not who I want to be," Dane said.

"Ouch," Josh said. "Sorry, bro." He embraced Dane. "Listen, if anyone can convince her otherwise, it'd be you. But before you even think about doing it, you might want to be sure that's what you really want to do."

Dane let out a breath. "Yeah. Thanks. I see the Braden grapevine wasted no time again." *What do you think I stayed up half the night thinking about?* "I think it's more than that, though. I think the panic attack had something to do with it."

"Can't you talk to her?"

He shook his head. "I've tried."

"Hey, Hugh was looking for you last night. You might want to ring him before you leave. He wanted to join you today down in Chatham. He said he needed a little more risk in his life."

Dane loved Hugh, but the idea of entertaining his self-centered younger brother when he was in such a crappy mood was painful. "I'll call him," he said.

After Josh left, Dane checked out of the hotel and texted Lacy again. *I'm sorry for everything. I hate how we left things and I miss you. Can we talk? Please?* He tossed his luggage in the trunk of the rental car, then texted Hugh. *I'm heading to Chatham. You up?* A minute later, his phone vibrated and a burst of excitement sent him fumbling with his phone. *Lacy?* His hopes deflated when Hugh's name appeared. He read the text.

My day freed up. Mind if I tag along on your trip? I'm taking off later tonight but I have a few hours to kill.

Great. Dane took one last long look at the dunes where he and Lacy had made love, remembering the way his brain hadn't zoned out like it had in the past with other women. With Lacy, he'd been both mentally and physically present. The feel of her skin remained on his hands, the taste of her on his lips, and the memory of those unfamiliar feelings pierced his heart like a spear.

He knew it wasn't fair to take his trouble with Lacy out on Hugh, and he didn't see Hugh often enough to warrant turning him away. Maybe the distraction would help him get through the day. He texted him back. *Sure. Meet me in pkg lot in 10 mins.*

Dane looked back at the hotel, a wave of sadness washing through him. He should stick around and say goodbye to his father and his siblings, who were all due to fly out over the next few hours, but the last thing he wanted was to hear them say they told him so. The last thing he needed was to walk back into that hotel and remember what he'd felt like the night before, knowing that he'd lost any chance he might have had with Lacy.

THE SUN HAD yet to ease the brisk New England morning. With coffee in hand, Dane pulled the hood of his Brave Foundation sweatshirt over his head, stuffed his wallet and cell phone into the pocket of his cargo shorts, and headed down the dock toward his slip with Hugh in tow. On a normal day, heading into New England waters would have his mind reeling with anticipation, his body infused with adrenaline. Today his mind was back in Wellfleet, stuck like a pig in mud in that moment at the park when he felt Lacy tear her heart away from his, when for the first time in his life he'd been unable to talk his way into a woman's arms.

"Where's Rob?" Hugh asked.

"Your guess is as good as mine." Maybe it was a mistake bringing Hugh with him. Dane wasn't even sure he could muster pleasantries or patience.

Dane eyed the sixty-foot lobster boat. *Sturdy. Seaworthy.* He checked his phone again. *Where the heck is Rob?* Rob had worked for Dane for the past ten years. He'd come on almost every assignment, and they were the safest and best team around. Hugh eyed a woman on a sport fishing boat a few slips away. *Come on. Really?* Dane didn't have time for this. He climbed aboard.

"Let's go," he snapped at Hugh.

"Chill, bro. I'm just taking in the eye candy. *Man.* You know she's hot beneath those sweats," Hugh said.

Two years ago, he'd have been right beside Hugh, drinking in the curves of some anonymous woman, but now the only woman he wanted to ogle was the one who wouldn't even return his texts.

Dane spotted Rob heading down the dock in rumpled clothing, his eyes locked on the ground and the temporary deckhand they'd hired to help them out following behind him.

"You all right?" Dane ran his eyes down Rob's clothing.

"Yup," Rob said. "This is Tim." Rob lifted his gaze to Hugh. "Hugh, good to see you, man."

"Rob," Hugh said. His eyes followed Rob's every move.

Dane watched Hugh scrutinizing Rob. He was surprised to see Hugh paying such close attention to someone other than himself. Hugh was usually too self-centered to worry about anyone else. Then again, Dane had learned about another side of Hugh on the boat yesterday, too. Maybe his baby brother was finally growing up.

Rob moved robotically through the motions of checking equipment. At five foot ten, Rob was a good five inches shorter than Dane. He was a burly man with an ever-present five-o'clock shadow and thick brown hair that had recently begun to gray at the temples. Rob was usually like a lion, strong and sure. Today he moved like a wounded housecat.

"What's up with him?" Hugh asked. "The last time I saw him, he was all big talk and false bravado."

"Dunno," Dane answered. Rob was a forty-four-year-old father of two, and Dane had always been able to count on him. Only over the past few weeks had he noticed a change in Rob's demeanor, but today was far different from anything he'd seen before.

Dane scanned the deck for the chum barrels. "Where's the chum?" he asked.

"Shoot," Rob said. "Tim, go get it ready. We'll come pick it up. It's down at the wharf."

"Dude, we were supposed to pull out of here half an hour ago." Dane shook his head.

"Sorry, man. I was up all night. Sheila and I are having a boatload of trouble," Rob said.

"Trouble?"

Rob put his hands on his hips and spit in the water. "Yeah. I didn't want to say anything, but she left me, Dane. She said she needed a break, to clear her head or some crap like that."

"You didn't want to say anything? Rob, you tell me when she breaks a nail," Dane said. "We just had dinner together a few weeks ago. You guys seemed fine. How does that happen after fourteen years of—"

"Fourteen years of marriage? You've got me," Rob said. "She took the kids and went to her mother's three days ago."

"What happened? Was it because of all the travel?" Dane asked. In all the years they'd worked together, Dane had never seen Rob do anything inappropriate with women. He'd always spoken highly of his family, and as far as Dane knew, he was a great father. He couldn't imagine him doing anything that would cause Sheila to leave.

Rob shook his head. "I just don't know."

Dane noticed the evasive shift in Rob's eyes, and he realized that Rob knew why Sheila had left, but he wasn't ready to share it with him just yet. "We can table this run." Dane put a hand on Rob's shoulder. "Take a day. It's no big deal."

Rob shrugged him off. "Yeah, right. I'm fine."

"Rob—"

"I'm fine. Let's do this." Rob turned and stalked to the far side of the deck.

Dane watched Rob walk away, wondering how fourteen years of marriage could end just like that. *How could months of—What? Long-distance flirting?—end just like that?*

DANE PILOTED THE boat out to sea, stewing over the way Lacy had ended their night. She hadn't wanted him to walk her to her room, and as he watched the elevator doors close, with

Lacy on one side and him on the other, he felt as if his heart had been cut in two. Now, as they raced out into the open sea, anger crept in. *Why hadn't I anticipated her panic attack? Why did I tell her about those other women? And why the heck didn't I go see her?*

"Excuse me, Dane?"

Dane spun around. Tim had tied a bandana around his head, reining in his blond hair, which stuck out below and hung down to his collar. He had a broad chest and a thin waist, and his bulbous biceps rivaled Dane's, though he was a good ten years younger. "Yeah?"

"It's just, uh, I don't mean to be disrespectful, but Rob's out there puking his guts up and I'm, uh, wondering if you wanted to go check him out. I can take over here."

"Freaking perfect," Dane said.

Tim took over, and Dane found Rob leaning over the rail. Hugh stood a few feet away with his arms crossed, shaking his head.

"You okay?" Dane asked.

"Yeah," Rob said.

"Why didn't you tell me you were sick? You could have stayed back onshore. I've got Hugh and Tim. We can afford to miss a day, too, Rob." Dane reached for a towel and handed it to his friend.

"I'm fine." Rob took the towel and walked away.

Hugh sidled up to Dane and whispered, "Hangover."

"No way. Rob would never be so careless." *Or fall off the wagon.* Rob was a recovered alcoholic, fifteen years sober. Dane had shared that information with Treat and his father, and now he wondered if the Braden hotline had fed Hugh that intel, too. Dane looked back at Rob, who was leaning over the opposite railing. He shook his head, not wanting to believe it. He pulled

Rob away from Hugh. "Something else you want to tell me?"

Rob grimaced. "No."

"Rob, we can't do this with you in this condition. I can't believe this, Rob. Why didn't you come to me?" Dane pushed aside his thoughts of Lacy long enough to really focus on Rob.

"I don't know what you're talking about. I'm just having an off morning," Rob said.

"Off enough that we should cancel the run?" He narrowed his eyes, but Rob met his stare and held it.

"No."

THEY'D BEEN CHUMMING the water and fishing for sharks for two hours. Dane watched Rob like a hawk, and he seemed to have pulled himself together. *Maybe it was just an off morning.*

"Fin!" Hugh yelled.

"Man, Hugh, why don't you call in the cavalry?" Rob snapped.

"It's about time," Dane said. Between Lacy and Rob, his patience had worn thin.

Dane and Hugh stood beside each other, arms crossed, watching the water expectantly.

Rob grumbled beneath his breath, "Come on, you beast. Take it."

The shark circled, then disappeared, and a few minutes later it reappeared.

"Son of a gun. Take the bait," Rob growled.

"Does it usually take this long?" Hugh and Dane stripped off their shirts. Their muscles already glistened with sweat.

"Yeah, this is nothing. Sometimes Rob and I are out here for four or five hours and we come up empty-handed. It's the nature of the beast," Dane said.

"Blasted beast," Rob said.

The more Rob grumbled, the more it rode Dane's nerves. Ever since Hugh had mentioned a hangover, he'd been watching Rob, and after seeing his bloodshot eyes, Dane wasn't so sure Hugh was wrong.

"They're so close. Look at that big one. When will they take the hook?" Hugh asked.

Rob leaned against the rail. "When they're good and ready," he snapped.

"He's having a hard time," Dane said to Hugh.

"Hey, whatever. I'm just glad I get to be here. I looked for you last night. I thought you left the resort early," Hugh said.

Dane gritted his teeth. The last thing he wanted to talk about was the previous evening. He was trying to keep his mind off of the fact that Lacy was ignoring his calls.

"Where'd you go?" Hugh asked. "I saw Lacy in the hall at the resort."

"You did? At midnight?" *What the...?*

"Yeah. I asked her where you were, and she said she thought you turned in early but that you might be with someone else." Hugh shrugged. "I figured something went down between you two."

"With someone else? Who does she think I—" The clicker on the fishing reel ticked repeatedly as the line was drawn out, catching Dane's attention. "Bite. We've got a bite."

Rob jumped to his feet and helped Dane strap the harness around his waist and legs. Dane scanned Rob's face. Whether it was the adrenaline rush that came along with tagging or the fresh sea air, Rob looked much clearer than he had moments before. The color had returned to his cheeks. They were done in seconds. Then Dane strapped himself into the fighting chair, or what Dane jokingly called the death chair. The death chair was constructed of wood and metal and secured to the boat deck. It had a foot plate that Dane used to further gain control while he reeled in the shark. The chair rotated with the movement of the fish, and Dane's legs strained against the pressure.

"You sure that's safe?" Hugh asked.

"It better be." Dane pulled back on the line until it was tight, then yanked three or four times—hard.

"Let him run with it," Rob said.

Dane was used to this part of the game. He could tell by the feel of the pull that this would be about a two-hour ordeal of wrestling to maintain control while tiring out the shark and finally bringing it in for tagging. He readied himself for a long, hot afternoon. *Good. It'll keep me from thinking about Lacy.*

An hour and a half later, the veins in Dane's arms and legs strained against his skin. His hands were locked to the reel and rod, his biceps bulging. Sweat drenched his forehead as he wrestled the rod and brought the eight-foot great white toward the boat.

"Rob!" *Where is he?* "Holy… Tim, grab the tail line. Hugh, where the heck is Rob?"

"I'll get him. He was in the head," Hugh said.

Dane kept his eyes trained on the shark. "What?" *No one goes to the head when a shark is on the line.* He couldn't whine about it now. He had a shark to tag. "This is the hardest part, Tim. Grab the tailer."

Tim picked up the long metal tool by the handle and scanned the flexible cable and strong line. Dane watched him run his hand quickly along the line and follow the loop back on the cable to the handle, checking the security of the D-shaped flexible loop. "Got it," Tim said.

Dane unhooked himself from the seat, working to keep the shark close to the boat. "Rob!"

"Right here," Rob said. His lids were heavy, and his cheeks were once again flushed.

"You okay to do this?" Dane asked.

"Heck, yeah." Rob carried the hand tools for tagging the shark.

Dane grabbed Rob's arm. "Dude. No risks. If you're not up to this, do not touch the shark."

Rob pulled his arm from Dane's grasp. "I got this. We're gonna have a good run."

"What can I do?" Hugh asked.

Dane watched Rob out of the corner of his eye. He recognized Rob's reaction to the shot of adrenaline that Dane knew all too well when a shark was finally within their grasp. Rob moved more confidently, and Dane wondered if—and hoped that—Hugh had been wrong after all. "Tim's going to hook his tail, and I've got the head. While Rob's securing the tag to the dorsal fin, you hold on to the fin too and hold him as still as you can," Dane said.

"What about that thing I read about...tonic immobility?" Hugh asked.

"You read about that?" Dane asked. Dane could hardly believe his brother had read up on what he did for a living. Tonic immobility was a technique used by several taggers—by flipping the shark upside down, they put the shark into a natural state of paralysis, or a trancelike state, for fifteen minutes, after which time the shark would right itself and swim away, unharmed.

"My life is more than racing and women," Hugh said.

"I never would have guessed," Dane said with a wink. "We use tonic immobility occasionally, but it's not our go-to measure." The shark fought and lashed from side to side, arching to one side and then the other. Tim struggled with getting the tailer on the shark.

Impressed with Hugh's knowledge, and trusting his strength and intelligence, Dane hollered to him, "Hugh, help him?"

"Got it." As if he'd been catching sharks forever, Hugh timed the action perfectly and secured the loop over the shark's tail on the first try. He pulled back, and the cable slid down and tightened around the shark's tail. "Ha-ha!" Hugh yelled. "That's a Braden for you."

Rob went to work tagging the shark. He positioned the hand tool on the dorsal fin and injected the one-inch tether, attaching the tag.

"Usually we like to get blood work, approximate weight, length, girth, but today we're just tagging," Dane explained to Hugh as he huffed and puffed, wrestling with the line to keep the shark reeled in close. "I hate to not get this sucker's length and girth."

Rob looked at him and smiled. "I got this."

"What?" Hugh asked, looking from Rob to Dane.

"Your brother wants to jump in and get a good feel for this monster's girth," Rob said.

"You wanna jump in?" Hugh asked.

Dane looked past his adrenaline and really studied Rob's face. "Man, you don't look too good."

Rob finished tagging the shark and wiped his eyes. "Go, will you?" he snapped.

"You look sick. Let's skip this one," Dane said.

"I'm fine," Rob said. "You going to do this or what? We got about seven minutes. Tops." They always kept their tagging and tests to less than fifteen minutes for the safety of the shark. "Enough of this. Get your butt in there. I'm fine. I told you—I was tired, but I'm fine now," Rob said.

"Tired doesn't equate to safe," Dane said.

Rob scoffed, stripped his shirt off, and jumped off the boat a foot from the shark's tail.

"For the love of... Hold that sucker tight, Hugh. Tim, gimme the tailer." *Idiot Rob. What the heck are you doing?* Dane's heart slammed against his chest as he searched the water for his friend while gripping the tailer with all his might. He knew Rob would swim under the shark and use his arms to estimate the shark's girth, but the water was too murky to see him.

Rob popped up beside the shark. "Got it." He had a grin on his face as he swam to the side of the boat. Just as he started to climb into the boat, the shark flailed, and Rob lost his balance and sank back into the water.

"Crap. Tim, get him in the boat!" Dane hollered.

Rob swam over, and Tim helped him into the boat. Dane began the process of freeing the shark from the line and the tailer.

"What was that? Rule number one: Never do *anything* un-anticipated. What the hell, Rob? What was that crap?" Dane yelled.

Rob sat with his elbows on his knees, wiping the water from a cocky grin. "A girth of about five feet."

"You son of a..." Dane said.

THEY PULLED INTO the slip around four in the afternoon and docked the boat. While Dane was pleased that they'd tagged a shark, he was livid. He watched Rob step off the boat and run the crook of his elbow down his face. For the first time in ten years, his faith in Rob faltered.

"What was that crap you pulled out there?" Dane asked.

"Hey, you know what? You only go around once, and living safe did me no good." Rob shrugged. "I needed a little adventure." He slapped Dane on the back. "We had a good run."

"A good run, my butt. You're worrying me, Rob. Wanna go grab a bite and talk for a bit?" Dane asked.

"Nah. I'm tired. I'm hitting the shower, then calling it a night," Rob said, waving to Tim.

Rob's trouble with Sheila and his behavior on the boat weighed heavily on Dane's mind. He needed to get to the bottom of whatever was going on. He didn't think Rob was drinking again, but he also had never seen Rob do anything that could jeopardize a mission—and today he was just plain careless.

Dane grabbed Rob's arm as he walked past. "Listen, I know you're having trouble with Sheila, but you can't pull that crap. You sure you don't want to talk about this?"

"I'm fine," Rob said through gritted teeth. "I'll see you tomorrow."

Dane watched Rob walk away. There was no way he'd take Rob out on the boat tomorrow after what he pulled today. He'd give him time to cool off and talk to him about Sheila and deal with the rest of his mess later.

"I gotta get showered and up to the airport in P-town,"

Hugh said. "Smitty's opening Treat's cottage for me to get cleaned up before I leave town. I'm flying into Boston, then to Cali. I had a great time today. Thanks for letting me tag along." He slung an arm over Dane's shoulder.

"I'm glad you came. What's up with the shark research?" Dane asked. He was distracted by Rob's behavior, and now that he was on dry land again, thoughts of Lacy stole his concentration, but he was curious about his brother's recent metamorphosis.

Hugh shrugged. "Just learning about all the crap my impressive older brothers do. I've been reading up on acquisitions, too. Treat got some big deals under his belt. What's up with you staying on Treat's boat tonight?"

"It feels more like home," Dane said. He withdrew his phone from his pocket and checked his messages. His gut clenched and he shoved the phone back in his pocket.

"No message from Lacy?"

"Nope."

"Drive me to Treat's?" Hugh asked.

"Absolutely."

They stopped at the Catch of the Day on the way and picked up crab cake sandwiches, then climbed back in the car and drove toward Treat's bungalow on the bay.

"Wanna talk about it?" Hugh asked.

Dane looked at his brother, surprised again that he was reaching out. He saw genuine concern in Hugh's eyes, then brought his own back to the road. "Not really," he said.

"Suit yourself, but I'm a good listener," Hugh said. "And I know women."

Dane laughed.

"Okay, so maybe I'm not a great listener, but I do know

women."

"Listen, little brother, so do I, okay? I know women; that's the problem," Dane said.

Hugh furrowed his brow. "So…she's upset because you sleep with too many women?"

Dane shot him a stern look. "I don't have a clue."

"Then you don't know women," Hugh said. He reclined his seat and sighed. "If you were me, you'd know exactly what was wrong. Could it have anything to do with her panic attack?"

"Hugh, I don't freaking know." Dane did not want to talk about Lacy. At best, it would make him angry. At the least, it would irritate him. There was no answer. He'd spent all those months living in denial about why he wasn't hightailing it to Massachusetts to see her, and by the time he realized why, it was too late.

"What? I'm trying to help. You're a big-time shark tagger, but you can't talk about some hot babe?" Hugh asked.

Dane veered over to the side of the road and slammed on the brakes. "Listen, she's not just some hot babe, and I don't know what's going on, okay? All I know is that when I was with her, I didn't want to let her go. And that's the first time I've ever felt that." His nostrils flared. He breathed in fast, hard bursts. "Darn it, Hugh. She wasn't just some roll in the hay."

Hugh brought his seat upright. "Chill, dude. That's not what I meant at all."

"Know why I didn't see her for all that time? I was stupid and afraid, okay? I never spend ten minutes getting to know a woman. Never. I hook up with women, pretend to listen to them for a few minutes, and the whole time all I'm thinking about is what their breasts will feel like, or how I just wanna get them in bed. But with Lacy, I spent every second I wasn't with her just thinking about her. I wondered what she was doing, who she was with." Dane slammed his back against the seat and let out a groan. "I cared about her *before* I ever touched her. And then we come here and she's more than I ever dreamed of."

"Dane," Hugh said.

"And then she has that stupid panic attack, which sends her into some weird I-can't-be-with-you state," Dane yelled. His chest constricted as he explained how far he'd gone trying to reach her. "I've spoken to Danica and Kaylie. I even asked Blake to try to convince Danica to convince Lacy to talk to me. She won't answer my texts or my calls." Tears of anger burned at the back of his eyes, and he turned away so Hugh wouldn't see them.

"Dane," Hugh said again.

"And then she ends it. Just ends it. She says while I was out sleeping with every girl that walks, she was waiting at home for me to show up on her doorstep. I killed it before we ever got started."

"Dane!" Hugh held his hands up in the air to get Dane's attention.

Dane shook the fury from his head. "What?"

"Do you want to be with her?"

"What kind of stupid question is that?" Dane asked.

"Do you?"

"Yes. I do, yes. More than you could know," Dane said. He scrubbed his face with his hand and groaned again.

"If she were a shark, what would you do?" Hugh asked.

"Whatever it took. I'd reel it in for days, weeks. Then I'd wrestle the thing to the ground."

"You really are messed up," Hugh said.

"You know what I mean. I wouldn't give up. Lacy's not a

shark. She's a woman. A bright, warm, charming, gorgeous, sexy woman who's not here and won't take the chum," Dane said. He pulled the car back onto the road.

"Sounds simple to me," Hugh said. "Didn't she say she worked at World Geographic? As a marketing rep or something?"

"Account manager," Dane corrected him.

"You own a foundation. Don't you need some sort of marketing program?" Hugh asked.

"No." *Marketing program?*

"You sure? I think you might," Hugh said with a coy smile.

"Marketing—" Dane smiled, then frowned. "Hire her? She'd never take the job."

"No. Hire the company. You're Dane Braden. You've got a reputation in oceanic research and a valuable company. Hire the company and stipulate that she takes the account. Seems simple to me," Hugh said.

"Simple? Then what? I go to her office and stare at the walls?" Dane asked.

"You're not this simple, Dane. Think."

Dane let out a loud breath. *Hire her company. Then what?*

"Dane, come on. She's afraid of sharks. You can help her with that. She can help you with marketing. Maybe your new account executive needs to come on a tagging mission with you for a week. Maybe she needs to immerse herself in your work to understand the project."

Dane pulled into Treat's driveway, shaking his head. "Farfetched."

"When has that ever stopped you from doing anything in your life?" Hugh asked. "Come in, shower, clean up, and then decide."

"It's insane," Dane said.

"So is diving with sharks."

TWENTY MINUTES LATER, Dane called and arranged an extension to the tagging mission. He'd need more time if he was going to follow through with his intentions. Then he called Rob and left a message. "Rob, take the next two days off. Rest up, and we'll pick this up on Wednesday. I have to head out of town for a day. If you want to talk about Sheila, call me. I'll keep my phone on and, buddy, after what you did today, I'm a little worried."

Dane called Danica and asked her to guide him through how to help Lacy with her phobia. He didn't tell her what he had planned, and it took some finagling, a good amount of begging, and assurances about his intentions toward Lacy, but forty minutes later he was armed with information on desensitization techniques and in vivo exposure for galeophobia. Dane was ready to help Lacy through her fear of sharks. He had one more phone call to make, and as he called 411, he knew he had made the right decision.

"The offices of World Geographic, please, just outside of Boston."

Chapter Eleven

LACY PUSHED THROUGH the glass doors of World Geographic Monday morning with a heavy heart. She hadn't returned Dane's calls, or his texts, and she'd purposely not checked her emails. The last thing she wanted to do was hear his voice or read a message that would soften her resolve. She knew it would send her heart into a tailspin. She hadn't realized how hurt she really was that he hadn't come to see her for all those months, and when he'd looked her in the eye and confirmed he'd been with other women, it had thrown her for a loop. Even so, she'd already rationalized that worry away—they hadn't committed to a monogamous relationship. She had no right to hold him to one, even if it hurt to accept. She held on to that rationalization and let out a loud breath. The whole mess had become too confusing, and Lacy felt like her head was spinning. *Being apart is for the best. No matter how much I ache to see him. Touch him. Kiss him. Oh, shut up!* She couldn't be a burden on his career. *A setback.* He deserved to have a relationship with someone who loved the sea and everything associated with his job as much as he did.

The previous evening had passed as if in slow motion. Everything reminded her of Dane. Every time she closed her eyes, she saw his face, his dark eyes pleading with her to stop being angry and talk to him. She'd surfed the Internet for a while, looking at People.com and then CNN, and she'd read an article about a great white sighting off Cape Cod. There was a reference to the Brave Foundation being summoned to tag and track the sharks, and no matter how hard she tried not to click that link, she couldn't stop herself. She'd spent hours watching shark videos and reading about the different shark species. The more she'd read, the more interested she'd become. With her head swirling with facts about sharks, she'd finally turned off her computer and collapsed into a fitful night's sleep.

At least here at the office she'd have projects to work on and clients to call. Her brain would be occupied. *Too occupied to think of Dane.*

She turned on her computer, and their internal message system dinged. She had a message from Fred, her boss. *New client meeting. Nonprofit, your bailiwick. Nine a.m., my office.* Great. Something to look forward to.

The second message was from Danica. *Ugh.* She'd dodged Danica's calls last night, too. She hadn't wanted to be consoled, and now guilt pressed in on her. She picked up her cell and called her sister.

"Lacy, are you okay?" Danica asked.

"I'm fine. I just needed to be alone."

"You're sure you're okay? What happened? I looked for you Sunday morning, but you had already checked out. Savannah said she heard there was trouble between you and Dane."

Lacy rolled her eyes in an effort to keep her tears at bay. "Is nothing sacred?" she managed.

"Savannah cares."

"Yeah? Well, she shouldn't," Lacy said.

"Oh, Lacy. You sound so sad. What happened?" Danica asked.

She didn't want to argue with Danica. She pushed the confusion she was feeling onto Danica, thinking she would agree and help her to remain strong. "Let's just say I realized that waiting so long to be with someone isn't right. I should have seen the red flags before. You were a therapist; you should have warned me." Lacy picked up a tissue and wiped her eyes.

"Really? So it's my fault? I thought you were okay with not seeing him for that long. You were crazy busy, too, and you said you understood. What happened?" Danica asked.

Lacy didn't answer. Lying was not her strong suit.

"Lacy?" When Lacy didn't respond, Danica said, "Lacy, listen, honey. If this is really about the panic attack, you can work through that. Your panic attack could have been caused by all of it—your heightened emotions for Dane, months of building up expectations and turning all that lust into real intimacy, and worrying about if you *were* afraid of sharks. Anxiety is a funny thing, Lace. It can be really powerful and fed by so many different things."

Lacy just wanted the whole mess to go away. She already loved Dane too much to be the woman he always had to worry about. Dane had been so attentive to her needs. She knew he would be the same way forever if that's what it took, and she couldn't let him mollycoddle her because of her stupid fears. He deserved to be with a normal person who wasn't afraid of the very things he worked so hard to save. It hurt to think about him, much less talk about him. She'd made up her mind already, and this time she was sticking to her guns, even if it meant leading her sister down a wayward path that she didn't really care all that much about...or maybe she did. She didn't really know, and it hurt too much to think about it, but it would definitely shut down Danica's attempts to push her toward Dane.

"He has women all over the world," Lacy said.

"So?"

"So? Danica!" Lacy lowered her voice. "What do you mean, *so?*" *Darn it. I thought that would shut you up.*

"What a person does before they meet the person they want to be with has no bearing on who they are going to be after they meet him…or her," Danica said. "Look at Blake."

"That's different," Lacy said. *Why is she so set on this relationship?*

"Really? How?" Danica asked.

It was no secret that before meeting Danica, Blake was a player of the worst kind. He'd have sex with any woman who wanted him.

"Most men aren't capable of change," Lacy said.

"Not true," Danica retorted.

"They have to want to change."

"True, and does he?" Danica asked.

"How should I know?" Lacy asked.

"Do you want him to?" Danica asked.

"I don't know." Lacy closed her eyes against another wave of tears. "None of it matters. I can't be around a guy who tags sharks if I'm afraid of sharks."

"It's a phobia, and you have no idea how bad it is. You've had one panic attack, and you had all those other anxiety-provoking issues rising at the same time. Once you and Dane spend more time together, your anxiety level might dissipate, and spending time learning about sharks and inundating yourself with them could lead you to conquer whatever fear is left. You can work through that if you want to, and it probably wouldn't be too difficult."

Silence filled the airwaves.

"What's your plan?" Danica asked.

"Forget I ever met him and go on with my life," Lacy said.

"And how did that go last night?"

Lacy looked down at her lap, remembering the box of tissues she'd gone through and the pint of ice cream she'd eaten.

"Lacy?" Danica said.

"Hmm?"

"Before you close that door, why don't you talk to him? It doesn't mean you have to be with him, but just clear the air. You waited more than a year. That's a long time to wait just to turn your back because of a panic attack. I can help you with that, too," Danica said.

"But doesn't it mean that he doesn't really like me, or that he's a user or something, because he didn't come see me in all that time? Think about it, Dan. Would you put up with that?" Lacy asked. She'd gone over their situation in her mind for hours the evening before. Every time he had free time, she'd said she didn't, because of that stupid promotion she'd wanted so badly, but the truth was, she'd been just as afraid as he'd said that he had been.

Danica sighed. "I don't know. You were so happy over that period of time. You weren't pining away for a man who was treating you badly. He called and texted you every time he said he would. He Skyped and FaceTimed, and he sent emails and cards. It's not like you were being neglected."

"You're not making this any easier," Lacy said. Her office phone rang. "Hold on." She lowered her cell to her lap and answered her office phone. "Lacy Snow."

"Our new client is here. Can you join me in my office now instead of nine?" Fred asked.

"Of course. Give me two minutes," Lacy said.

"Sure."

She hung up the phone and returned to the conversation with Danica. "I have to go. My boss wants me to meet a new client."

"Okay, but listen, Lacy. Maybe you shouldn't make any snap judgments about Dane. I can help you work through your phobia, and you can figure things out with him slowly," Danica said.

"I don't know. I think it's for the best if we're not together. I've been ignoring his calls and texts, which, let me tell you, was the hardest thing I've ever done. I'm so used to hearing his voice almost every night that last night was torture. I wasn't ever lonely before meeting him and now, after talking to him almost every night and then seeing him again"—*and touching him*—"I'm so lonely. How can I be lonely after seeing him for only one weekend?" Lacy groaned. "I have to believe it's for the best." *And I'll just live with a broken heart forever.*

DANE SAT ACROSS from Fred Wright, managing director of World Geographic, focusing on the ruse he'd initiated. Lacy could avoid his phone calls and his messages, but she couldn't avoid a man who was standing before her. His feelings for her were too strong to let them fall away like all those months of getting to know each other—of falling for each other—meant nothing. In many ways, those long-distance conversations had been more intimate than the night they'd spent together in

Wellfleet. They meant everything to him, and the changes he was seeing in himself were all because of Lacy. There was no way he'd just let her walk away. He had to at least try to get her to recognize and accept the man he wanted to be, and part of who he wanted to be was the man to help her with her fear of sharks.

His stomach had been tied in knots since he'd settled on the idea. He was taking all sorts of risks. Lacy might go off on him the second she saw him, exposing his ruse and finalizing their breakup all in one fell swoop. Dane hung on to the tiny shred of hope that her job was too important to her to do that.

Lacy walked through Fred's office door, wearing a white scoop-necked blouse and a pair of fitted black slacks and flashing a businesslike smile. Dane's heart leaped into his throat. Her eyes swept the room, landing on Dane. It pained him to watch her professional greeting morph into a confused gape. Her finely manicured eyebrows drew together. Her eyes darted between the two men.

"Wha…" she managed.

"Lacy, this is Dane Braden. He's the founder of the Brave Foundation, and he's hired us to handle his marketing campaign for the upcoming year." Fred was a diminutive man with narrow shoulders and a thick waist. He motioned toward Dane with a smile. "I'm sorry I didn't give you time to prepare. Mr. Braden called the service last night and had me paged. It was too late by the time we wrapped things up to call, and we've been working all morning to coordinate a plan."

"Uh…hello?" she said.

"Lacy." Dane stood and shook her hand as if he'd never met her, much less ravaged her body a few nights earlier. He'd take his lead from Lacy, play the game her way…sort of. Her hand trembled within his, and Dane put his other hand over it, hoping she'd take comfort in the small embrace and maybe even ease the darts she was casting his way.

Lacy lowered herself into the chair beside Dane with a confused gaze.

Dane breathed a sigh of relief. *At least she didn't call me out right away.* He knew he shouldn't smile, because she might think he was gloating, but he couldn't wipe the stupid grin from his face. Just seeing her again made his heart sing. It was all he could do not to reach out and touch the soft skin of her cheek.

"As I explained, the Brave Foundation has hired World Geographic to develop their marketing program, promote the brand, and get their name into new media channels. Lacy, Mr. Braden has—"

"Dane, please," Dane said.

Fred smiled. "Dane, thank you. Dane has requested that you head up the efforts."

Dane saw her flinch, and the light that her smile brought to the room was sucked away with the confusion and hurt in her eyes.

"But...I'm on an assignment already. And I've got—" she said in a thin voice.

"Already taken care of," Fred interrupted. "Tasha is going to take over your other accounts for the foreseeable future while you immerse yourself in the Brave Foundation activities and get to know their focus and marketplace."

Lacy drew her eyes to Dane and pursed her lips.

"I heard you were the best," Dane explained.

"You did?"

He heard the annoyance in her voice.

"From whom?" she asked.

Dane had spent the morning researching Lacy's previous clients and had come away even more impressed with her abilities than he'd already been. "Oceanic Research, and a good friend at the Boots for Boys Foundation said I couldn't find a more qualified person for the job."

Lacy clenched her jaw, but beyond the tension in her face and behind the angry stare, he recognized sadness. The redness beneath her lashes told him that she, too, had had a difficult evening. *I'm doing the right thing.*

"Dan—"

"Dane," Dane corrected her, smiling to himself at her attempt to rile him. *That's the Lacy I know and love.* Dane loved Lacy's femininity, but her strength was equally as appealing.

Fred interrupted. "Lacy, Dane is currently on assignment in Chatham, and as of this afternoon, so are you."

"Excuse me?" Lacy asked.

"It's exciting, I know," Fred began. "This is a brilliant idea. Immerse yourself in their work for a week or two. Strategize. See who they talk to, how they present themselves—really get involved. Become one of the team." Fred looked at Dane. "She's incredibly talented. Our best account manager."

"One of the team? Sorry, *Dane*, but doesn't your company handle shark research? Unfortunately, I'm afraid of sharks, so this is probably not the best match." Lacy flashed a gloating smile.

Dane had anticipated such a reaction. "Yes, we do, and that shouldn't be an issue. I will ensure that you are not put in any uncomfortable situations," he said.

Lacy narrowed her eyes. "But being near that activity is uncomfortable for me."

"In that case, I will ensure that you will not be near any of that type of activity." Dane felt the burn of Lacy's stare. As much as he cared and as much as it sent a pain through his gut to see her squirming in her chair and to know her brain was working to figure out a way to disengage from the assignment, he had to believe that they deserved this chance to see if that one night was a precursor to a fulfilling and happy life together, or if he'd been altogether wrong about them.

Dane stood and extended his hand across Fred's desk. "It's been a pleasure, thank you. I look forward to a mutually beneficial business relationship." *And so much more with Lacy.* He turned to leave and extended the same handshake toward Lacy with just as professional of a tone in his voice. "I'm driving to Chatham this afternoon. Would you like to ride with me?" He couldn't imagine his life without Lacy in it, and he wasn't leaving anything to chance. He knew that Lacy would worry about being pressured into being intimate with him, and he'd already come up with a plan to help her feel more at ease. He would assure her that he would not fall any deeper in love with her. She didn't need to know that he already felt as though he'd fallen to the center of the earth.

"I have a car, thank you," she answered with an icy stare.

Chapter Twelve

"I'M THE WRONG person. I'm afraid of sharks. I have too much other work to do. Please give it to Tasha." Lacy had been trying to convince Fred that she was the wrong person for the job for five minutes, and she felt like she was banging her head against the wall. *I'll kill Dane.* Why was he doing this? He could have any woman he wanted. Why her? *I'm not anything special.* Even as she thought the words, she knew it wasn't about her being special. It was about how what they had together was special. She knew that because she felt it, too. It was too powerful to deny, which was why she bolstered her resolve to ignore it.

"I have faith in you, Lacy," Fred said. "This is a major account for World Geographic, and I expect you to treat it with the same diligence and professionalism as you would any other assignment. Your job depends on it."

Fred had supported her vehemently in the five years since she'd worked under his supervision. He'd pushed her to work harder and reach her potential at times when she thought she already had done just that. He urged her down the right path to secure the promotion she'd been working so hard toward. Was he really going to pull that out from under her? He had to believe this stupid ruse was what would seal the deal for the promotion, or he wouldn't threaten her. *Darn it.* "My job depends on it? Are you telling me that you'll fire me if I don't take this assignment?" Lacy broke out in a sweat. *Lose my job?*

"No. You're a valuable employee, Lacy. But we both know you have higher aspirations than account manager, and you've proven that you have the skills and the dedication. If I give this to Tasha, you could be swept under the rug for that senior account rep promotion you've been vying for."

"This account is that important?" Lacy asked.

"This account will bring in an enormous amount of revenue for us. Lacy, senior account rep will mean that you call the shots. You decide who you take on as a client and when. You'll have underlings to do your research and administrative work. This is big, Lacy. Besides, going to Chatham for a week or two? Not a rough way to earn a living. Dane Braden seems nice and professional. He's agreed to an excessive travel budget for you, too. You'll be well taken care of," Fred assured her.

I bet I will. That's what I'm afraid of. She couldn't afford to lose her chance at the promotion. She'd worked too hard to maintain a lead in the running—and she'd missed out on seeing Dane for all those months. She silently groaned inside. As much as the idea sent her heart and her head into fits of confusion over working with Dane, she reluctantly relented.

"Fine," she said. "Thank you for the opportunity." *The opportunity to fight my freaking urges to smack Dane upside his head and follow it up with a kiss on those luscious lips. Stop it. Stop it. Stop it.*

Lacy grabbed her cell phone and stormed out of the building. She dialed Danica's number, pacing the parking lot, feeling as though fumes were coming out her ears.

After Danica's voicemail picked up, she left a message. "He was here, Danica. He showed up at my work and hired my company, and now I have to go to Chatham and work with him or I'll lose my chance at the promotion. Where are you?" She lowered the phone and then quickly put it back to her ear. "I'm sorry. I didn't mean to rant. I'm just so frustrated. Call me? Please?" Lacy ended the call and stared at the building. Too angry to return to work, she stalked to the edge of the parking lot and continued pacing off her frustration. She stepped to the side to let a car pass, and when it stopped beside her, she spun around.

Darn it, Dane.

He sat in the car with a smile on his lips. "Sorry," he said with a shrug.

"Sorry? You come into my office and demand that I follow you to Chatham, and all you can say is sorry? What do you think is going to happen, Dane? That I'll be swept off my feet? Nothing's changed. This was a big mistake." She planted her legs in a determined stance and crossed her arms, willing the tears in her eyes not to fall.

"That's kind of what I'm hoping for," he said.

Lacy groaned. "Not happening. You can't buy your way into someone's heart."

"A heart that can be bought is not a heart worth pursuing. Lace, I've experienced your heart, and I've never seen anything so pure."

"Stop it," she said.

"What?"

"Being so stinkin' nice to me."

Dane smiled again. "We should really talk about the details of the assignment, don't you think?" Dane parked the car and opened the door.

As soon as his foot hit the pavement, her heart skipped a beat. She dragged her eyes down his body, remembering the feel of him on top of her. Inside of her. *Don't. Don't. Don't.* Lacy took a step backward.

Dane reached into his pocket and handed her an envelope. "This has the address of the cottage I rented for you. It's right in Chatham, so you won't have to travel far each day. It's nice—right on Cockel Cove. I think you'll enjoy it."

She took the envelope. *You rented me a cottage? On a cove?*

"Directions to the marina are in there, as is a list of local restaurants, stores I thought you might enjoy, and the address of where I'm staying in case you need anything. You have my cell number, so…I guess I'll see you tomorrow morning at eight?"

Lacy stared at the envelope. This was all happening too fast. *I'm going to Chatham with him. He rented me a cottage.*

"Eight," she said. Maybe she should be alarmed at his assumptions and his planning, but she had just the opposite reaction. Dane was right there. He'd not only come for her, but he'd made all of the necessary arrangements to ensure they'd spend time together. After hoping he'd do just that for so long, now that he finally was, it was hard for her to turn away from it. She felt her eyebrows return to their rightful places. The tension in her jaw released.

"There's an itinerary in there. I'm not going to pressure you, Lacy."

"Like this isn't pressure?" Lacy rolled her eyes.

"This is a nudge in what I hope is the right direction. But don't worry. While I might nudge you to spend time in my presence, I'll never pressure you with regard to anything physical. In fact, let's make a pact, Lace." He smiled, his eyes dancing over hers.

I love when you say my name like that.

"Let's agree not to fall madly in love with each other. Okay? Because that would just be too much pressure," Dane said.

"Not to…" *No pressure. No falling in love. I already love him.*

"Yes, I think it's best. Let's just see if we can be friends. I felt something up on that dune that I still don't understand, and last night? Last night was torture. I'm so used to hearing your voice at night, even if by phone, that it was awful. I kept hearing the elevator doors shut and picturing your face, so upset, so angry." He reached out and ran his finger along her cheek. "I don't want to lose your friendship."

"Friendship." *Geez, get a grip. Say something intelligent. Do you really just want to be friends?* She was too confused to decipher if he was doing this as a safety net so she wouldn't feel pressured, or if he truly wanted to hang on to their friendship above all else. Either way, she was going to agree to whatever he asked because being near him only made her want to see him more. "Okay." *Ugh.*

"Okay?" His eyes lit up. "Okay, you agree not to fall in love with me?"

Lacy felt a smile push its way across her face. "I agree not to fall in love with you, but it's a two-way street. No falling in love with me, either." *What am I doing?*

"Deal," he said.

She watched him pull away and dialed Danica's number again, leaving another message. "You'd better call me. I think I'm in trouble."

Chapter Thirteen

"SO LET ME get this straight. You're in a cottage that he rented for you, in Chatham, and you're going to do what? Follow his itinerary for the next few days? And your boss let you go?" Danica asked.

It was nine o'clock in the evening, and Lacy was sitting out on the deck of the cottage that Dane had rented for her, the sound of waves breaking and the cool air coming off the water, sending memories flittering through her mind.

She pressed her cell phone to her ear. "Yup," she said. "He's got really good taste, too. This place is amazing. There are two bedrooms, two bathrooms, and—"

"Lacy," Danica interrupted.

"Yeah?"

"You left me a message like you were in real trouble. What am I missing?" Danica asked.

Lacy sighed. "I can't decide if this is all crazy. I mean, am I ignoring all sorts of red flags? Who does this type of thing? Rents a house, arranges for a week or two away from the office—and pays for it—for someone they like?" She walked down the steps to the beach and ran her toes through the sand. "I can't decide if this is incredibly romantic or insanely postal."

Danica laughed. "If it were a guy from any other family, I might agree with you, but the Bradens tend to do things all the way. Remember my wedding? The spa morning? The *island*, for Pete's sake?" Treat had arranged for Danica and Kaylie to have exclusive use of an island for their wedding.

"I guess. Yeah, you're right."

"Lacy, tell me what you're thinking. This morning you wanted nothing to do with him, and now you're down in Chatham. I know you had to go in order to save your promotion, but what does your heart tell you? What about the other women you were worried about?" Danica asked.

Lacy sat on the bottom step and buried her feet in the sand. She'd been thinking about that very same question all afternoon, and no matter how many times she put Dane's face with another woman, it never stuck. It didn't feel real. Sure, she felt a tiny pang of jealousy, and she'd love to know if he was with other women up until the day of the wedding, but in her heart she knew that even if he were, he'd made it clear that she was all he wanted now. She'd used the other women as an excuse, an easy way to end their relationship.

"I don't know. I've been thinking about what you said. Everyone has a past," Lacy said. "Am I being stupid? You can tell me if I am. I can take it. And I'm not saying that I want to jump into bed with him, either. I just feel like maybe..." Lacy didn't know what followed *maybe*, but she felt something there, and it felt a lot like hope.

"What about your fear of sharks?" Danica asked.

Shootshootshoot. "Ugh. You're right. There are too many obstacles. Signs. Whatever." Lacy climbed the stairs back up to the deck and watched a man walking toward the water. She settled into a chair and kicked her feet up on the railing.

"That's not what I'm saying. The therapist in me thinks you need to keep all of your worries in the forefront of your mind so you aren't driven by your emotions and you can make a rational decision. The sister in me wants to jump up and down, hug you, and celebrate the intense romantic nature of the whole thing. I'm riding a fine line here, Lacy," Danica said.

Her admission made Lacy smile. "That's exactly what I'm feeling."

"Listen. One thing you should think about is that phobias are usually irrational fears," Danica said. "Your case is different, of course, after what happened when you were little, but you can still manage that fear. When you feel that prickling of anxiety, you can remind yourself that you're fine and that you're in control, assuming you're in a safe place, of course, like on a boat. You have the power to control that anxiety. It might not feel like it right now, but you really do."

"The thing is, I know all of that. I get it. But when that panic attack hit, there was no talking myself out of it," Lacy said.

"I know, but you can still try. I also think you should take stock of your emotions. If you think about it, all those months of buildup leveled itself last weekend, and that, too, probably heightened your anxiety. Even if you don't think it did, I'd put my money on it. And to some extent, the only way to overcome your fears is to face them."

"Face my fears. Do you mean with sharks or with Dane?" Lacy asked.

"That's for you to decide. My gut says both," Danica answered.

"Maybe you're right. I don't know," Lacy said.

The man who had been walking sat in the sand, looking out

at the water. She went to the edge of the railing and looked more closely. Her pulse sped up. She sat back in the chair and whispered into the phone. "He's here."

"Who?" Danica whispered back.

"Dane. He's here, on the beach. He's sitting in front of the house." Lacy peeked at him through the slats in the railing.

"Are you sure?" Danica asked.

"Totally sure. Creepy or romantic?" Lacy asked.

"I don't know. Maybe he saw you on the phone and decided to wait until you were off. Where'd he come from?"

"I don't know." Lacy put her hand around her mouth to keep the sound from carrying. "Is he a stalker?" *Yeah right. It's my heart that I don't trust.*

"You're so weird. No, Dane Braden is not a stalker." Danica laughed. "Go out and say hello."

"Okay, thanks, Danica. I'll call you later." Lacy held the phone by her side and walked tentatively down each step to the sand below, then approached him. Dane leaned back, supported by his palms, his feet outstretched before him, crossed at the ankles. Her hands sweat despite the cool breeze coming off the water.

"Hi, Lacy," he said.

"Hi." Goose bumps raced up her arms.

Dane cocked his chin to the side, and the sweet look in his eyes softened her nerves. "Want to sit down for a sec?" Dane asked.

Yes! Lacy contemplated Danica's advice. *Keep all of your worries in the forefront of your mind.* She still felt pressured to be there, but as she looked back at the cottage and then at Dane, she couldn't maintain her anger.

Dane stood. He was wearing jeans, a T-shirt, and a thick

cardigan sweater. He reached for her, then pulled his hands back. "Lace," he said. His eyes caressed her; his voice soothed her. "I'm sorry that I've upset you. I just couldn't let us go that easily."

Us.

"I'm not here tonight to pressure you any further. I tried to call you several times, and when you didn't return my calls, I thought I'd just come over and make sure you got in okay."

"I...I've been on with Danica for a while, and before that I was showering, getting groceries. Sorry I missed your call." She chided herself for not checking her voicemail.

"No worries. Did you find the grocery store okay? Do you need anything?" he asked.

"I'm fine." She looked away, trying to ignore the pull in her stomach that was drawing her toward him. He'd forced this situation on her, and she struggled to remember that, to use it as a crutch to lean on when she felt herself being wooed by him.

"I know you're probably mad at me for pulling the whole thing with your boss, Lace, but I couldn't think of any other way to get you to even talk to me. You ignored all of my attempts to reach you, and I don't blame you. I mean, I know you're worried about the panic attack, and I know you're worried about what I said about other women."

Lacy's legs became weak. Fear crept up her limbs. "I don't want to talk about them."

"I know, but I do."

No, no, no.

"Can we sit? Please?" Dane motioned to the sand.

Lacy's heart was beating so fast that it stole her ability to think. She lowered herself to the sand and wrapped her arms around her legs.

"Lacy, if I were a woman and met a guy like me, I'd probably run the other way. I know I look like a player. Maybe I was one. I don't know. But I never thought of myself that way. I'm a guy who couldn't settle down. I've never had any interest in settling down. But things have been changing over the last few years. I've been changing. And when I met you, it was like I ran face-first into a brick wall. For the first time in my life, I stepped back and took a good look at my life. And I wanted to change, Lace. Because of you."

"I don't know what to say to that." In an effort to keep herself from falling into his arms and kissing him until she couldn't breathe, she said, "It seems rather convenient."

"Convenient?" He laughed. "Nothing about our relationship has been convenient. Look, I guess you'll either accept me for who I am...as a friend...or you won't. I was *that* guy. The keyword being *was*," Dane said.

"What does that even mean?" Lacy asked.

"It means just what you think it means. I was the guy who powered a boat into a new port, found a ready, willing, and able woman for a day or two, and then never looked back until the next trip. I can't change what happened in my past. I can only try to be the person I want to be moving forward," Dane said.

"I didn't know you were like that when we were talking for all those months. I wondered, but I didn't really know." As much as she thought she was past being hurt by that, once again she felt sick just thinking about him and other women. *What is wrong with me? Let it go!* She didn't want to have this conversation, and now she was stuck in it, and her frustration came out in her words. "That's just gross. How could you be like that?" Lacy asked.

"I don't know. I just was. But, Lacy, the last few months as we were getting closer, things changed," he said. "I'm not proud of what I did, but if we're going to move forward, even as friends, you have to accept all of me, the dirt along with the shine. I'm not that man anymore, Lacy, and had I met you ten years ago, I probably never would have been that man. You're the only woman who has ever had this effect on me. But this is me, Lace." He drew her chin up so she was looking into his eyes again. "The man who wants nothing more than to explore what's between us—even if we've agreed not to fall in love. I'm still the guy you talked to all those months. I'm the one who sang to you in an off-key voice when you didn't feel well and the guy who laughed with you while we watched *Young Frankenstein* on your television together on Skype."

Lacy dropped her eyes. Everything he said made her want to embrace him. She needed to forget about those other women. She cared about what she and Dane had, and what they had was turning out to be too big for her to walk away from.

"Look at me, Lacy. Please."

She met his gaze.

"It's me, Lace. I'm the same guy."

He was pouring out his heart and soul, and it dawned on Lacy that what he was doing wasn't easy. He looked at her with tenderness, and all those months of falling for him, phone call after intimate phone call, came rushing back and gripped her heart.

THE LOOK ON Lacy's face stopped Dane cold. She furrowed her brow, and her mouth was stuck in a half smile, half worried upturned line.

"That's who I was, Lace. Then I met you, and then those other nights, well, they became few and far between," Dane said.

"Okay. Can we change the subject?" Lacy asked.

"Yeah, I didn't come here to make you feel uncomfortable. I can go." He pushed to his feet again.

She looked up at him. "No, you don't have to go. I just don't want to talk about you and other women. Even if we're agreeing not to fall in love with each other, I don't want to be the friend that you tell about your…trysts." The pain in her eyes was palpable, and she shivered against the cold.

He slipped off his sweater and draped it around her shoulders. "Fair enough," Dane said. "I just want to be honest."

"Thank you," she said, pulling the sweater around her.

"Want to go inside to warm up?" he asked.

"Not really. I like it out here, but maybe we can move to the deck. A glass of wine might be nice. I bought some earlier," Lacy said.

They made their way up the deck, where they filled their glasses and settled onto the deck chairs. Dane felt like he was doing a balancing act. He'd restrain his desires to hold her, to touch her hand, or stroke her face if that's what it took to spend time with her, but there was no way he wouldn't try to get her to look past who he had been and see him for the man he was now, or the man he intended to be in the future.

"You know, you made a big mistake bringing me here. I'm not going to watch you catch sharks," Lacy said.

The defiance in her voice startled Dane, until he caught sight of the tease in her eyes.

"If you'd looked at the itinerary, you'd have seen that there is no shark catching on it. Tomorrow we're going to the library," he said.

Lacy finished her wine and Dane refilled her glass. "You're not getting me drunk, either. At least not drunk enough to do anything I'll regret tomorrow."

Dane's stomach sank. "You regret being with me?" he asked. He expected a lot of things, but regret for their evening together was not one of them. "Lacy, maybe I made a mistake bringing you here. I never imagined that you felt that way."

She tucked her feet beneath her on the chair. "I don't regret that evening," she said. "I'm just not going to jump into bed with you again."

"That's fair. We're not heading that way anyway. No falling in love, remember? And I don't sleep around anymore, so..." Dane said with a smile.

"I have to admit, I did miss talking to you last night," Lacy said. When she looked up at Dane, the moonlight caught her big baby blues.

"I did, too." He needed a safer topic to talk about. Talking about missing each other and jumping in bed together made his body crave her. He needed to talk about something that didn't make him think about what her lips tasted like or the way her eyes fluttered closed in the throes of passion. "Fred seems like he's a pretty nice boss."

"Yeah. He's great." Lacy laughed under her breath. "He's so smart, but really nerdy in that endearing sort of way. I can't believe you were able to rope him into sending me on a vacation."

"Oh, is that what you think this is? A vacation? You, my dear, are mistaken. This trip is to immerse you in the life of a Brave Foundation employee. This trip is to show you what we do, so you can sell us to the world." *And hopefully you'll find me irresistible along the way.*

Lacy emptied the remaining wine into their glasses. "Really? I had you pegged all wrong," she said with a smile.

"I doubt that. You probably had me pegged pretty close," Dane said. *Unfortunately.*

Lacy rested her head back on her chair and closed her eyes. Dane had the urge to pick her up and carry her inside, tuck her into bed, and let her fall asleep in his arms, safe and warm. Instead he pushed to his feet.

"I think I'd better go," he said.

Lacy sat up. "You don't have to go."

"I do. I promised you that I wouldn't fall in love with you, and spending too much time with you isn't going to help me keep that promise." Dane took her hand and helped her to her feet. Her body swayed with fatigue, and when she settled herself on her legs, her lips were inches from his. Dane inhaled the clean, fresh scent of her shampoo. His hands ached to touch her hips and pull her close, to draw her chest against his, his mouth to her lips. She looked up at him with wanting eyes, a look that was seared into his memory from their night on the dunes.

"I have to go," he whispered.

She licked her lower lip.

Dane stifled a groan. *Walk away.* "It was nice to"—*Man, I want to kiss you*—"see you." He shoved his shaking hands into the pockets of his jeans and took a step back through the doors that led from the deck into the house. "I'll see you tomorrow, Lacy."

She arched a brow. "Tomorrow," she said.

"Sleep tight." He walked backward through the living room, knocking into a chair and stumbling over it. Lacy raced to his side, catching his arm. They stood at the same time, measured movements, each watching the other. Need flashed in her eyes. *I'm not blowing this.*

"Thank you," he managed, then turned and headed for the door. "Tomorrow. Eight o'clock. See you then."

THE SECOND THE door closed, Lacy groaned aloud, then threw herself onto the couch.

"Shoot. *Shootshootshoot.*" She rolled onto her stomach and buried her face in the pillow. *What am I going to do? Go get him!* She ran to the front door and peered out the sidelight window, but he was gone. She leaned her back against the door and sank down to her heels. She'd wanted to kiss him so badly that she could practically taste the sweet wine on his breath.

Her phone vibrated. She read the text from Dane. *Good night, Lace.*

He was doing exactly what he promised. *No pressure.* She wanted to tell him to come back, but she sat frozen, staring at the text. Should she tell him to come back? Tell him she didn't want that promise?

After several painful minutes, she finally replied with a simple, *Good night.*

She stood in the center of the living room, waiting for another text. After ten silent minutes, she threw her phone on the couch. Then, spotting Dane's sweater on the chair out on the deck, she went to retrieve it.

The cool breeze felt good against her skin, which had become far too warm in anticipation of his touch. She lay back on the lounge chair and brought his sweater to her nose, inhaling deeply. She moaned at the delicious reminder, then inhaled his scent again. She settled his sweater over her chest and spread it out so it covered her whole torso. *He's so big.* The thought sent a shiver down low, and her mind conjured the image of him, his chest a wall of muscle as he lay perched above her. Naked. She lay there now, under the cover of the night, her mind playing with thoughts of the man she swore she'd never kiss again and wondering what tomorrow might bring.

Chapter Fourteen

THE NEXT MORNING, Dane popped out of bed with renewed energy. He moved through the plush cabin of Treat's forty-two-foot sailboat and into the galley, where he brewed a pot of coffee. Then he showered and called Rob. He raised an eyebrow when it went to voicemail.

"You lazy dog, asleep at seven. Enjoy your day off and call me if you want to talk. I've been thinking about you and Sheila, and I wonder if you shouldn't just take a day or two and go to her parents' house. Talk to her. Clear the air of whatever's going on. Anyway, man, I'm around. I'm here if you want to talk."

Dane's next phone call was to Lacy. He pushed her speed dial number on his cell phone, whistling as it rang. Then he hung up quickly. He didn't want to seem like he was hounding her. He hadn't been able to resist stopping by the evening before, and leaving was about the toughest thing he'd ever had to do. But a promise was a promise, and there was no way he'd be the one to break it. He had to prove himself to her, and he wanted to help her through her fear of sharks. He wondered if Hugh had been right and that her fear was really the crux of what was keeping her from accepting him back into her life. *At least last night was a start.* He loved Lacy, and he hated knowing that anything could steal her confidence. Sharks and the oceans had always been his passion, but what he felt for Lacy was far stronger than the love he felt for anything else. He was the perfect person to help her through this, and in the end, maybe Lacy would finally see him for the man he was trying to be. *The man I am.*

His phone vibrated with a text from Lacy. Dane smiled as he scrolled to read it.

Did you just call?

He laughed and texted back. *I called, then remembered ur not supposed 2 fall in love w/me so...*

He drank his coffee on the deck and stretched out in the morning sun. When his phone vibrated again, a thrill ran through him.

A hang-up will def keep me from falling in luv w/u. See u in 20 mins.

Dane watched Lacy walking toward the dock. Her blond curls hung thick and wild around her nicely tanned face. Her hips swayed as she walked in a short white skirt, and the navy sleeveless blouse and white sneakers she wore gave her a nautical look. Dane smiled. Every time he saw her, she looked even prettier than she had the time before.

She looked at the itinerary he'd given her, on which he'd written, *I'll be in the third slip from the left.* She wrinkled her nose, looked to the left, then to the right, then checked the paper again and scanned the boats one more time. She was so stinkin' cute that he was tempted to watch her for a few more minutes as she figured things out, but the urge to be closer to her was greater than his desire to watch her.

Dane stood and waved. "Lace!"

She waved and approached the boat with a smile. "This is

like the boat we were on in Wellfleet."

"Sort of. It's much smaller. Treat has great taste," Dane said.

"You stayed here? Why am I not surprised?" she asked.

He kissed her cheek. "Friends greet that way, so that's within my rights," he teased. He reached for her hand to help her aboard.

"I'm not going out with you to hunt for sharks," she said.

"I know. There are no sharks in coffee, and I don't think there are many sharks at the library, so we should be safe." He helped her onto the boat. "Home away from home," he said. "Coffee?"

"No, thanks," Lacy said, eyeing the cabin. Her cheeks flushed.

"Don't even think about it. I'm not going down in that cabin with you. The last time I did, you took advantage of me." He winked and was relieved when she smiled.

"Does the library open this early?" she asked.

"No, but I thought we might go to the fish pier, then maybe take a walk through town, and by the time the library opens, we'll be right there."

"Don't you have to work?" she asked.

"We tagged a big one Sunday, and yeah, I have to work, but I've reprioritized my duties, and I've dedicated the next few days to ensuring that you get a proper education on all things Brave." Dane finished his coffee and went belowdecks to wash his coffee cup while Lacy relaxed in the sun.

"Ready?" he asked.

"As ready as I'll ever be, I suppose," she said.

A few minutes later, they climbed into Dane's car and drove down to the Chatham fish pier. It was too early to see the fishermen bringing in their loads for the day, but Dane had already spoken to the pier manager and he had something else in store for Lacy.

They parked by the road and walked down a steep hill toward the pier.

"This is so cute," she said as they passed the fish market.

"That body of water is Aunt Lydia's Cove, and see that little island? It's Tern Island Sanctuary." He took her hand in his. "Come on." As they climbed the steps to the second-story deck of the fish pier, Dane let go of her hand, not wanting to push the limits.

It was harder than he thought it would be to not reach for her again. He had to remain strong. *No pressure.* He pretended not to notice the questioning look in her eyes.

She went to the far side of the upper deck. "Seals," she said, pointing to the little dark heads popping in and out of the water by the island.

"Yup. That's why they called the Brave Foundation. In the last decade, this area has gone from a seal population of two or three thousand to more like fifteen or sixteen thousand. Seals came, sharks followed," he explained.

"To eat the seals," Lacy said.

Dane shrugged. "They have to eat." They descended the stairs and walked toward the beach. "Are you okay to go out on the floating dock?" He watched her for signs of nervousness.

"Yeah. I should be fine," she said.

A fisherman stood on the edge of the dock with a bucket. He tossed fish into the water as Lacy and Dane approached, and within seconds, there were three seals arching their slick backs out of the water, then poking their enormous heads up and looking at the man with the bucket. He tossed a few more fish into the water, and the seals dove under the water to catch them.

"They're so cute!" Lacy said. "Look how big their eyes are. And look at that one over there. See how it's staring at us?" She moved closer to the fisherman. "Can you toss him one, please?"

Dane loved her enthusiasm, and as she moved toward the edge of the dock, he stood protectively by her side. She crouched down, and he knelt beside her.

"Dane, by saving the sharks, you're allowing these cute creatures to be their meal tickets," Lacy said.

"Lace, what's in the bucket?" he asked.

"Fish?" she said.

"Right. Are fish more important than seals?" he asked.

"Well, no."

"It's the natural food chain, babe. Seals eat fish, and sharks eat seals. We eat cows and chickens. It's the way nature works. Oceans are the most important ecosystem on the planet and our best defense against global warming. Sharks play a vital role at the top of the food chain by maintaining the oceans." He dipped his fingers in the water. "Did you know that oceans absorb most of the carbon dioxide that we put into the atmosphere?"

Lacy shook her head.

"The oceans convert that carbon dioxide into a large percentage of the oxygen we breathe. Destroying the sharks could destroy our oceans and our life support system," he explained. "That's just one example. There are a million reasons to save sharks, just as there are a million reasons to save seals."

"Thanks, Caleb," Dane said to the fisherman. Caleb waved, and Lacy and Dane headed back up the hill to the car.

"Don't you ever feel guilty saving sharks when you hear

about shark attacks?" Lacy asked as they climbed into the car.

"Nope. I feel horrible when someone gets bitten by a shark, but sharks are not looking for humans to eat. If they were, there would be a lot more fatalities," Dane explained. He drove around the corner and into Chatham.

"So you buy into the whole thing about sharks thinking humans on surfboards are seals?" she asked with a touch of sarcasm.

"Not at all. If sharks thought people were seals, they'd attack with torpedo-like speed. They're curious creatures. When they appear in stealth mode, their goal is not predation. They use their teeth like we use our hands. When they bite something unfamiliar, whether it's a person, a surfboard, or a license plate, they're looking for tactile evidence about what it is. It's like a test, a sniff from a dog. When they attack seals, they attack fast and hard, tearing them to shreds. It's a different approach. So, yeah, I feel terrible when someone gets bitten by a shark, just like I feel terrible when a person gets bitten by a dog, stung by a bee, or hit by a car, but you don't kill all dogs, snuff the bees, or dismantle the cars, right?"

Lacy nodded. "I guess I can see your point."

"I sound like I'm lecturing. I'm sorry. I get a little passionate about what I do," he admitted. "Rob and I spend a lot of our free time convincing people of the innocence of sharks. It's a tough business." Dane parked the car and they walked through the parking lot to Main Street.

"Where is Rob? I thought he was arriving Sunday," Lacy said.

"He's going through a hard time with his wife right now. To be honest, I'm a little worried about him." Dane thought about Rob's behavior on the boat. He'd have to remember to call him again later and see if he could get him to open up a little more about what happened between him and Sheila.

"Gosh, you've told me so much about him over the last year and a half that I feel like I already know him and his wife. If you're worried about him, maybe you should be with him instead of me."

"The enormity of your heart never fails to amaze me," Dane said. "I'll call him later. I left him a message this morning. You'll get to meet him when we go out on the boat later this week."

Lacy's eyes widened.

"Don't worry. We're not catching sharks," he assured her.

Lacy looked up and down Main Street. "I can't remember if I have ever been here. It looks familiar, but..." Lacy said.

Despite the early hour, tourists walked along the sidewalk of the small town. Lacy and Dane peered into the shop windows as they passed. Unlike other parts of the lower Cape, Chatham was known for its predominantly preppy undertone. Pink Izod shirts and lime green shorts were displayed in almost every clothing storefront window. They looked over the books in front of the used bookstore, then headed across the street to Kate Gould Park, where Lacy walked through the plush carpet of grass with wide eyes.

"I've been here. I know I have," she said.

Dane pointed to the white gazebo at the far end of the field. "To a band concert?" he asked. The Chatham Community Band had played every Friday night during the summers since just after World War II.

"Yeah," she said. "I remember old men in red outfits, I think. Gosh, I must have been so young. I haven't thought of that in...forever." Lacy smiled. "Come on." She took off running down the lawn to the gazebo and flew up the steps, then twirled around on the empty stage.

Dane jogged after her, watching the smile spread from her lips to her eyes.

"You know what?" she asked.

"What?" He wanted to touch her hand again, something, anything to let her know he was there for her, ready, willing, wanting to listen to whatever she wanted to share.

She sat down on the steps of the gazebo. "I don't think happiness is based on the amount of time you have with someone. I think it's all about how you spend that time and the enjoyment of each other while you're together," she said.

"You're thinking about your dad," he said.

"My dad wasn't around a lot because he had another family, as I told you," she said. "But when he was with us, me and my mom, he was present. He was there. Emotionally and physically *present.*"

"Lace." He wondered if she was making the same connection he was between her father's attentiveness and his own. "I'm sorry if it was difficult for you when you were growing up, and I'm sorry I wasn't physically there for you for so long." Dane watched her nod, then pull her knees to her chest. *The heck with keeping my distance.* He wrapped his arm around her and pulled her against his side.

"Thank you. You've heard me say it all before. I had a good childhood, but it was kind of weird knowing I had sisters that I had never met, and the kids at school thought I was making up stories." She sighed. "But my dad loves all of us, and I never had any hard feelings toward Danica or Kaylie even though he spent most of his time with them. After I met their mom, I felt horrible about what he had done, but he loves us all. Even their mom, I think. And my mom was always there for me. I guess that really made things okay for me." She touched his hand. "Even when you weren't physically there, Dane, I still felt your presence as if you were."

Dane closed his eyes, relishing in the confirmation of his attentiveness. He needed to hear that she at least recognized the efforts he'd made. It was another step forward.

"I think you're right, Lace. It's not how much time we have. It's how much we enjoy the time we have with others that matters." *Like spending time with you right now.* Her body was warm against him, and he had to remind himself that she was not his girlfriend. He hated that invisible line in the sand that he had to try not to cross.

"Are you thinking about your mom?" she asked. "You must miss her very much."

Dane's chest tightened. A familiar lump formed in his throat. He pushed past it and smiled down at her. "I do, Lace. Some days more than others."

She smiled up at him.

Not wanting to push his luck, Dane withdrew his arm from around her shoulder and pushed to his feet.

"Library?" he asked.

"Sure." She reached for his hand, and he helped her to her feet. Lacy didn't release his hand. Dane didn't pull away; he didn't grip her hand tighter. He let her control the connection between them.

When they reached the stone wall in front of the library, Lacy walked up the edge of the grassy lawn and balanced as she crossed the wall like a balance beam, still holding on to Dane's hand.

"I would bet that I did this when I was here, too," she said with a laugh. At the end of the wall, she released his hand as she stepped onto the grass and he climbed the steps.

"This is gorgeous," Lacy said as they passed through the entrance, lined with rich, dark wood, and crossed the Oriental rug to the hardwood of the library's main room.

Dane waved to the women behind the desk and then guided Lacy to a particular aisle and began pulling books from the shelves.

"What are we doing?" she asked.

"You got the itinerary," he said with a smile.

"All it said was, *library therapy.*"

"That's what we're doing. Come on." He carried a stack of books to a table in the back of the library and sat beside Lacy. "Here. Take a look at this and tell me three facts about tiger sharks."

"Tiger sharks?" She crinkled her nose.

"You're awfully cute. You know that?" he asked.

"I haven't been called cute for years. Thank you. You're not so bad yourself," she said.

He pointed to the book. "Tiger sharks." Dane watched her open the book, mumbling, *Tiger sharks,* under her breath. He opened another book and ran his finger down the index, then opened to a page and set the book aside. He did the same thing with the next three books in his stack.

"Okay, I've got it," Lacy said.

"You're a quick study. Let's have it." Dane sat back, expecting Lacy to rattle off the first three facts in the book.

"They grow to be fourteen to twenty feet. They're the fourth-largest species of shark; they're solitary creatures living primarily alone—which is really sad. They must get lonely. They can live almost one hundred years. They sleep with their eyes open." She stopped to take a breath, and Dane cut her off.

"Lace, their sleeping habits aren't in that chapter," he said. A flash of excitement ran through him. Maybe she wanted to overcome her fear as much as he wanted to help her.

"Oh, sorry," she said, biting her lower lip.

"If I didn't know better, I'd think that you have been researching sharks." Dane took the book from her and set another one in front of her.

"I might have read a few things about them," she admitted.

He pushed another book in front of her. "Have you read up on these?" he asked.

"Basking sharks?" She clenched her eyes shut, and when she opened them again, she let out a breath. "The *Cetorhinus maximus* grows to a length of thirty-five feet; their mouths can reach three feet in diameter, and—this is cool—they swim with their mouths open because they eat zooplankton. I would think they'd eat seals, fish, gosh, anything, but they don't. That's weird, right?"

Dane was still hung up on the fact that she knew the genus of the species. "Yeah, that is weird," he managed.

"And they're known as sunfish because they like to swim up by the surface. I swear, if I saw one, I'd be scared to death, but they have these tiny little rows of teeth." Lacy shook her head.

"Lacy, what's going on?" Dane asked.

"What do you mean?"

"Why do you know so much about sharks?" he asked. "I wanted to help you to understand sharks, but it sounds like you do understand them." He crossed his arms over his broad chest and leaned back in the chair.

"Oh, that," she said. "I sort of stayed up all night Sunday night reading about them. It was an accident. I was reading about a shark sighting off the Cape, and they mentioned Brave, and then I clicked around, and you know how the Internet is. A few hours later, I was neck deep in shark facts."

"Amazing," Dane said. The right side of his mouth lifted. "You are full of surprises. How do you feel about them now?"

"About sharks?" Lacy's eyes darkened. "What do you mean?"

Dane leaned forward and rested his elbows on his knees. His hands stilled a few inches above her leg. He was careful not to touch her, though he wanted to take her in an embrace and kiss that confused look from her lips. "In here." He touched his chest, just above his heart.

"I don't know. I guess I hadn't thought about it that way. I mean, until we were out on that boat together, I didn't even know how scared of them I really was. Now that I'm thinking about it, when I was reading about them, I had started out feeling a little creeped out by the pictures. But then, by the time I was ready to go to sleep, I was actively searching for more." Lacy looked at the books that lay on the table. "You know, I think it helped."

"You beat me to the punch," he said. "There's a new aquarium about half an hour from here. Would you like to go?" Dane asked.

"I don't know. It's one thing to see them in pictures and a whole other thing to see them up close and personal," Lacy said.

"It's up to you," he said.

Lacy's eyes met his and held his gaze. "You brought me here to try to help me understand sharks to help me with my fear, didn't you? Not to learn about Brave."

Bingo. "Is that such a bad thing?" he asked.

"It's about the sweetest thing a guy could do." Lacy reached over and touched his thigh. "Really sweet."

The muscles in Dane's legs twitched. "Babe," he whispered.

Lacy leaned in closer. "Yeah?"

Don't kiss her. Do not kiss her. Dane leaned forward. *No. No. No. No.*

Her perfume permeated his senses. Dane held his breath and pushed away. He moved her hand from his leg.

"I'm sorry, Lace. No pressure. We have a pact," he said. He leaned back, giving himself enough space to clear his mind. He was only human, after all. How close could he get without giving in?

"The pact. Right." She straightened her back. "Okay, Mr. Braden, what's next on the Brave tour?"

My lips on yours, my tongue in your mouth, my hands—Uh oh. Stop it. "Aquarium?" he asked.

"You're the boss," she said, holding his gaze.

They returned the books to the shelves in silence and left the library. Every glance stoked their fire, radiating tense, stifled passion between them as they made their way down the street toward the parking lot. Dane felt Lacy stealing glances his way, and it was all he could do not to turn and kiss her right there in the middle of the sidewalk. Instead, he picked up his pace. *Get to the car. I need a distraction.*

Minutes later, they were back at the car. Dane opened Lacy's door for her. She leaned her back against the car, fiddling with the edge of her blouse.

"I don't know what you're worried about. I'm not going to fall in love with you," Lacy said with that same dark challenge he'd seen the night before in her eyes.

Dane held the door with his right hand and clenched his keys in the left. He held her stare. Every breath pulled at his groin; every thought tightened the string of nerves that ran through his hard body.

Lacy looked up at him through a handful of curls that had fallen into her eyes, looking devastatingly sexy.

"Maybe you can't help yourself from falling in love with me…but I'm strong. You can put that hot body of yours against me every night of the week, and I'll be able to resist," she said.

Dane took a step closer to her. His mind raced, his body revved, and his hands had a mind of their own—reaching for Lacy, grabbing her by her slim waist and holding her tight, then pulling her hips against his. He leaned down and opened his mouth to settle it over hers. He couldn't fight the feelings any longer, especially when she was flashing a green light with every breath.

His lips hovered over hers. Lacy arched against him and wrapped her arms around his neck, pulling him closer. Her breath was hot; her chest pressed against him.

"Test me, baby," he whispered, and then he strutted to the other side of the car, gritting his teeth against his raging desires. Anyone looking would have seen a confident man in control of his emotions. Dane could barely see past his intense yearning for her or hear past the curses he tossed at himself for not kissing her. He slid into the driver's seat.

Lacy threw herself into the passenger seat and clicked her seat belt in place. She crossed her arms and stared straight ahead.

"You okay?" Dane asked in entirely too light a tone.

"Perfect," she said.

"You look…frustrated." He smiled to himself as he started the car. At least she was thinking about him now. His cell phone rang, and he let out a breath and answered the call from the unfamiliar number. "Excuse me," he said to Lacy.

"Dane Braden."

"Dane Braden? This is Officer Eaton of the Chatham police. Do you know of a Robert Mann?"

"Yes, he works for me," Dane said. Fear flattened his desire. "Did something happen?"

"We've detained him for disturbing the peace. Are you willing to come get him?"

Rob, what did you do? "I don't understand. Disturbing the peace?" Dane shot a look at Lacy, who watched him out of the corner of her eye.

The officer explained, "He was provoking a group of college kids."

"That doesn't sound like Rob at all. Are you sure you have the right guy?" Dane asked.

"Robert Mann, thick brown hair, graying. Stocky, five ten, mid-forties. Says he works for the Brave Foundation," the officer said.

"I'll be right there," Dane said. He ended the call and tried to mask his worry and irritation and tuck the guilt that was brewing inside him away. He should have forced Rob to talk and gotten to the bottom of this mess.

"I'm sorry, Lacy. I have to table our aquarium date. I'll take you to your cottage."

"What happened?" She'd switched out of frustrated mode, and now her eyes were laden with concern.

"My buddy Rob. He's at the police station. I guess he was provoking some college guys or something. I don't really know," Dane said.

"Want me to come with you?" She reached over and touched his arm.

"You don't want to deal with this stuff," Dane said.

"You probably don't, either. Maybe I can help in some way. Besides, I wouldn't want to go to a police station alone, and I don't mind going so you don't have to either."

He closed his eyes for a breath while he thought it over. When he opened them, Lacy was still looking at him, her hand still holding his arm. "Lacy, I don't know what to expect. This has never happened before," Dane said. "But he's been pretty out of it lately."

"I'd like to go. I'd like to be there for you."

Chapter Fifteen

AS THEY DROVE toward the Chatham Police Station, Lacy wondered if she was doing the right thing by tagging along. She wanted to support Dane, and she wouldn't want to face something like this alone, but as they neared the station, she envisioned all sorts of derelicts hanging all over her, groping her, reaching for Dane from within their meth-induced stupors.

One look at the benign nature of the police station and all that worry fell away. The station looked more like a school than a place for wayward criminals, with big white pillars holding up a newly painted and finely constructed A-frame porch, cream-colored siding with white trim, and beautiful gardens out front. Now more relaxed, Lacy followed Dane into the lobby, where he spoke to an officer through a glass window. They showed their identification; then he and Lacy were escorted down a hallway to another room. They sat beside a small table and waited.

"Why are we in here?" Lacy asked.

Dane shrugged. "I've never been through this before, so I have no idea, but I'd expect they need to go through some sort of out-processing procedure."

Lacy wondered how she would feel if Danica or Kaylie had

been detained by the police. Would she be mad that she had to come down and claim them? Embarrassed? Worried? Scared? Dane's mouth was pinched tight. Worry lines crossed his forehead. He leaned forward and steepled his hands over his mouth and nose and closed his eyes. Dane's concern for Rob's well-being was written not only in his face and evident in his actions, but the air around him was becoming heavy, too. Lacy wanted to reach out and touch him and remind him that he wasn't alone. She held back. She was so confused about what she should or shouldn't do with him, how she should act. She'd been the one to break away, and now she was the one wanting to come back together. In the Chatham parking lot, Lacy had wanted to kiss him so badly that she was sure she'd attack him if he didn't kiss her first. When he didn't, she was hurt, and that hurt turned to embarrassment, which had quickly morphed to frustration at being played for a fool. All those emotions running together and fighting to be heard didn't come close to the worry that consumed her heart right at that moment.

Her need to comfort him was too great. She touched his arm. "Are you okay?"

He nodded, then lowered his hands and shook his head. "I'm worried about Rob. He's drinking again. I should have seen it. The other day, Hugh thought he was hungover when he came to work, and I didn't want to see it. In all the years I've known him, Rob's never done anything irresponsible. Now this. I'm just worried about him. He's a good man. He's my friend, and I feel like he's slipping away. I wish I knew what to do."

"Let's find out how he is and what happened; then we can deal with the rest."

"We?" Dane asked.

Lacy shrugged. "Friends help friends."

He smiled. "Yes, they sure do. Thank you."

The door opened, and an older officer came in, followed by Rob and another, younger, officer. Dane shot to his feet and went to Rob's side. Rob's clothes were disheveled. He had a small cut beneath his eye, and he was favoring his left side.

"Rob, what happened?" Dane ran his eyes over Rob's face, holding tight to his arm. The veins in Dane's neck rose like thick snakes. His biceps flexed, and Lacy heard the silent accusation in the stare he pinned against the officer.

"He provoked a pack of college kids, got into a fight, and he lost," the older officer said. "We didn't book him, but we kept him overnight until he sobered up."

"You were drunk?" Dane asked. "Rob…"

Although his voice was harsh, the way he handled Rob, with one hand on his forearm, the other around his back, was gentle and nurturing. The word *protective* came to Lacy's mind.

Lacy had seen enough photos of Rob to know how out of character he looked now, unsteady on his feet and leaning against Dane.

"What happened to the other guys?" Dane asked. "Were they detained?"

"One of them, yes, but the others were released. Mr. Mann provoked the group. We don't take this type of thing lightly around here, and if it happens again, we will book him."

"Understood," Dane said. "May I take him home now?"

"Yes, sir. And, Mr. Mann, I suggest you steer clear of trouble, you hear?"

"Yes, sir," Rob said.

Before they walked out the door, the officer said, "Lemme ask you a question. You're the Brave Foundation guys, right?" He didn't wait for a response. "Don't you worry, going in the water with those sharks?"

Dane spoke to the officer, but his attention was still focused on Rob. "It's less risky than driving down the street. You know, you could choke on a chicken bone."

IN ROB'S MOTEL room, Rob stretched out on the bed with a groan. Lacy watched Dane pacing the small, tidy room. He ran his hand through his hair, glanced at Rob, and shook his head.

"Aren't you going to say anything?" Dane finally asked.

"I'm sorry, Dane. It's all this stuff with Sheila."

"I could have helped you, taken you to AA meetings, stayed with you, given you time off, whatever it took, Rob. How could you let it go this far?" Dane's deep voice softened, and his worried eyes washed over Rob.

"It sent me off the deep end, I guess. Those guys were talking about how they were going to go…" He glanced at Lacy, then back at Dane. "They were gonna go hook up with a few unsuspecting women, only not in a consensual sense. I lost it. I kept thinking of Katie and how I'm not there to protect her."

"Katie? She's four," Dane said. "You can't go around busting on guys. You've never done something like that before."

"No, I haven't, but I've never been separated before either," Rob said.

"You know, I didn't want to believe it when Hugh said you were hungover." Dane crossed his arms over his chest.

Lacy watched Dane's jaw clench as he stared down the man she knew he loved like a brother. The tension between the two multiplied in seconds; then Dane let out a sigh, and the tension deflated like a popped balloon. He sat beside Rob on the bed and reached for Rob's arm, meeting his friend's eyes with a softer gaze.

"Buddy, let's get you to a meeting. Is this why Sheila left?" Dane asked. He squeezed Rob's arm.

The harshness in his tone fell away, revealing the empathetic and genuinely caring man that Lacy had come to know. She felt a fissure in her resolve.

Rob shook his head and sat up. "I didn't start drinking until after she left. We were arguing a lot. I guess I hadn't realized how much. You know she's been all over me to stop tagging. I can't give it up. I can't do it, but..." His eyes welled with tears. "I can't lose her, man. She's everything. My kids...I can't lose them."

Dane wrapped Rob's burly body in his arms and placed one hand on the back of his head as he held him. "It's going to be okay. She loves you, Rob. This'll work out. You said you had all that stuff worked out about work. I never gave it another thought. Listen, take the week off, go to Connecticut and see her. Talk it out. She knows how much you love what you do."

You're holding him like you held me. She loved the way Dane and his family weren't shy about their emotions, and as she watched him with Rob, she sensed that Rob really was family to him, which endeared Dane to her even more.

Rob pulled back. "I can't. She said she needed space, but I'll call her."

"And a meeting?" Dane pulled out his phone and typed something in. "I'll find a local meeting we can attend."

"I went last night. I just messed up afterward," Rob said. "I can do this. I did it fifteen years ago, and I'll do it again."

"I'll go with you. You need support," Dane offered.

So available, willing to be there no matter what. Lacy felt her heart opening like a flower in bloom.

"Nah. This is something I have to do alone. It's all out in the open now, Dane." He looked away as a flush crept up his cheeks. "I'll call you if I feel like I'm falling off the wagon. I promise. I've only been back on the bottle for two days. I'm sorry, man. You don't deserve this," Rob said. He turned to Lacy. "I'm sorry, hon."

"Please don't apologize. I'm sorry you're having such a difficult time," Lacy said.

Dane pulled Rob close again and whispered, "I have faith in you. Just promise me this will be a good run, because I can't walk out that door knowing I could lose my best friend."

A good run. She'd come to know that expression from Dane, and she knew it meant he trusted Rob to make it through this. She swallowed past the lump in her throat and suppressed the urge to open her arms and join the closeness that was coming together before her.

"I promise you, Dane." Rob held his stare.

"And if you need me, I'm a phone call away. I can be here in minutes."

Dane closed his eyes and Lacy opened hers.

Chapter Sixteen

DANE'S EYES WERE still damp as they pulled away from the motel. Lacy looked away, not wanting to embarrass him and not really knowing if it was her place to say anything at all.

When Dane finally spoke, his voice was soft and his eyes were contemplative. "I never would have guessed that Rob would drink again. He was sober for fifteen years. Fifteen years. He had everything. They had everything. I just don't understand it."

"He did say something about Sheila wanting him to stop tagging, and love is a powerful thing," Lacy said. "People do stupid things to try to get the attention of those they love." *Or to protect them.*

"He'll never give it up. But she won't leave for good, either. She adores him. I've seen them together, and you can't fake what they have. I'm sorry about all of that."

"There's no need to apologize. Rob's your friend, and he's obviously having a hard time right now. Do you think you should stay with him? I can catch a cab back to the cottage. I really wouldn't mind," Lacy said. She felt as though she were seeing Dane through new eyes. The way he'd put away his initial anger and stepped up to the plate for Rob, willing to give up whatever he'd had planned to go with him to a meeting, and the way he embraced and comforted him, wasn't so different from the way he was with her. Where he had empathy for Rob, he had tenderness for Lacy. Where he had love for Rob, he had something strikingly similar, it seemed, for Lacy. She was beginning to see the man beneath the sexy exterior, and the man that was emerging was inching his way into her reluctant heart.

"I'm glad you came. It helped to know you were there," Dane said. "Do you want me to take you home or…?"

"I'm fine with whatever you want to do. If you want to be with Rob, I'd understand that. Don't plan around me; plan around him. He needs you," Lacy said.

Dane pulled over to the side of the road and leaned toward her. "Thank you," he said and pulled her close. "I'm lucky to have you as a friend."

Friend? Lacy was beginning to loathe that stupid pact. She put her arms around him, trying not to inhale his raw, masculine scent.

"Rob wants to be alone. He knows this route, and he knows what works best for him. I have to respect his wish to be alone." He pulled back onto the road. "We could still go to the aquarium if you're up to it."

Aquarium. A nervous flutter danced in Lacy's chest. "I'm not sure I can accomplish whatever it is you have in mind for me, and I know I don't want to go near any shark tanks, but short of that, I'd love to."

THE LOBBY OF the new aquarium included several life-sized models of different species of sharks. *Perfect.* Dane didn't intend to push Lacy past her limits, but Danica had told him that immersing her in as many shark-related activities as possible while watching her for signs of distress would help her overcome her fears. He knew several of the research staff, as they'd moved from other research facilities to open the new site, and he'd made arrangements for a private tour of the research area for Lacy. As much as Dane hated the idea of sharks being taken from their natural habitat, today he was thankful for the convenience.

"Lacy, we haven't spoken about what happened on the boat very much, and I'd like to understand what you're feeling," Dane said.

Lacy crossed her arms. "It's so embarrassing."

"Babe, everyone has fears. There's nothing to be embarrassed about."

She looked at him through her long lashes and said, "You don't seem to."

"Oh, yeah I do," Dane said with a laugh. *Like my fear of losing you.* "I never made it to see you. That was fear driven, even if I don't really understand it. It couldn't be driven by anything else. And every time I dive into the ocean with a great white shark, there's a type of fear that settles in. It's not all-encompassing, but it's there in the back of my mind."

"You were afraid to see me?" Lacy asked.

"I sort of explained that to you already. I was afraid of what I was feeling, and I didn't want to face you knowing the kind of guy I had been and knowing the type of man you deserved. But we're not falling in love, remember? So let's not go down that road. I want to know about you, Lace, not rehash who I am. I want to know what you're feeling…" *About me.* "About the panic attack you had."

"The more I read about sharks, the calmer I felt, but I have no idea if that was just the fact freak in me taking over or if it was something more," she said.

"But how do you feel, Lace? When you think of a shark, what do you feel?" Danica had told him to be hypervigilant about understanding where Lacy's emotions were during the desensitization process, and she'd been sure to throw a sisterly warning or two in for him as well. She'd said that with some patients who have hidden from their fears—or repressed them—for long periods of time, the actual fear might return fast and furious, but it can also fade quickly as the person comes to grasp the realization of how unfounded their fears are. Dane wasn't so sure it would be that easy.

"I guess I don't feel much. But that's probably going to be different if I go out on a boat and actually see a shark in the water. Danica says she thinks the panic attack might have been from more than just the shark, that I was probably anxious about seeing you after building up all those expectations. I need to face the fear." She shrugged.

The tension in his shoulders relaxed. "Well, we won't push things," Dane said.

"You're supposed to be immersing me in Brave's scope of work," she said.

Dane smiled. "I am; trust me. You'll see it all. I'll just make sure you're comfortable along the way. If you feel uncomfortable at any time—whether it's with me or just being here—let me know, okay?"

LACY WAS AWARE of being under Dane's scrutiny from the

moment they walked into the aquarium. The entrance was lined with models of different species of fish. Lacy ran her hand over each of them, feeling the cool ceramic beneath her hand, the roughness of the etched scales and the smooth glass of the eyes. She wanted to work through her fear, but the truth was, she was already feeling uncomfortable—and she didn't want to leave his side.

"A little different from the ones at the Frying Pan, huh?" Dane asked.

"Yes, these are more calming," she said. She felt Dane's eyes on her, watching her facial expressions, and when she approached the larger models, he moved a little closer to her. While the models of the fish didn't cause a rush in anxiety, having Dane beside her with his hawk eyes watching her sure did. Each time he moved closer, butterflies took flight in her stomach.

She looked down the hallway and noted that the models got successively larger as they neared the room with the main aquarium exhibits. She moved on to the next model. *Am I going to freak out when I reach the sharks?*

Dane stood before a fish that looked to be around three and a half feet long. "That's a tuna, believe it or not," Dane said.

"They're kind of cute, actually."

His arm grazed her shoulder, and Lacy looked up at him. She loved how tall he was, how thick his chest was, and when he reached for the fish, she remembered how good his strong hands had felt on her body.

"I don't think too many people would call this fish cute," he said. "But then again, you're not like anyone else I know."

Lacy felt her face flush. She looked down.

"Sorry, Lace. I don't mean to embarrass you. We're going to

be getting to the models of sharks next. Are you okay? How do you feel?"

"I'm okay," she said. She contemplated reaching for his hand. Even if she wasn't nervous yet, she could say she was.

"You sure?"

His eyes were so sincere that she couldn't breathe. She smiled. "Yeah, I'm okay."

"The next one is a black-tip reef shark," he said. He put his hand on the small of her back and guided her forward.

When the warmth of his hand touched her back, she realized how much she enjoyed his nonsexual touch. Who was she kidding? She enjoyed everything from the way he looked at her to the way he'd had to grit his teeth earlier in the day to keep from kissing her.

"See the distinctive black markings? These guys are fast," Dane said.

Her heartbeat sped up as she touched the model, but Lacy couldn't tell if it was from the model of the shark or from her thoughts of Dane.

Dane ran his palm over the model beside Lacy's hand. Their thumbs touched, and he looked down at her.

"You still okay?" he asked. His eyes darkened seductively as he held her gaze.

"I think so," she said. *This is harder than the darn sharks.*

"Should we move forward?" Dane asked.

Yes. Gosh, yes. His eyes held her captive.

He motioned to the next model, and Lacy let out a breath she hadn't realized she'd been holding. She forced her legs to move toward the next model. *Get a grip. He's doing something nice for you and you're acting like a schoolgirl with a crush.*

Lacy followed him to the next model, and when she reached

for his hand, it was to settle her nerves.

"I'm right here. You're okay." Dane held her hand tightly and took a step closer so his chest was against her back.

Lacy nodded. She leaned back enough to feel the security of him. She stared at the model of the massive bull shark.

"That's a bull shark. They're very aggressive," Dane said.

I'm okay. I'm okay. I'm okay. "One of the most common sharks," she said.

"Yeah, they're pretty common in warm waters," Dane said. He put his hand on her shoulder. "Are you okay?"

"Yeah, I think so," she said. "It was easier to deal with the smaller ones." She turned to face him. Her eyes were an inch from his chest. She looked up. "I know they're not real. I'm not sure why I'm so nervous." Lacy wondered if what Danica thought was true. Was she nervous because of Dane *and* the sharks, or was her heart beating double time solely because of one or the other?

"Let's not push it," he said. He nodded down the hall.

Lacy followed his gaze to a sign that said, MEET THE SHARKS. She had to know if the issue was Dane or the sharks. She hadn't had a panic attack yet, so maybe it had less to do with Dane after all.

"I want to try to go in, but I can't make any promises," Lacy said.

"I don't know if it's a good idea, Lace."

She drew on the advice Danica had given her. *I'm fine. They're in tanks. It's okay.* "I don't have to go all the way in if I get too nervous, but I think I want to try."

He held her hand. "It's your call, but if you feel anything bad, you have to clue me in."

"Dane, you've been watching me like a hawk. You'll know,"

she said with a smile.

He nodded. "Sorry."

"It's okay. I appreciate it."

"Okay." He took a deep breath, as if he were the one who was afraid of sharks. "You okay?"

"Yeah, I'm good," she lied.

He must have heard the hitch in her voice, because he squeezed her hand. She was thankful for the strength of his grip and the surety of him.

"You can hold my hand, but remember, no falling in love," he teased.

She nodded, unable to pry her voice from her lungs. *I'm fine. I'm fine. I'm fine.*

They walked past the last two models without stopping and followed the signs to the shark exhibit. Beneath the arched entrance, Lacy came to an abrupt stop. Before them was a wall of glass, behind which were three sharks passing in quick succession. Lacy held her breath and looked around. The tank wrapped around the room, and the sharks followed a pattern around the room and then back again.

"They can't touch you, Lace," Dane assured her. "I'm right here, and I'm not going to let anything happen to you."

Lacy's eyes were locked on the sharks as they swam a streamlined path around the tank.

"Lace?"

"Yeah?" I can't do this. "I think I'd do better if they weren't so big."

"Let's go, Lace. No need to push it," he said.

Face your fears. Lacy closed her eyes and said, "Ask me questions."

"What?"

She looked up at him, trying not to allow her urge to bolt to take over. "I can't walk in there, but ask me questions about them. If I'm concentrating on facts, it'll help." She held his arm with her other hand. "They can't touch me. I know that. But my heart is thundering, and I feel like I want to run away. Danica said to face my fears, and I'm trying my best. Please ask me questions."

"What kind of sharks are they?" Dane asked. His eyes never left her face.

He stepped closer, and Lacy leaned against his side to settle her shaking body. *Ohgoshohgoshohgosh.* "Um…" She squinted, concentrating on defining the species. She looked at their shapes, their noses, the breadth of their bodies, their tails. "Is that a sand tiger shark?" She couldn't release his arm to point to the shark as it glided past. She heard the trembling in her voice. *I'm fine. I'm fine. I'm fine.* "Right there, that one."

"That's my girl. Yes, a sand tiger shark," Dane said.

My girl. Lacy tried to concentrate on what he'd said instead of the anxiety that prickled her nerves. She narrowed her eyes and scrutinized the sharks.

"That one there, I know what that is." Lacy looked at Dane, then back at the tank. "That's a…Oh my goodness, I know this. Oh, oh, a nurse shark, and probably a female, based on the size."

"You're right on target, Lacy," Dane said.

When she looked up, she was met by his proud smile. She couldn't force a smile to her own lips, but she felt a swell of pride for not running away—or passing out.

"Are you okay?" he asked.

"I think so. If I'm distracted, it's much easier," she said.

"I'll try to remember that," Dane said.

She didn't miss the flirty note to his words.

"I think that's enough torture for today." It was a statement, not a request.

Dane guided Lacy down the hall. The minute they passed the large models, she felt the tension in her limbs ease.

He grabbed her arms with a beaming smile on his lips. "That was huge, Lacy. How do you feel?"

She blinked away the fear she'd felt when she was in the room with the sharks. "I…good, I think."

"I'm so happy for you."

He embraced her, and in his arms, the rest of Lacy's anxiety dissipated. *I love when you hold me.*

"Since you did so well, I want to show you something really special." Dane guided her away from the shark area, through another corridor, and stopped by a door marked PRIVATE.

"I'm not sure we're supposed to go in there," Lacy said. *If he thinks I'm going to make out in the aquarium, he's very wrong. I think…*

Dane knocked on the door, and a tall, thin woman with short brown hair opened the door.

"Dane Braden!" She opened her arms and Dane hugged her.

Lacy felt a pang of jealousy. Was this one of his other women? *No. He wouldn't bring me to meet someone he'd slept with.*

"Sara, this is Lacy Snow," Dane said, placing his hand on the small of Lacy's back. "Lacy's the one I told you about."

Told her about?

"Hi," she said. Dane's hand remained on her back as they followed the woman into what appeared to be a laboratory, and the intimate touch made her feel special.

"Sara and I have worked on several research projects together. She has the greatest job," Dane explained.

"So you're the one who turned Dane's heart into mush?"

Sara said with a bright smile.

Lacy felt her face flush, and when she looked at Dane, she realized that he was blushing, too. The streak of jealousy she'd felt fell away with the love in Dane's eyes.

"Yeah, I do have a pretty great job," Sara said with a bright smile. "Lacy, come look at this tank." She motioned to a tank that was about ten feet by six feet and the height of Lacy's chest.

Lacy peered into the tank, aware of Dane's hand, which now touched her shoulder blade. Inside the tank were two baby sharks. Lacy gasped.

"Dane, look," she said, reaching for his hand.

He came to her side. "I know. Incredible, right?"

"It's rare for shark pups to be born in captivity, and they usually perish, so we feel very lucky to have our newest little additions. These are sandbar pups. We're cautiously optimistic about them," Sara said. "I get to spend my days monitoring these little rascals."

Lacy didn't realize she was holding Dane's arm until they stepped back from the tank. "Can I touch the skin of one? I read all about how thick their skin is, and…" She looked at Dane and drew in a deep breath, still holding his arm. "I think I know how rough it is, but can I just touch it with one finger?"

Sara and Dane exchanged a glance. Dane nodded.

"Normally we wear gloves when we handle the sharks, but Dane explained to me what you've been through. I'm glad to see you are interested in understanding our misunderstood friends. If you wouldn't mind using that special soap"—she nodded at a sink to her left—"then yes, of course you may."

Lacy's heart raced. *I'm going to touch a baby shark. A shark!* She was surprised by her lack of fear. There were no tremors running through her, her nerves didn't feel like live wires, and when she looked at Dane and saw the concern in his eyes, she couldn't help but feel proud.

"Okay. I'm ready," she said.

Dane held out his hand, and Lacy took it, then went to the side of the tank. Dane's eyes never left her face, and knowing he was beside her gave her strength. *I'm fine. I'm fine. I'm fine.* Lacy held her breath. She reached her hand toward the water, and it began to tremble. She took a few deep breaths. Dane let go of her other hand, enabling her to hold the edge of the tank; then he rested his hand firmly on her lower back once again.

"Go slow, Lace," he whispered.

Lacy nodded, reaching forward again. She broke the surface of the water with her index finger as the pup swam beneath, brushing its rough skin against the pad of her finger. She pulled her hand back to her chest with a gasp, her eyes still trained on the water.

Dane leaned in closer. She felt his warm breath on her cheek. "I'm right here."

She nodded, then looked at Sara. "May I? One…one more time?"

Sara nodded.

Dane stepped closer, his body against her side, one hand on the small of her back, the other on her hip. She reached in again as the pup swam below, and this time she reached down and closed her eyes. She shivered as the unfamiliar roughness marred the tender tip of her finger; then she drew her hand out of the water slowly.

"You're trembling," Dane said. He wrapped her in his arms and held her against his chest. His heart beat against her cheek. Lacy closed her eyes, and pride filled her heart. *I'm fine. I did it, and I'm still okay.* Dane pressed his arms tighter around her back, and when she looked up, his eyes were suspiciously damp.

Chapter Seventeen

"THAT WAS THE most incredible afternoon. I touched it, Dane. I touched the baby shark, and I didn't panic. I didn't pass out or run away in tears. I did it," Lacy said.

They had spent another hour at the aquarium, and now they were on their way back toward Chatham. The sun hovered just behind the tree line, casting a pinkish gray over Route 6. Lacy hadn't stopped talking since they'd left the research area, and to Dane, it was music to his ears. The enthusiasm in her voice mirrored the enthusiasm she'd had when he'd first met her in Nassau.

"I'm so happy for you, Lacy," he said.

"For me? How about for you?"

Dane glanced at her. She'd bundled her blond curls in one hand and secured it with an elastic band at the nape of her neck. The blue of her eyes was vibrant and alive with hope. "Oh, Lace, you're so beautiful," he said, and instantly regretted it. He was afraid she'd pull away from him and quickly got back on track. "Sorry. What do you mean *for me?*"

"Dane, you can tell me you think I'm pretty," she said. "Thank you. I was surprised that you had told her about me."

"You've been my world since the day we met. I told everyone about you, Lace," he admitted.

For a minute she just looked at him, like she didn't know how to respond or was waiting for him to say more. When he didn't say anything more, she said, "This means I can probably get over whatever fear rattled me so badly on the boat."

Dane wanted to take her in his arms and allow the joy he felt about her progress to sweep them both away, but he didn't trust himself not to get carried away with her and push their friendship into a relationship, and that was not his call to make. He was determined to let her make that decision without any pressure.

Instead, he said, "That's true. As I said, I'm happy that you're conquering your fears. It will allow you to have a fuller, richer life, not hamstrung by fears."

"Thanks…I think," she said.

He could feel her eyes on him as he drove toward town. "Should I drop you at your cottage?" he asked.

"I guess."

He heard the disappointment in her voice. *How am I supposed to navigate this? I want you to fall in love with me, but if I act on my feelings, I'll scare you away.*

"I want to check on Rob," he said.

"Oh, good idea," she said. "I hope he's doing okay."

"Me too," he said.

They drove in awkward silence to Lacy's cottage. He walked her to her door, wishing he knew how to bridge the gap that had formed between them over the past twenty minutes.

Lacy's keys hovered over the lock. She spun around and looked up at Dane. "So, what now? I just follow the itinerary tomorrow?"

"Yeah, that works." He tried to sound nonchalant, but he

really wanted to take her in his arms and kiss her until she couldn't speak.

She nodded. "Tomorrow's the Brave Exhibit?"

"Yeah," he said.

She nodded again, looking down at her keys. "Dane," she said.

"Hmm?" *Invite me in. Let's have some wine, laugh, talk. Anything. Just don't say good night.*

"I have to check in with my boss tonight. I'll tell him that it's a good fit after all." She turned and unlocked the door.

Dane's eyes dropped to the curve of her hips, but his mind was still playing over her words. *A good fit after all.* "Thanks, I appreciate that. I know today was stressful, but if overcoming fears was easy, no one would need immersion therapy." Dane cringed.

"Immersion therapy?" Lacy drew her eyebrows together.

"I might have called a friend and asked her how to help you through your fear." Dane looked away, focusing on a tree in the front yard. The muscles in his arms and neck tightened, as he expected her to be angry.

"You did that?" It wasn't an accusation.

He turned to face her. A breeze swept curls across her cheek, and he reached up and tucked them behind her ear. She closed her eyes for just a second as his finger brushed her cheek, and she smiled, easing his worry.

"I did. I wanted to help," he explained.

"Dane, I can't believe you did that. That's really thought-ful."

She touched his arm, and his body cried out to embrace her again, but he was too nervous now. *Baby steps.* "I'm glad you're not upset with me."

She shook her head. "Just the opposite."

He smiled. "Good. Tomorrow we're going to see the Brave Exhibit. No live sharks. I promise," he said. He kissed her cheek, trying to ignore the pull in his groin caused by the scent of her. "Good night, Lacy."

He turned to leave, and as he descended the front steps, she called his name.

"Yeah?" he asked.

She held his gaze for so long that Dane almost crossed back the way he'd come to kiss her again.

"Thanks," she said. "For everything."

He nodded. "Sure. I only want you to be happy." He went to his car and watched as she went into the cottage and closed the door behind her. He hated the idea of leaving her again, but he took solace in the fact that he'd helped her today. *At least that's something.*

He started the car, and before he drove away, he called Rob.

"Hey, Dane," Rob said. He sounded rested and much stronger and clearer than he had when Dane had left him earlier in the day.

"Hey, buddy. How are you feeling?" He rubbed his temples with his thumb and index finger in an attempt to focus on Rob instead of how much he longed for Lacy.

"Fine. Good, in fact. I called Sheila. She's going to bring the kids to the Cape," Rob said. "And I went to an AA meeting earlier. I really appreciate your help, Dane, and I'm not going to let you down. I know how to slay this monster."

Thank heavens. "That's great, Rob, and I'm here if you need me. All you have to do is call. Day or night. I've got your back," Dane said.

"You always do. Thanks, buddy. Are we sailing with your

pretty lady tomorrow?" he asked.

Dane smiled and looked at the cottage. "Why don't you spend tomorrow with Sheila and the kids. Get on better footing. We'll go out the next day."

"Man, that would be great. I'll call Sheila now and let her know. All this came on so fast and stole my feet out from under me, Dane, and I'm really sorry. Actually, it seemed to come on fast, but as Sheila pointed out, she's been after me for two years to leave the business. I've just been ignoring it," Rob said.

"And?" Dane had the feeling Rob was about to drop a bomb he didn't want to hear.

"Nothing. We're working it out."

Dane let out a relieved breath and pushed away the part of him that wanted to nag him for a clearer explanation. He knew when Rob was ready, he'd clue him in on the details.

"Hey, Dane."

"Yeah?"

"Here's to a good run," Rob said.

"Yeah. A good run." *With Lacy and with you.*

LACY'S STOMACH WAS doing flips. She'd hoped that Dane was going to at least try to kiss her goodbye, but he made no move toward her. He was a perfect gentleman. She hated the stupid promise she'd made. Why had she ever agreed to it? But she wasn't going to be the one to break it.

She sent an email to her boss and let him know that things were going well and she was enjoying the assignment. Then she took a quick shower to clear her mind. Everywhere she looked, she saw Dane. She checked her phone for messages, but he hadn't called or texted. *Shoot.* She had to stop thinking about him. Lacy took her phone out to the deck and called Danica.

"Hey, sis, how's it going?" Danica asked.

"Great and sucky at the same time," Lacy said. She flopped onto a deck chair.

"Give it to me straight," Danica said.

"Oh, Dan. Dane's wonderful. He's so darn nice and, well, you know how he is. That's not new. We agreed not to fall in love with each other, and now it's all I can think of. He had to bail his friend out of jail and—"

"What?" Danica said.

"Yeah, remember I told you about his best friend, Rob? You saw the pics. I emailed them to you months ago."

"Oh, yeah, the brown-haired shark hunter guy," Danica said.

Lacy looked out at the water, remembering the other night when she'd found Dane sitting in the sand. She smiled at the memory.

"Yeah, well, he's going through a rough patch with his wife and he's a recovered alcoholic—well, he was. His wife left him, and he started drinking again. He started a fight and got picked up by the police. The whole thing was really sad. The guy's in his forties, and he's so broken over things with his wife. But Dane was so emotional. He's always said that Rob was like a brother to him, and today I saw it. He was so careful with him. Protective. He even offered to go to AA meetings with him," Lacy said.

"I think Dane's a good guy, Lace. It sounds like he's really trying all around, but I thought you were supposed to be learning about his business."

"I am. He took me to the library, and he was so cute. He

had all these books about sharks, and he wanted me to read them, to get familiar with the sharks. But, Danica, I'd stayed up all Sunday night reading about sharks for some stupid reason. Anyway, he took me to a new aquarium, and I pet a baby shark. You'd be so proud of me. I couldn't go into the shark room, though. Totally freaked me out. I stood in the doorway, clinging to Dane's arm," Lacy said.

"No panic attack?"

"No, but I wasn't in the room with them. I stood in the doorway."

"That's awesome, Lacy. That's a big step, but don't be surprised if you have another panic attack at some point. It would be surprising if you were able to desensitize yourself in a day," Danica said.

"Oh, and he got advice on immersion therapy to help me through my fear."

"Yeah, about that..."

"Danica Joy, please tell me that you did not do what I think you did." Lacy was angry and overjoyed at the same time.

"I didn't do anything but answer a phone call...and maybe give a little advice," Danica admitted.

"He called you?" Now the picture was becoming clearer. "So you were the friend he mentioned. And you didn't call me and tell me? How could you?"

"Lacy, if I had told you, you'd have been angry with me, and it's obvious how you feel about him and how he feels about you. Besides, I did more than just give him advice. I told him that if he hurt you, Blake would kill him."

She heard the smile in Danica's voice. "That's just great. So he went behind my back to my *sister*." Lacy wanted to be furious at his sneakiness, but she couldn't. No one would do what he did unless he really—*Oh wow*—loved her.

"Lace, not many guys would go that far. I was impressed," Danica admitted.

Lacy sighed. "Yeah, I guess I am, too. He's not like any other guy I know. That's kind of what I wanted to ask you about. I've been thinking about everything, and I wonder if you might be right, that my panic attack wasn't just about the shark. Could it really have been about *everything?* The shark, the memories, and the idea that after all that time I was finally with Dane? Could it have scared the crap out of me?" Lacy asked.

"It could have, but, Lace, you have to be careful. You can't just assume you'll be fine on a boat when he's tagging. That's really dangerous," Danica reminded her.

"I'm not going tagging with him. Don't worry. Danica?" Lacy asked.

"Yeah?"

"I really, really like him. I feel like all that time apart set us up to just fall in love the moment we saw each other face-to-face. I know that's crazy." Lacy leaned against the deck rail and ran her finger over the rough wooden edge.

"It's not so crazy. You guys shared your lives. You just did it from afar. You shared your secrets, Lacy. You shared your hearts. So in a way, you did set yourselves up for just that," Danica said.

"But shouldn't I feel something about the fact that he was with other women during that time? How can someone be intimate with another person when they have feelings for someone else? I just don't get that," Lace admitted.

"Oh, Lacy, intimacy is so different from what you're defining. Sex is sex. It can be meaningless, filling-a-gap or easing-a-frustration sex, or it can be intimate and loving sex. Sex is not exclusive to love," she said.

Lacy sighed. "I know, but…"

"From what you've told me, he's not trying to hide who he was. He's being honest and, Lacy, honesty is the most important thing in a relationship." Danica paused, then said, "Haven't you ever done anything in your life that you would be mortified if someone found out about?"

"No," Lacy said.

"Nothing? Ever? You never cheated on a test or made out with a teacher? You never had sex on the roof of your high school? Or fantasized about your best friend's father?" Danica asked.

"Geez, Danica, what kind of people did you help when you were a therapist? No, I haven't done those things," Lacy said, then flopped into a chair.

"Well, you really are perfect, little sister," Danica teased. "Listen. Maybe you're right. Maybe you're not cut out to be with him no matter what you feel for him. It takes a really strong, special person to forgive a past that is so different from her own."

"You make it sound like I'm conceited or I think I'm above him somehow," Lacy said.

"No. I'm just being realistic. If you had done some of those things, you might understand the whole using-sex-as-an-escape thing, but you didn't, so to you it's foreign. How did you ever forgive Dad?"

Lacy pictured Danica's serious dark eyes watching her, waiting for an answer. "He's my father. I didn't forgive him so easily, and I'm not sure I have completely forgiven him yet. I have my moments when the whole thing still upsets me, but then I realize that he just happened to love two women…at the same time."

"But isn't that worse than not loving any and being honest about it? He's not living a double life, unless…did you guys say you were exclusive for all those months?"

"No, Danica, you know we didn't." Lacy stood and paced.

"Then it sounds to me like you need to make a decision. You're either in the relationship and willing to forget his past—really forget it, as in, not bring it up every time you have an argument—or you're out and you let him go and move on."

"Sheesh, sometimes I hate you," Lacy said.

"That's what big sisters are for. What are you doing tonight?" Danica asked.

"It sounds like I'm making a life-altering decision."

Chapter Eighteen

BACK ON TREAT'S boat, Dane stepped out of the shower, wondering if he should have made a move toward Lacy. Her comment about her boss gave him hope, but she hadn't invited him in after they spent the day together. She hadn't made any innuendos either. Now he was stuck on the boat missing her. Dane wasn't used to having to chase women, much less having to refrain from chasing them. *Enough of this.* He picked up his keys and headed for the car. He was the man in the relationship, and it was time he acted like it. If she didn't want to be with him, she'd have to tell him to his face. Tonight. *Now.*

His phone vibrated. He snagged it, hoping it was Lacy, but it was from Hugh.

Dane read the text. *Did u fix things w/Lacy?*

Dane smiled and texted back. *Trying. Thanks 4 pushing me.*

He climbed into the car and a few seconds later his phone vibrated again.

Can I come over? Confused, he scrolled back on the message and realized it was a text from Lacy. *Lacy!* He texted back. *Of course. What's wrong?*

Another text rolled in from Hugh. *She'll come around.*

Dane didn't answer his text. He was too worried about

Lacy. He pushed speed dial, and Lacy answered on the first ring.

"What's wrong?" he asked.

"Nothing...I just...I didn't feel like eating dinner alone," she said.

He leaned back against the seat and closed his eyes, sighing with relief. *You won't fall in love, huh? I must be doing something right.* "Why don't I come get you and we'll go grab a bite."

"You were just here. I can come there," she offered.

Waiting will be torturous. "I'm in the car. I'll be there in a few minutes." He put the phone on speaker and turned the car around. "What are you hungry for?"

"Your company."

DANE STOOD ON Lacy's front porch with a bottle of wine and his leg bouncing with too much nervous energy to calm. He smoothed his black, short-sleeved button-down shirt against his stomach and checked the drawstring on his linen pants. *What is taking her so long? Maybe she's in the shower. Maybe she changed her mind.*

He knocked again, and the door swung slowly open, revealing Lacy in a dark blue, off-the-shoulder minidress and sandals, a nervous smile inching across her lips.

"Hi." She leaned against the door, looking up at him through wayward curls that hung in front of her eyes.

"You look beautiful," he said. *Why am I so nervous?* He kissed her cheek and couldn't miss the coconut scent of her shampoo. "Mm. You smell nice, too."

"So do you," she said, closing the door behind him.

The glass doors to the deck were drawn wide open; the sheer

curtains blew in the breeze.

"You brought wine," she said, eyeing the bottle. "Let's open it."

He followed her through the living room to the connecting kitchen. His eyes were drawn to the fabric stretched across her hips, the fine outline of a thong evident beneath the sheer material. He felt a familiar tightening between his legs, and he drew his eyes away from Lacy, settling them on the counter beside her.

"I'm glad you called," he said.

She handed him a corkscrew, and he went to work opening the wine, a much appreciated distraction.

"I can never open those things. The corks just get me all befuddled," Lacy said. "I'm always afraid I'll drop the bottle or I'll stab myself with the corkscrew."

"Well, consider me your personal cork remover," he said, trying not to stare at the silky, tanned skin of her shoulder. "How did you open the wine last night?"

"Screw top," she said.

He lifted his eyes and met hers. She shrugged. "A girl's gotta do what a girl's gotta do."

"I guess so," Dane said. He filled their glasses, and they went into the living room and sat on the couch. When Lacy sat, her dress hiked up even farther, revealing the crests of her thighs. She angled her knees toward Dane, and he stretched one arm over the back of the couch.

"I was really proud of you today," he said. "I'm sure that wasn't easy for you, seeing the sharks, touching the pups."

Lacy looked at her glass; then she looked up at Dane through her curls. He reached over and used one finger to draw the curls from in front of her eyes.

"I was proud of myself, too," she said. "So...you called Danica?"

Dane closed his eyes. Danica had promised not to tell Lacy unless she asked. *I guess she asked.* He took a deep breath, ready to be chastised for going behind her back—again. He looked her in the eyes. "Yes. I'm sorry, Lace, but I wanted to help and she knows you so well and she was a therapist. I know you trust her, so…"

Lacy smiled, then looked down. "It's okay." She lifted her eyes to his. "I'm glad you did. That means you care, but just so you know, I don't like things to be done behind my back. Next time, just tell me or suggest it to me."

He let out the breath he'd held in as she spoke. "I talked to her before you even agreed to see me. I couldn't have mentioned it to you, but I probably should have mentioned it before you found out on your own."

"Dane, you do all these wonderful, romantic things for me, and honestly, I love them. But if we ever…you know…move past our friendship to something more, then I won't ignore your calls and you can't go behind my back. Deal?"

He'd agree to just about anything for Lacy, and the fact that she even mentioned moving past their friendship gave him hope. "Absolutely."

"And I'm not mad, so there's no reason for tonight to be weird." Lacy took a sip of her wine.

Dane wasn't used to anything even closely related to real dates, and even though this wasn't a traditional date, it was still completely different from anything he was used to—and now, no matter what she said, it had a layer of discomfort added to it. Dane was used to showing up, making a move, and moving on. He wanted so much more with Lacy, and if that meant facing the things he'd done, like calling Danica, then so be it. The silence in the room was broken only by the swishing sound of the curtains and the faint sound of the waves breaking on the shore, and it was heightening his nerves.

"Want to turn on the stereo?" Dane asked.

"Yeah, sure." Lacy turned on a local station, and when she returned to the couch, she sat closer to Dane. "I was hoping we could talk." She ran her finger around the rim of the glass, then stuck her finger in the wine and brought it to her mouth. She licked the sweet nectar from her finger, then drew it out of her mouth slowly.

Dane bit back a groan. When she licked her lips, he let out a heavy breath.

"Talk?" Dane repeated. *You're killing me.*

"Yeah." She shrugged. "We know so much about each other, but there's stuff we don't know. It might be fun to find out more about each other." Lacy placed her palm on the couch and leaned toward him. "Unless there are skeletons in your closet, of course."

"I'm an open book, Lace. I'll tell you anything." He downed the rest of his wine. If she moved any closer, he'd have to kiss her. The blouse of her dress bloomed open, and Dane couldn't stop his eyes from dropping to the groove between her breasts. She leaned back, just enough to right the neckline. Dane knew just how good her body felt, and knowing she wasn't wearing a bra made it even more difficult for him to quell the urges that had been building all day.

Dane refilled his glass and Lacy threw her head back and finished hers in one swift swallow, then held the empty glass out toward Dane.

"Okay, here goes. Truth or dare?" she said.

"Truth or dare? I thought we were talking." He arched a brow. *I like where this is going.* He could think of about ten things he'd like to dare her to do.

"This is more fun. I just thought of it. Okay, truth…or dare?" She finished the wine he'd given her, and he took his cue and did the same.

This is getting interesting.

Before he could reach for the bottle, Lacy had it in her hand and refilled their glasses.

"Truth," he said, although he was dying to know what her dare might be.

"Okay, this is an easy one. Favorite ice cream?" she asked.

"That's not as easy as it sounds. My favorite depends on where I am. If I'm at Ben & Jerry's, it would be Cherry Garcia, but if I'm at Baskin-Robbins, it's definitely mint chocolate chip."

Lacy twisted a lock of hair around her finger. "Good choices," she said. "Your turn."

Dane watched Lacy finish her wine. "Are you okay, Lace?"

"Yeah, just a little nervous. Wine helps," she said.

"Why are you so nervous? We just spent the day together," he said.

"Truth?" she asked.

"That's what I'd prefer," he answered.

Lacy slipped her feet from her sandals and used the toes of her right foot to scratch the top of her left. "Because I'm trying really hard not to fall for you."

He finished his wine in one gulp. Too nervous to figure out if he should tell her that he felt exactly the same way and too afraid that if he did, she'd get scared and send him away, he said, "We have a deal. No falling."

"I know," she said.

"That wasn't my question, right? Truth or dare?" Dane couldn't think of a single appropriate question. He mulled over the ones that were racing through his mind. *May I kiss you? Can I run my fingers through your hair? How long do I have to wait to touch you?*

"Dare," she said, narrowing her blue eyes in a seductive, wanting gaze.

Oh, man. Dare? What was appropriate for a dare? All Dane could think of were the dares they used to give each other as kids. *I dare you to streak across the yard. I dare you to peek into the girl's locker room shower window. I dare you to steal a beer from Dad's stash.*

"Dare it is," he said. "Lace, I'm not very good at these games." She'd turned into some type of seductress, and now that the tables were turned, he was afraid to dare her to do the wrong thing. Should he ask for something sexual? Is that what she'd expect? Or maybe she was just acting sexy but didn't want him to go that far.

"Go on, but be gentle. I haven't played this in twenty years," she said.

"Okay. I dare you to get another bottle of wine from your fridge." *What the heck was that?*

Lacy smiled. "I can handle that."

Good. Now I can choose dare and see where we're headed. He watched her carry another wine bottle back to the living room. Each sway of her hips pumped more desire through his veins. She sat beside him, her leg touching his thigh.

She filled the glasses and handed him one.

"I thought you wanted to eat dinner," Dane said.

"I do," she answered. "Okay, your turn. Truth or dare?"

He locked his eyes on hers and said, "Dare."

Lacy pointed at him and lowered her chin, looking at him with a seductive leer. "Oh, you naughty boy." She scooted away from him and set the heel of her foot in the space between his thighs. "Foot rub?" she asked.

Dane could hardly breathe. Who was this little sex kitten that had inhabited sweet Lacy? "Foot rub?" he repeated.

She smiled. "Yup. That's the dare."

That tells me nothing. Dane took her petite foot between his hands and began to knead the arch of her foot, pushing his thumbs up the center of her arch, then massaging the sides and tops and moving his hands up her ankle. Lacy leaned her head back on a pillow.

"Oh yeah, that feels good," she said in a throaty voice.

He moved his hand up, caressing the soft skin of her calf beneath his strong hands.

"Lace?"

"Yeah," she whispered, her eyes still closed.

"Truth or dare?" he asked. *I'm not going to be the one to break the pact.* She had to make the first move; otherwise he'd always wonder if he'd pushed himself on her.

"Truth."

"Why did you ask me here tonight?"

Her smile faded, and she lifted her head. Her dress bloomed open again as she leaned forward and took a long drink of her wine. "I changed my mind. Dare," she said.

"I'm not sure changing your mind is fair," he said.

"You can dare me anything you want," she said with a flutter of her lashes.

Dane clenched his jaw. He had a heck of a list for her. He moved his hands up her calf, past her knee, to the warm skin between her thighs, and caressed her there. She leaned back on her elbows, her body open to him. Her head fell back, and Dane crawled over her. She opened her eyes, and he lowered his face until her exhalations became his oxygen.

"I dare you to tell me what you really want from me," he challenged.

"Everything," she whispered. "Everything, Dane. I want everything from you."

He lowered his mouth to hers, kissing her ravenously. She tasted so sweet and familiar, all his pent-up desires rushed forth, leaving him breathless. He reached over his back with one arm and tugged his shirt over his head. His body was on fire as he lowered his mouth to her chin, nipping at the hard edge of her jaw.

A bold look rose in her eyes, and just as quickly, it turned dark and seductive. "Truth or dare?" she said in a sultry voice.

"Truth?" he asked.

"How long has it been since you were with another woman, exactly?"

He closed his eyes. He knew exactly how long it had been. He'd stopped sleeping with other women three months after meeting her. But he couldn't tell her that. What kind of man relies on self-gratification to satiate a need that's driven into him night after night by a woman who's too far away to touch?

"Lace, please," he said.

"I could give you a dare," she said. "But I prefer the truth."

A defeated sigh escaped before he could stop it and he said, "More than a year."

"More than a *year*?" she repeated incredulously. "You can be honest with me, Dane."

"It's true. Remember that night you told me about your

father? The night you cried?"

She wrinkled her forehead. "Yeah." Her voice was just above a whisper.

Dane remembered it like it was yesterday. He'd wanted to climb through the computer and hold her until her tears dried and she felt safe. "I knew that night that I couldn't be with anyone else. Not while my heart was becoming yours." He looked away. "I'm sorry, Lace. You're the last person on earth I ever wanted to hurt." He reached for his shirt.

"Dane…"

His heart ached for the hurt in her eyes and the embarrassment that rose on her cheeks. But mostly, he hurt for himself and the reality that who he had been would never change—even if he'd stopped being that person months ago.

"I'm sorry I killed the mood," he said softly. "My history is always going to be between us. It's the one thing I can't change." He went to the glass doors and closed and locked them. "You don't have to stay for the rest of the week, Lace. Nothing I do will ever change the man I was."

"Wait, please," she said, stopping him in his tracks. "The other night, when you said you had women all over the world, I thought you had been with them more recently. More than a *year*, Dane, that's a *really* long time."

"I'm well aware of every day, every second, every hour." Dane's heart was shattering. He didn't need to remember all the nights he'd longed for her touch, or the multitude of midnight hours he'd spent staring at the photos she'd texted him, wondering what it would be like to kiss her.

He needed to go away. Far away. Someplace he wouldn't see her face in every cloud.

"I'm not judging you, Dane," she said. "I asked that question expecting an answer of a few months, maybe two or three. I don't know. That would have made me feel better. I never imagined it had been that long."

"Now you know." He couldn't change the fact that he hadn't gone to see her in all the months since they'd met, and he couldn't change the number of months and years he'd slept with other women—all of which made him too upset to think clearly enough to comprehend what she was trying to say.

He looked away, and Lacy wrapped her arms around him from behind, resting her cheek against his back.

"Thank you," she said.

"For?"

"For liking me enough to be faithful even when I was too far away to know if you weren't."

Dane clenched his eyes shut as relief tore through him. His shattered heart began pulling itself back together, piece by fragile piece. He'd completely misunderstood what she'd said, and the realization knocked the air right out of him. He turned and reached for her, as much for stability as for the need to feel their connection.

Everything he'd wanted for so long was right there, coming together, and he couldn't find the words to tell her how much it meant to him. Instead, he looked into the sea of love in her eyes, and he lowered his mouth to hers, kissing her until his heart reassembled, until the pain of thinking he'd lost her melted away and the desire to love her back to being *his* took over.

He lifted her into his arms and carried her toward the bedroom.

"You're staying," she said with a wide smile.

"Babe, we have a lot of making up to do."

THE NEXT MORNING Lacy danced around the kitchen, humming as she made coffee, eggs, and toast. She'd gotten up while Dane was still sleeping and picked wildflowers from the garden. She arranged them in a vase and set them in the center of the table.

"Breakfast? This was not on the itinerary," Dane said as he came out of the bedroom in only his boxer briefs and wrapped his arms around Lacy's waist from behind. He kissed the back of her neck and slid his hands beneath her satin camisole.

"Neither was last night," Lacy said, turning to kiss his cheek.

He pulled her close. "I don't think I've ever wanted anything as much as I wanted us to get back together. I can't change my pa—"

Lacy covered his lips with her finger. "Shh…I didn't know how much I had been wondering about your past until the words left my lips last night and, Dane, I couldn't have asked for a better response. No more talk about your past, okay?"

"You won't get an argument from me." He kissed her neck.

"And I won't ever bring it up again. That's done, and I'm working on my fear of sharks, but I think my fear was bigger than just sharks."

"Bigger?" He kissed her shoulder, her breastbone, her neck.

Lacy closed her eyes, her body purring from his touch. "Yes," she said in one long breath. "Danica said…Oh forget it." She turned and kissed him. "I swear I feel like a nympho with you."

"Good." He narrowed his eyes and lowered his mouth to hers, taking her in a possessive kiss. He swept her off her feet and carried her back into the bedroom. "I haven't had a chance to spoil you yet."

"Didn't you spoil me last night?" she asked as he laid her on the bed.

"Heck no. Last night I *devoured* you. There's a difference."

He stood beside the bed looking more handsome and virile than he ever had. Sunlight spilled into the room through the sheer curtains, casting a streak across her stomach. Dane's hand disappeared into the streak as he lowered himself to the bed beside her.

"What do you want, Lace?" he whispered.

He looked at her with so much love, she felt it like a presence in the room. "You. I want you."

He kissed her lightly on the lips. "Let me in, baby. Trust me. Tell me what you like so I can be your perfect man."

Her pulse quickened at the thought of actually saying what she wanted, but his eager eyes, and the way he was caressing her cheek, opened the door, and she walked right through, telling him what she liked as he stripped off her clothes. And the more he gave, the bolder she became. Heat blazed through her with his every touch, his every passionate kiss. Just when she thought she might lose her mind, he drew back and whispered, "I love making love to you, Lacy Snow."

She closed her eyes, taking pleasure in the masterful, loving attention he gave her, and wondering how she could have ever walked away from him in the first place.

Chapter Nineteen

IT WAS THREE in the afternoon by the time Lacy and Dane arrived at the Salt Pond Visitor Center in Orleans. Lacy couldn't remember a time when she'd felt happier. Dane had spent the last twenty-four hours helping her through her fears, taking care of his friend, and showing her just how much he loved her. He'd weaseled his way right back into her heart, and as he reached for her hand with a warm smile, she realized that even if she was never able to overcome her fear of sharks completely, they just might be able to be together after all.

In the center of the lobby was an exhibit featuring the Brave Foundation, complete with a reduced-sized model of a great white shark and several billboards of information and photographs.

"This is all about Brave," she said.

"Yeah. We want the community to understand what it is that we do," Dane said.

"Speak of the devil," said a tall woman from behind the reception desk. She smiled at Dane, revealing deep grooves across her forehead and around her mouth. Her skin had a leathery look, as if she'd spent every free moment in the sun.

"We'll look at it in just a sec," Dane said. He turned to the woman behind the counter, who looked to be in her mid-forties, with short, sandy blond hair and green eyes. Beside her stood a tall, lanky young man with short brown hair, wearing a park ranger uniform. His eyes locked on Dane.

"Shelley, how are you?" Dane led Lacy to the desk. "This is my girlfriend, Lacy Snow." He squeezed Lacy's hand.

Girlfriend? The term took her by surprise, then settled around her until it felt like a second skin. *Girlfriend.* "Nice to meet you," Lacy said.

"Hi, Lacy. Nice to meet you, too. I was just telling Tom all about you, Dane," Shelley said. "He wanted to meet the shark hunter."

Dane smiled. "That would be me, but I prefer researcher or tagger. Hunter sounds like I might hurt the sharks." He extended his hand, and Tom's eyes grew wide.

Tom pulled his shoulders back and said, "Yes, sorry. Researcher. Got it. It's so nice to meet you. I was looking over the exhibit and…wow. That's all I can say. Pretty cool stuff."

"Yeah, it's pretty cool. We tagged an eight-footer the other day. Hopefully, we'll gain valuable data and tag a few more over the next week or so. It's nice to meet you," Dane said.

"I won't hold you up," Tom said. His eyes moved to Lacy. "Enjoy the exhibit, Lacy."

"Thank you," she said.

They crossed the room, and Lacy scanned the large orange, black, and blue sign that read BRAVE FOUNDATION, which hung across the top of the exhibit boards with photographs of Dane and Rob lining them. Dane's dark eyes smiled in every one, his tanned, muscular arms glistening in the sun. In most of the photographs, he was on a boat, leaning over the side, holding the fin of a shark or crouching over a shark that was lying in the center of the boat. She could almost feel the wind blowing his hair askew.

"This is from nine years ago," she said, pointing to the information posted below the picture of a younger Dane wearing a bathing suit and tank top at the helm of a boat.

"That was a great day. We tagged three sharks that afternoon in Maui. You can just see the edge of Rob's arm." He pointed to the right side of the picture. "He was gloating. I remember it like it was yesterday."

Lacy noticed one common thread in each picture; the exhilaration that radiated from Dane's eyes was palpable. There was no doubt that the man in those pictures loved what he was doing. She looked at Dane now as he stood beside her studying the pictures, and she knew that he could never give up what he did for a living—and for the first time, she wondered if she could, or if living a life of continuous travel would be overwhelming for her.

"Excuse me, mister?"

Lacy and Dane turned toward the child's voice.

"Hi there," Dane said. "My name's Dane and this is Lacy."

You included me. I love that.

"I'm Ashton and I'm six. My mom said you were the shark guy, and I wanted to know what you're tracking on the television. All I see are red dots." Ashton's barely there blond eyebrows were pulled together above his startling blue eyes.

Dane glanced at the little boy's parents standing behind him with wide smiles. He leaned down so he was eye level with Ashton. "Come with me, buddy. I'll show you." He guided him to the monitor. "This is what we call a live-stream monitor. We put tags on sharks, and if the shark has a satellite tag, then that tag sends a signal to a satellite way up in the sky, past the clouds, and we get to see what that signal means here on the monitor."

"Why do you need a satellite?" Ashton asked.

"Well, you know how you have to plug your television into the wall to get electricity? The satellite is sort of like that for our tags. We need it to read the signals. You wanna know what we track, right?" Dane asked.

Ashton nodded.

He pointed to the monitor. "Those dots that you see, those are sharks. This monitor shows us where the tagged sharks are swimming. See the different colors?"

"Yeah," Ashton said. His eyes followed Dane's finger to the colorful dots.

"Each color tells us how long ago the shark appeared in that location. We call that a *ping*."

Ashton laughed.

Lacy watched Dane as he taught the little boy. She swore she could feel her heart opening wider with every word he spoke. *He'd make a great father.*

Dane continued. "We can track the temperature of the water and the depth where the tagged sharks swim, and we can even track their swim patterns."

He looked as if talking about sharks and teaching the little boy came both naturally and comfortably.

"I'm afraid of sharks," Ashton said.

His father put a hand on his shoulder.

"I have a good friend who's afraid of sharks, too." Dane winked at Lacy. "But if you try hard enough to understand sharks, you might realize that they're not really that scary. They're just trying to live in the world they've been given, just like we are."

Lacy's mind took a different turn. She began thinking of ways to wrap the educational side of Brave into their marketing, reaching out to schools and even aquariums, science museums, and the like.

"Do you wear one of those wet suits? My dad says the shark thinks people are seals when they wear them, and that's why they get bit," Ashton said, looking at his father.

How often does he have to field the same questions, and how can he answer them over and over without any irritation?

"We do wear wet suits, but not for the reasons you think. You see, Ashton, sharks aren't interested in eating humans, but they've been known to bump their noses into anything they see as potential prey." He used the back of his hand to lightly tap Ashton's arm. "Like that. When they do that, they emit electrical signals, like little shocks, and human skin makes those shocks conduct. That's probably hard for you to understand, but if a person's skin sends a certain signal to the shark, the chances are greater of an attack. Since wet suits don't interact with electrical signals like animals and human skin does, we wear them to minimize those chances."

Ashton's eyes glazed over, and he reached for his father's hand.

Ashton's father stepped forward. "That might be a little over his head, but thank you," he said.

"No problem. I'm always happy to explain what we do. I'm Dane Braden," Dane said and extended his hand.

"Craig Knoll. Nice to meet you."

"If you stop by that table, one of the Brave volunteers can give you an educational pamphlet. You'll find a list of books that you can read to Ashton, so he can better understand sharks and maybe even work on overcoming his fear of them."

"We'll do that," Craig said. He reached his hand out to the woman beside him. "This is Kathie, my wife."

Kathie stepped forward, her cheeks flushed. She looked a little older than Lacy, and Lacy knew that part of that flush was due to the incredibly handsome man standing before her. Her eyes drifted back to Dane. *And he's all mine.*

AFTER WATCHING A movie that explained how four decades of federal protection was the cause for the expanding seal population, Lacy and Dane left the visitors center and headed toward Provincetown.

"So if they protect the seals, won't the sharks just keep coming as more seals are born or move into the area?" Lacy asked.

"That's the issue. Part of what Brave does is to gather research about swim patterns, mating grounds, things like that. Something will need to be done, but the answer isn't killing the sharks. We think the answer lies in somehow getting the seals to migrate elsewhere. But like anything else, politics take precedence, so decisions are slow, and meanwhile, great white sightings are increasing." Dane glanced at Lacy and could see the gears in her mind working. He loved knowing that she was becoming interested in the process and reasoning surrounding what he did.

Dane pulled into the parking lot of PB Boulangerie, a little French bakery in Wellfleet.

"What's next on our agenda?" Lacy asked. "I didn't see anything else on the itinerary."

Dane lifted the left side of his mouth in a smile. "You'll see. I have to run in and pick something up. I'll be right back," he said. He left Lacy in the car to wonder what he was doing, and he went inside to collect the dinner basket he'd called ahead and ordered when Lacy had been in the ladies' room at the visitor center. He'd felt closer to Lacy in the past day than he had even over the months they were video chatting and talking over the phone. It was like their hearts had just clicked into place beside each other. As Dane returned to the car, he saw Lacy through the passenger window. Her neck was arched, her eyes were closed, and her lips were slightly parted as she rested against the headrest. They hadn't gotten much sleep the night before, and as he took in her long, graceful neck and those lips he couldn't get enough of, he was reminded of the sexy little whimpers she'd made when he was loving her the previous night. *Loving her.* He had no doubt that he was moving in that direction. Heck, he was probably already there. The thought moved around his mind like a cloud, seeping into every crevice until it was no longer separate from his other thoughts. It was in everything he saw, in the smell of the lobster in the bag in his hands, in the breeze as it mussed his hair. It was even in him. He closed his eyes and reminded himself that she'd been back for only twenty-four hours and that telling her how he felt might send her running right back out of his life.

It was nearly sunset when they turned down a narrow road just before Pilgrim Lake. Lacy carried a blanket and Dane carried the package he'd picked up at the market as they walked down the peaceful stretch of beach. With his free hand, he reached for Lacy's hand.

Dane saw the pod of seals before Lacy noticed them. She squinted as they neared.

"What...Oh my gosh. Are those seals? There must be hundreds of them." Lacy's eyes grew wide as she turned to face

Dane.

"When the tide goes out, the seals come in. I wanted you to see just how many seals there might be in any one place," Dane said.

The seals covered every bare spot of a sandbar about fifty feet from shore. The tide was already starting to roll back in. Dane spread out the blanket and stood with Lacy at the edge of the water.

"They're magnificent," she said. "I never imagined how big they really were. They must weigh hundreds of pounds. Look how many there are."

Dane nodded. "And this is just a fraction of the seals that are around the Cape."

"No wonder there are no more fish around. They have to eat," Lacy said.

He took her hand and led her back to the blanket. He withdrew plastic wine glasses, a bottle of wine, a loaf of French bread, and a variety of cheeses from the package.

"When did you have time to arrange this?" she asked.

"I can't tell you all of my secrets," he said as he poured them each a glass of wine. "I figured I'd have to feed you at some point, and what better place than while we enjoy the tide as it rolls in?"

She leaned her head on his shoulder. "This is very romantic," she said.

Lacy felt so good against him. He could sit right there next to her on the beach forever and never feel like he was missing a thing. He put his arm around her shoulder, and they watched the seals disappear with the rising tide.

"You'd never know they were there," Lacy said.

"I think the silence of mammals is part of their beauty. We

humans are loud. Everything about our lives is loud and creates havoc. Take a look around after we leave the beach. From our cars to our lawn mowers, we put things into the air that shouldn't be there, and we leave so big of a footprint that..." He looked down at Lacy, who was gazing up at him with a tender smile. "I'm sorry. I'm lecturing again."

"You're passionate. I like that," she said. "I can't help but wonder, Dane. Why are you compelled to be the one to make a difference with something as scary as sharks?"

He kissed her forehead. "They don't scare me. I could die driving—"

"I know, driving down the street," she said. "But why? Why not do something safer? Be an advocate for living green or something."

Dane shrugged. "Everyone has a calling. Sharks are mine." He put his hand beneath her hair and brushed his fingers along the fine hairs on the back of her neck. "Just like you're my calling, Lace. I want to be with you, and I want to protect you." He didn't know how it had happened so fast, but Lacy owned a piece of his heart as big as any piece his family ever had. "I never want anything to hurt you, and I never want to cause you any pain." The sun set behind the dunes, casting a blue-black haze over the water. He leaned down and kissed her, hoping that in that kiss, Lacy would feel the three words he couldn't yet say.

LACY GIGGLED AS Dane kissed the back of her neck while she tried to concentrate on finding the right key on her key chain to open the door. The porch light was off and she couldn't see anything. She swatted playfully at him with a feigned sigh. He slid his hands around her waist and up her belly. Lacy leaned against him, feeling his heart beat against her back.

"Dane," she whispered through a smile.

He dragged his tongue along her neck. "I've waited all day," he said.

He spun her around so she was facing him and pressed his hips into hers, then backed her up against the door. With his hands on either side of her head, he pushed her hair to the side.

"I so love your face," he said, then settled his lips over hers.

Lacy dropped the keys and wrapped her hands around him, pulling him even closer. He smelled like ocean air and tasted like wine. The combination was intoxicating. Well…that and the bottle of wine they'd shared. He moved his hands up her rib cage, kissing his way down her neck. A rush of heat moved through her.

"We should go inside," she managed.

"Okay," he whispered, but he made no move toward the door and took her in another deep kiss. His kisses alone were enough to send her into fits of heart-quaking lust, but his hand wandered, driving her out of her mind. She went up on her tiptoes with a little mewl of desire. If they didn't go inside, she was going to rip off his clothes right there!

She tore her mouth away, picked up the keys, and fumbled them as fast as she was able, not wanting to waste a second. She shoved the key into the lock and pulled Dane inside, kicking the door shut behind them. The cottage was dark, save for moonlight coming through the glass doors in the living room. He knew just how to make her body sing, and now it was her turn to learn to do the same. She pushed his back against the front door—*not so* playfully.

"My turn," she said huskily.

His eyes turned dark and lustful. He reached for her, and she stepped back, then grabbed his fly at the waist and ripped it to the side, sending the button flying across the room.

He pulled her close, ravenously kissing her. She nearly melted into a submissive kitten, but she held strong to her resolve to give him as much pleasure as he'd given her. She drew back from that delicious kiss, and with one palm on his chest, she pinned him against the door.

"You know what I like," she said. "Now teach me." She unbuttoned his shirt and ran her hands along his chest.

"Lace," he whispered. "You don't have to. Let *me* love *you*."

She lowered her lips a breath away from his, the smell of wine mingling between them. "I'm an eager student," she whispered, enjoying the rush of control sweeping through her. "Tell me what you like."

She grabbed the back of his neck and pulled him into another deep kiss. In the next second, she was in his arms and he was carrying her to the sofa. Breaking their connection was the last thing she wanted, but her desire to master his pleasure was stronger than the need to be taken by him.

"Dane! It's my turn."

His eyes turned volcanic. "Darn right, baby, and I intend to make sure you enjoy every second of it."

"No. I want to learn to touch *you* the way you like it."

"I like every way you touch me," he said, lowering her to the couch.

How could she argue with that? And when he said, "But if you want me to tell you what I like, I'm all in, baby. Class is *in session…*"

Chapter Twenty

ROB HAD THE boat ready to go when Dane and Lacy arrived at the marina the next morning. Dane handed Rob a warm to-go cup of coffee, noticing his eyes were clear and his skin color looked healthy. He was relieved to see that Rob's strength and confidence had returned, but he'd be sure to keep an eye on him just in case. He helped Lacy aboard, then pulled her into a hug. Today they were going to troll for sharks so Lacy could see one in the water.

Dane whispered in her ear, "You sure you want to do this? It might be ten times harder than the aquarium, and you had a hard time there."

"I know. I do. I really, really do," Lacy said.

He knew this was going to be difficult for her, but Danica had stressed the importance of Lacy facing her fears, and apparently, she'd told Lacy the same thing. He felt the fast pace of her heart against his chest, and Dane wondered if he was doing the right thing.

"You two must have had quite a night. I almost never beat Dane to the boat," Rob teased.

"Yeah, about beating me to the boat. You look pretty chipper," Dane said. "I take it things are better with Sheila?"

"Much. You were right. We needed to talk, and now that we have, we've got it all under control. That was three days of misery that I never want to go back to. Hey, why don't we all have dinner tonight? Sheila and the kids would love to see you, Dane, and she's heard about Lacy for so long she feels like she knows her already."

"Lace?" Dane and Lacy had spent the night in each other's arms, and now, looking at Lacy's gratified grin, he knew the worst was behind them.

"Sure. Sounds great," she said. Lacy zipped her sweatshirt over her bikini and stretched out in one of the deck chairs. They were taking Treat's boat out today instead of the work vessel. Dane had wanted Lacy to be comfortable, and if she had a difficult time, she could escape to the cabin below.

"I guess it's a date," Dane said to Rob. "You had me worried, Rob. I want you to know that if you need me, I'm here. I'll go to meetings. I'll let you stay on the boat. I'll stay at your motel. Whatever you need. I'm here for you."

"I know, Dane, and I appreciate it. I went to a meeting yesterday morning and another last night. I figured *immersion therapy* might be a good thing." Rob winked. "I did fine last night. I had them move me to another room. I didn't want any reminders of how far I'd fallen."

Dane glanced at Lacy. "If there's one thing I've learned, Rob, it's that we can always change. We make mistakes and we learn from them; then we move on. There is no hard-and-fast point of no return."

THE AFTERNOON SUN beat down on them as they sailed

through Chatham Harbor. Dane was relieved to see Rob back to his old self again. His energy was high and the camaraderie they'd shared for so many years fell right back into place. Dane silently vowed to keep a better eye on Rob. What kind of a friend was he if he didn't notice when his best friend's life was upended?

Dane laughed at a joke Rob made and cast a glance back at Lacy, stretched out on the deck cushions with only those tiny triangular patches of cloth covering the parts of her body that were so fresh on his mind. Beneath her head was the sweatshirt she'd had on earlier. Her curls fell away from her face like heavy twine. The evening before, he'd wrapped his fingers deep in those curls. He'd never met a woman whose desire to please was as strong as her desire to be pleasured. Then again, Lacy was like no other woman he'd ever met, and he knew she'd be the last woman he invited into his bed.

Now, looking at her lying in the sun, the curve of her belly moving up and down with each peaceful breath, all he wanted to do was love her. *Need* felt too shallow for the emotions that were burying themselves deeper in his mind with every thought. His feelings for Lacy encompassed love, adoration, inspiration, respect, gratification, and yes, *need* was a part of those feelings, but they were not the driving force of his emotions toward her.

"What's the plan for tomorrow?" Rob asked.

"Tomorrow?" Dane pulled his attention back to his friend.

"We're supposed to go free diving, remember? You delayed the tagging, but I got a message from Carl today, and he said our equipment would be ready for the dive," Rob said.

Damn. He looked at Lacy. She might be fine lying out in the sun on a luxury boat, but he doubted she'd be okay on a dive boat while he was underwater looking for sharks.

"Yeah, I did forget, but I'll be there," Dane assured him.

"Great. So, what's the deal with Lacy? Is she everything you hoped for? She seems like a really nice girl," Rob said.

"The deal?" Dane looked at Rob's expectant stare and shook his head. "Every time I think I have her figured out, she throws me for a loop."

"That's women for you," Rob said.

"I think it's more than that," he said. "I don't know."

Lacy came up behind the men. "Are you talking about me?" she asked. She put her arm around Dane's shoulder and kissed his cheek.

"Not you—all women," Rob said.

"That's worse," she said with a feigned pout.

Dane pulled her onto his lap. "Did you enjoy the sun?"

"Mmm. It was glorious, and I'm not the least bit anxious," she said.

"There are no s-h-a-r-k-s here either." Dane kissed her cheek.

"Rob, I'm glad things are going better for you and Sheila," Lacy said. "I look forward to meeting her."

"And you'll meet my kids, too. They're so cute, but they'll pester you. Katie loves anything girlie—hair, nails, makeup—and Charlie is pretty quiet, but if you get onto a subject he likes, he'll talk forever."

"I love kids. I'm sure we'll get along just fine," Lacy said.

"So you work for World Geographic? You think you can help us get people to fund our research? It's a tough job," Rob said. "It's like asking Hansel and Gretel's parents to fund the wicked witch's cooking classes."

In addition to Dane and his siblings having very successful careers, they each had trust funds. Their father would never have allowed them to grow up acting as if they'd had silver spoons in their mouths. He'd instilled in them solid morals and work ethics, and to this day, Dane tried not to dip into his trust fund to subsidize the Brave research. He was emotionally and physically invested, but he knew the only way to get the public to care about the oceans, and the sharks that lived within them, was to educate them and enlighten them to the value of protecting the sharks and, in turn, the oceans.

"I think we'll find a way to make it appealing. I've actually got a few ideas up my sleeve."

"Have you?" Dane arched a brow. *You've thought of something other than me?*

"That is what I'm here for," she said, leaning in to his chest.

"That's great. I don't know if Dane told you, but there's some question about whether the Cape has become a shark breeding ground the last few years, so we're also looking for residency hot spots, which we hope will give us enough information to help keep the sharks and the public safer," Rob said.

"I think you can use that angle with your marketing, too," Lacy said.

They talked about Brave and marketing strategies for the next hour. Rob pulled Dane aside and said, "She's a bright woman. I thought you said she was afraid of sharks. She seems comfortable talking about them."

"She is afraid. Talking and seeing are two different things," Dane said with a smile.

Rob looked at his watch. "You wanna bag the sighting then and go back in?"

"I'll leave that up to Lacy," Dane said. They went back to the seating in the rear of the boat, where Lacy was sitting in the sun. Dane sat beside her. He put his hand on her knee and looked her in the eyes.

"Lace, we can take this next step toward helping you overcome sharks if you are ready, but if you're not, we can go back in." Dane searched her eyes, recognizing the flash of fear that she was trying to hide with her rapidly blinking lashes. Her leg went rigid beneath his palm.

Lacy nodded. "I think I want to try. I just need to remember that I'm not going in the water with them."

"You control your safety when you're in the boat, and I'm right here. I'll be holding you tight, but we don't have to do this. There's no gun to your head, Lace. I'm so proud of everything about you. That won't change at all if you decide we should head in. I don't want you to feel any pressure," Dane assured her.

"I know. Thank you."

Dane took her hands in his. "Let's go over again what to expect." He couldn't shake the worry that this would be too difficult for her. She couldn't go near the sharks in tanks. How would she handle seeing them over the side of the boat? He took a deep breath and continued. "Rob will throw chum into the water, and you'll see it. You'll see fish, blood, and a trail as we go, okay?"

Lacy swallowed and set her lips in a tight line. Her eyebrows drew together and Dane felt tension stiffen her arms.

"We may or may not see a shark, Lace. I don't know if we will. Sometimes it takes hours, and other times…" He shrugged. "It could happen really quickly."

She nodded again.

Rob put a hand on Lacy's shoulder. "Dane and I are right here, Lacy. We would never let anything happen to you."

Now, that's the Rob I know and love.

She smiled, and Dane knew it was forced. "I know. Thank you," she said. "Let's do it."

Dane's heart thumped against his chest so hard he was sure he was more nervous than she was. He moved closer, pressing Lacy's body tight against his side, one arm around her shoulder, the other covering both of her hands in her lap. He nodded to Rob, and Rob went to work chumming the water. Lacy sat rigidly beside him. He kissed the side of her head. "I'm right here. Nothing is going to happen to you."

She stared straight ahead as she nodded, but it was her silence that worried him.

"Lace, look at me, babe." When he saw the fear in her eyes, it was all he could do not to turn the boat around and head for shore, but this was Lacy's choice, and he respected her decision. "I just want you to know that even if you are never comfortable on a boat when I'm working, we can make this relationship work. That doesn't worry me one bit."

Lacy let out a breath. She lifted her lips into a nervous smile, and an ounce of fear disappeared from her eyes. "Thank you," she whispered. "But I want to do this anyway."

"Okay." He nodded. "Okay. I just wanted you to know."

Forty-five minutes later, Rob gave Dane a silent signal, indicating that he'd spotted a shark. Dane looked over the side of the boat and spotted a five- or six-foot shark just below the surface in the chum trail.

"Babe, do you still want to do this?" Dane asked.

She nodded, her eyes wide. "Is there a shark?" She grabbed his hand.

"There is. It's a small one."

She licked her lips, then pressed them tightly together and

nodded.

Dane helped her stand, his arm wrapped around her shoulder, her body pressed to his side. Rob came to her other side and put a hand on the small of her back. Then he and Dane both took a half step forward, so Lacy was tucked safely between and slightly behind them.

"We've got you, Lacy," Rob said.

Lacy stared straight out into the water, but Dane knew her eyes were riding the surface.

"Lace, to your right about fifteen feet from the boat is where the shark is," Dane said. "I've got you, and the shark can't hurt you. You're safe in the boat."

She nodded and dropped her eyes to the water. Dane watched as she dragged her eyes in a slow line toward the chum trail. She sucked in a breath and pushed her body closer to him.

"You're okay," he said. "He's a small one, Lace. He's too far away to hurt you. You're safe."

She nodded. Her fingers dug into the waist of his pants.

"You did great, Lacy. I think that's enough. You saw it. Now let's sit back down and head in," Dane said. He nodded toward Rob.

"Wait," Lacy said, grabbing Rob's arm. "Wait. I want to look again. I need to do this." She whispered, "*I'm okay. I'm okay. I'm okay.* I'm safe. I'm in control. One, two, three..."

Her shoulders were pinched tight and high, just below her ears. A deep vee had formed between her eyebrows. Dane held his breath as she stared at the shark, whispering her mantra and counting to ten into the breeze. Her heart thundered against his side.

"Ten. Okay," Lacy said. Clutching Dane's side, she walked backward two steps. The words tumbled from her mouth.

"Okay. Can you please get me to the seats? And can we leave?"

Dane led her to the seats as Rob took them toward shore. Dane didn't let out his breath until Lacy was settled safely on the aft seating. He knelt before her and rested his hands on her thighs.

"You okay?" he asked.

She nodded, and let out several loud breaths through puckered lips. "I'm good. I did it. I'm okay."

The trembling began in her legs and wound its way up her body until she was shaking like a leaf in the breeze. Dane wrapped a blanket around her and pulled her into his lap.

"You're safe, baby. I'm right here, and I'm so proud of you."

She clutched the ends of the blanket and turned damp eyes toward Dane. "I'm not sure I will ever be able to be on a boat when you're down underwater with a shark. I'm not just afraid for me, Dane. The risks…I'm afraid for you. But I can be on a boat when you're not actively seeking sharks. Then I'm fine."

"Lacy, I'll take you with me any way you'll let me. We can make this work." He kissed her forehead and held her against him, with one hand buried in her curls and the other around her back, until her body stopped trembling and his own breathing calmed.

By the time the marina was in sight, Lacy was back to her normal self. She'd shed the blanket and stood in the middle of the deck with her shoulders back and a gleaming smile across her lips.

She placed her hands on her chest and proclaimed, "I did it. I didn't freak out."

"You sure did, Lacy," Rob said. "We're so proud of you."

"You never fail to amaze me, Lace." Dane swooped in and twirled her around with a kiss. "You ready to blow this taco joint?"

Lacy flashed a flirtatious smile at Dane. "You lead; I'll follow."

She'd whispered those words into his ear last night in bed, and hearing them again sent heat to his core. "I've got some *studying* I want to do before we go to dinner."

The flush on Lacy's cheeks told Dane that she was thinking the same thing.

Chapter Twenty-One

STUDYING. THAT WAS all Lacy could think about from the second the line flew from Dane's lips. He was a fast learner, too. She stifled a smile as the memory of the night before came back to her. She walked away from the men, wanting to clear her head. If she didn't hear his voice, she wouldn't think about the things he'd said to her the night before, in the throes of passion.

The dock was not coming into focus fast enough. Her body was pumping with adrenaline from seeing the shark. Thoughts of touching Dane were sending her heart into a state of desperation. *Hurry up. Hurry up.*

Once they reached the marina, it seemed to take forever to bring the boat into the slip. Lacy went to Dane's side, and he reached an arm around her, stroking the bare skin of her waist beneath her T-shirt. Every touch made her mind wander to sensual places. Every minute was a slow, treacherous drag of time. She didn't understand why she was so sexual with Dane, but she didn't want to question it, either. Once she'd found out how long he'd gone without touching another woman, her whole outlook had changed. When he'd told her, she'd wanted to dance around the room singing, *He feels it too! He really, really likes me!* And now, as she watched Dane and Rob, laughing,

215

patting each other on the back, all Lacy wanted to do was get him into the cabin and show him that she'd been worth the wait.

Lacy watched Dane and Rob secure the boat to the dock, and when they were done, she touched Dane's arm. His skin was hot from the sun. She wanted to run her tongue up his rock-hard abs and taste his saltiness. He flashed an urgent, hungry look from the dark shadows of his eyes, and the word *savage* came to mind.

Rob gathered his stuff and stepped to the edge of the boat. "Thanks for a great run," he said with a smile. "I loved your ideas for Brave, Lacy. I can't wait to see what you come up with for the strategic marketing plan."

Oh, I have a few strategies up my sleeve. "I can't wait to meet Sheila."

"We'll see you tonight," Rob said as he stepped onto the dock.

Lacy watched Rob get into his car and drive away. She turned around and bumped into Dane's chest. He didn't give her time to recover. In the next breath, his mouth was on hers, his hands pressed to her bottom, pulling her hips against his. He kissed her passionately and came away breathing hard.

"I thought we'd never get back," he said breathlessly. He pulled her toward the cabin, tugging her shirt over her head as they stumbled down the stairs.

"I know," she said between hungry kisses. "All I could think about—"

He hauled her in for another kiss.

"Was *studying*," she said breathily.

He stripped them bare, and then he gathered her close again. "Lacy," he whispered as he backed her up against the wall.

"Touch me," she commanded, and he did.

"When did you turn into such a temptress?" he whispered.

She felt her cheeks flush. "I don't know." Her breath came fast and hard as his hands roamed over her body. "I realized my fear was probably more of everything…" She paused, trying to gain control over her breathing. "Not just sharks. And when I let go of that, and let you into my heart, everything changed."

He leaned his forehead against hers. "You own my heart, Lace. I want only to protect you."

His heart beat rapidly against her chest. She never considered herself to be a woman who needed protecting, but as the words fell from his lips, she couldn't think of another person she'd rather have watching out for her.

Chapter Twenty-Two

AFTER DANE DROPPED Lacy at her cottage to get ready for dinner, she showered, dressed, and read an email from her boss advising her of the status of her previous work and congratulating her on solidifying Brave as a client. *You have no idea how solid Brave is.* She called Danica to fill her in on how things were going.

"I'm seriously the worst sister ever, and I'm sorry," Lacy said when Danica answered the phone.

"I don't know. Kaylie has her moments," Danica teased.

"I'm sorry I haven't called. So much has happened, and I don't know where to start, but I know I owe it to you, Dan. I thought about what you said about letting his past go, and it's like the minute I did that, all the fear and anxiety fell away." Lacy put the call on speaker and began applying eyeliner beneath her lashes.

"That's the funny thing about anxiety. You never really know what it stems from," Danica said. "So, tell me what happened."

"I don't know. I tried to seduce him, which, by the way, I think I suck at, but anyway, one thing led to another, and he told me that he hasn't been with another woman for more than a year. More than a *year*, Danica. It's been longer for me, but how can a guy even do that?" Lacy finished putting on her makeup, picked up the phone again, and walked into the living room, where she sat down at her computer.

"The heart is a powerful thing," Danica said.

"We went out on Treat's boat and looked for sharks."

"Lacy, what did I tell you? Holy cow, talk about pushing the limits," Danica chided her.

"I know, but you also said to face my fears, and I was pretty much okay. Your advice really helped. We saw one shark that Dane said was small but looked huge to me. I didn't panic. I didn't like it, but I didn't lose all of my faculties either, so I feel like that's a big step."

"That's a huge step, Lace. All you need to do is be okay on the boat and, Lacy, you know that even if you can't overcome this, you and Dane can still have a relationship. He's the one in the water, not you," Danica pointed out.

"True, but I don't want him worrying about me when he needs to be concentrating on the sharks and doing his job. Given what I've seen so far, he'd worry about me every second he was underwater if I was on the boat. He doesn't need that distraction, and as a couple, we don't need that stress."

"You're not going to end it again, are you?" Danica asked.

"No. I don't mean it like that. I think I'm figuring all this stuff out, and actually, I'm excited about doing marketing for Brave, too. Oh, and don't forget that I touched a baby shark at the aquarium, remember? At first it freaked me out a little, but then I was okay and went back to touch it again." Lacy sat down on the couch.

"I didn't forget. I'm really proud of you. I'm sure you were scared to death. Just be careful, Lacy. You could still have a panic attack, so be sure that if you do go with him when he's looking for sharks, you have a safety net for yourself. Someplace to escape. I don't know where that would be, a cabin in the boat maybe?"

"I will, but I don't plan on going on any shark finding missions with him. Thanks, Danica, for everything. I'm glad you talked to Dane, and I'm even kinda glad you didn't tell me. You're probably right. I would have felt added pressure or something." For the millionth time, Lacy was thankful to have her sisters in her life.

"You know that if I thought he wasn't worthy of you, or if I thought it would hurt you, I never would have talked with him, right?"

"I know. I trust you. Oh, I almost forgot to tell you. We're having dinner with Rob and his wife tonight. I really like him." Lacy wondered what Sheila would be like.

"He's the one you picked up at the police station?" Danica asked.

"Yeah. He's back at AA and he seems to be really trying and sincere in his efforts."

"That's good. I hope he can stay on the right path. I've been thinking. Have you and Dane talked about what happens next?" Danica asked.

"Next?" *Gulp. Next?*

"After Chatham? You do have a life, you know, and so does he. Are you going back to Skype and phone calls?"

"Gosh, we haven't talked about it. Oh, Danica, I don't know. I can't go months without seeing him, not now that we've become so close." Lacy stood and paced. "Darn it. I have no idea what we'll do. His schedule isn't going to change." She dropped back onto the couch. "Great, another nightmare."

"This isn't a nightmare, Lacy. You sound like Kaylie, drama girl. You'll figure it out. It's just a...setback," Danica assured her.

Setback? A chill ran up Lacy's spine. "How can we figure it out? Geez, Danica. I wish you hadn't brought that up."

"Sorry, Lacy, but you only have a few more days with him before real life steps in. I always want to know where I'm heading," Danica said.

"I was kind of enjoying my little nympho stage. I've never been so spontaneous. I've never felt like my heart might explode if I didn't touch someone before, and now...Oh, Danica. For the love of..." Lacy lowered her forehead to her hand.

"Lacy, honey, calm down. Where there's a will, there's a way. Look at Max and Treat, Josh and Riley. You'll figure it out. It might take some time, but it'll come to you, and you won't always be on a sexcathalon, either. At some point, that'll slow down, and then, if you see each other every two weeks or something, it could work."

"Thanks, sis. Maybe you're right. I guess I have a lot to think about tonight, and I can't even have a glass of wine with Rob's recent misstep. There's nothing worse than trying not to have something that's flaunted before you. When I first came back, it was like that with Dane. I wanted him, but I couldn't— or wouldn't—let myself have him."

"You don't need wine, although it does help, and now you can have as much of Dane as you want. All you need is to think past your raging hormones and the illusion that romantic getaways can last forever. I'm a big believer that the universe will step in when we need it to. We have to rely on our resources and our minds, but I have faith that you'll see some kind of sign and it will push you both in the right direction.

Call me if you need me," Danica said.

"Thanks. I will. Tell Kaylie I'm sorry I haven't been in touch lately. I'll call her when I have my head on straight. How are the twins?" Lacy went to the window and looked out at the water, thinking of how much Trevor and Lexi would love the cottage and the beach. "I miss them."

"They are so freaking cute, and I swear Kaylie is the best mom I've ever known. She's wrestling with going back to work. I'll send her your love, and we'll all get together again soon. Love you," Danica said.

"You too."

After ending the call, Lacy sat on the couch mulling over what Danica had said. *How will we work out our lives?*

Chapter Twenty-Three

THEY HAD DINNER at a family-style restaurant and sat outside on the patio, giving Rob's two children, Charlie and Katie, space to walk around if they got antsy. Charlie hadn't left his chair all evening. He sat beside Rob with his arms crossed. Even at seven, he had the sullen teenage stare down pat, while Katie wore a perpetual smile and hung on to the arm of Lacy's chair, blinking thick lashes over her big brown eyes.

Lacy touched her nose. "You are the cutest four-year-old I've ever seen."

"Can I touch your hair?" Katie asked.

Lacy smiled. "Of course you can, sweetie."

Katie petted Lacy's curls. "Pretty," she said.

Lacy leaned down and whispered, "Can I touch your beautiful hair?"

Katie nodded. A wide, crooked smile graced her cheeks.

Lacy stroked Katie's hair, then opened her eyes wide and feigned surprise. "Oh, Katie. I've never felt such softness. You're so lucky to have your mommy's hair."

Dane had never given much thought to having children of his own, and now, watching Lacy with Katie, he had a fleeting thought about how good Lacy was with them. She was patient and kind and attentive to everything they said. He briefly envisioned what she might be like as a mother.

Katie ran to her mother and climbed into her lap. She rested her head against Sheila's chest. Sheila stroked her hair.

"Say thank you," Sheila said, planting a kiss on Katie's head.

"Thank you," Katie said.

Charlie sat beside his father, watching Lacy like a hawk, narrowing his dark eyes and looking up through the bangs of his wavy dark hair.

"You know what I think?" Lacy asked. "I think Charlie is going to be even more handsome than your daddy when he grows up." She winked at Rob, who smiled and put his arm around Charlie.

Charlie's eyes opened wide. He looked at his father. Rob nodded, and Charlie sat up straighter, smiling for the first time all evening.

Dane reached for Lacy's hand and squeezed. He loved watching Lacy's warmth and attentiveness to Rob's kids. Their relationship was moving fast, but it felt too right to slow it down. Lacy brought her hand to her lap, and Dane drew his eyebrows together.

She smiled, but he sensed a hesitation in her eyes. He leaned toward her and whispered, "Is everything okay?"

She nodded. "Fine."

He didn't miss the thread of tension in her voice.

"Lacy, since the men are going diving tomorrow, I was thinking that maybe we could spend the day together, take the kids to the fair or something," Sheila offered. She brushed her long hair behind her shoulders. "I mean, if you don't mind hanging out with a couple of kids."

"I'd love that," Lacy answered.

Dane watched Sheila place a hand on Rob's arm and could almost feel the wave of love that passed between them.

"I also wanted to thank you guys for helping Rob the other day," Sheila said. "Marriage can be hard sometimes, and we kind of fell down the rabbit hole for a few days. It can be hard when you're separated for long periods of time. But Robby's working on his...stuff, and I'm working on mine." She smiled at Rob. "We both realized how much we didn't want to lose each other." Sheila turned back to Dane and Lacy. "Thank you for being there for him."

"Rob's like a brother to me." Dane looked at his best friend and diving partner; one tree-trunk arm rested across the back of Charlie's chair, the other on his lap. A five-o'clock shadow peppered his tanned cheeks. He looked strong and healthy, so much different from when Dane had picked him up at the police station.

"I'd walk to the ends of the earth for him," Dane said. "He's a good man, Sheila, and I'm just sorry that I didn't notice that things were falling apart so I could step in and help."

"Thanks, Dane," Rob said with a flush on his cheeks.

"We all have our rough patches. We'll work on schedules, Sheila. I know it's rough with the kids, and I appreciate you allowing Rob to travel so much. I don't know what I'd do without him," Dane said.

"Neither do we," Sheila said, turning a warm gaze to Rob.

DANE AND LACY said good night to Rob, Sheila, and the kids, and then they drove to the cottage to take a walk along the beach. The temperature had dipped as the evening wore into night, and they snuggled against each other as they walked on the cold sand.

"I really like Sheila a lot. I'm looking forward to hanging out with her and the kids tomorrow," Lacy said.

"I'm glad. She's a really nice person, and Rob's a great guy, despite his recent issues," Dane said.

"I know. You don't have to try to sell me on him. I like him a lot, and it's obvious how close you two are," Lacy said.

"Were you okay back there? I thought I picked up on something…" Dane let the sentence hang in the air between them.

Lacy wrapped her arm in his and rested her head against his shoulder. "I had a talk with Danica tonight. She brought up some stuff that's probably way too early to be thinking about, but now I can't stop thinking about it."

"What kind of stuff?" Dane asked.

"Like what happens when this trip is over." Lacy looked up at him.

Dane stopped walking and faced her. Her eyes were wide and worried as they searched his. He held on to her, probably too tight, but the thought of losing her again rattled his nerves.

"I've been thinking about that, too," he admitted. "I don't know if it's too early to think about it or not, but it's where my mind traveled…" He shrugged. "Lacy, seeing you with Rob's kids made me think all sorts of things that are probably wrong to think about so soon."

"Yeah? Like what?" she asked.

Kids, marriage, growing old together. He didn't want to scare her off, but he wanted her to know how immense his feelings had grown.

"The same kind of thing. What's next. Kids."

Lacy touched his chest and smiled. "Kids? Really?"

He shrugged. "I don't know. I was watching you with Katie and Charlie, and for the first time ever, my mind put me and children together in the same sentence, led by you."

"I love kids." Lacy's eyes lit up. "Gosh, you're thinking even further ahead than I am."

Dane pulled her close and kissed her lightly on the lips. "I don't know what it is between us, but I can see us together when we're old and gray. What I can't imagine is a life without you by my side."

"Me either," Lacy said. "It's the in between I can't figure out."

"I'm not sure what the answer is. I know you love your job. You came here to save your career."

"I came here to be with you," Lacy said.

"I'm just a bonus to your fluffy little vacation on the Cape. Oh, and a path to a promotion," he teased.

"You've got me all figured out. So, Mr. Braden, what happens after the fluffy little vacation is over?"

I wish I knew.

They walked hand in hand. The sounds of crashing waves filled the gap in their conversation.

"We'll have to make better travel plans," he said. "See each other at least once each month."

"Once a month?" Lacy shot a worried look at him.

"Lace, I travel all the time. You know that. I want to be with you every second, but short of you quitting and traveling with me…"

She turned away.

He'd been afraid to even approach the subject because she'd been adamant about how much she loved her job, but now, he couldn't *not* ask.

"Would you consider that? Coming with me? I'd like nothing more than to have you by my side every second—I know you can't be on the boat while I tag, but every other second."

Lacy's arm stiffened. She bit her lower lip, and when she turned to face Dane, it was sadness that he saw, clear and present, in her heavenly eyes.

"It's okay, Lacy. We'll figure something out," he assured her, though he had absolutely no idea how they ever could.

"Can we see each other more often? Once every two or three weeks? I can come to you once each month and you can come to me."

Her pleading tone pulled at his heart. "We can try, but realistically, going to Maui or even Florida for a weekend can be exhausting if you're doing it all the time, just like flying from those places to Massachusetts would be."

"Do you want to see me more often?" she asked.

Dane dropped to one knee and held her hand in his.

"Dane?" Lacy's other hand flew to her mouth.

"Lacy Snow, I want you by my side every second of every day. I know you promised not to fall in love with me, so will you *friend me*?" He smiled, then added, "Will you *friend-with-benefits* me? Forever?"

Lacy laughed. "What does that mean? Like on Facebook?"

Dane stood again and brushed off his slacks. "Come with me. You don't ever have to admit to falling in love with me. Just live with me. Be with me. Be my *friend-who-can't-be-in-love-with-me* forever." He was sure they both were way past the friendship pact, but he was afraid a real marriage proposal might scare her off. Still, hope soared through his chest as he thought about the possibilities. "We'd wake up together every day, Lace. Spend our free time knocking around villages or reading, or whatever. I don't care what we do. I just want you there with me. What do you say?"

Her smile faded, taking Dane's hope with it.

DANE'S FRIENDSHIP PROPOSAL stole the wind out of Lacy's lungs. Was he serious? Give up her job and travel with him? What would she do all day? She couldn't go on the boat with him when he was working. What about all the years she'd worked her butt off for World Geographic? That meant something to her. It meant a heck of a lot to her. She looked at Dane's hopeful eyes, the way his chest heaved up and down with each excited breath. She wanted to jump into his arms and say, *Yes! Yes! I'll be your friend-who-can't-be-in-love-with-you* forever! But how could she do that?

"I never expected a friend forever proposal," she said.

"I didn't expect to give you one," he admitted. Dane touched her cheek. "A pact is a pact," he teased.

"Like blood sisters when you cut your palm and mix your blood with your best friend's," Lacy joked, but inside she wasn't laughing. She didn't know how to navigate their relationship into the future, even though she wanted to do exactly that. "Dane, would you give up your career for me?"

"Come on, Lace. I built an entire foundation from nothing," he explained.

She nodded. "I know."

"Think of the life we'd have together. We could go anywhere," he said.

"As long as there are sharks," she pointed out.

"Okay, you have a point, but, Lace, the alternative is being together part-time," he said.

"What if something happened to you? What if I gave up

everything and, I don't know, you get eaten by a shark or something?" Lacy realized the viability of her question, and she clenched her jaw to keep the new worry from taking over.

"Lacy, that's not going to happen. I told you, my job is less risky than driving down the street."

"But what if?" she asked. "Then I'd have given up everything, and I'd have no home, no stability. No job." *No Dane? No, just no.* She didn't even want to think about that.

He stepped closer, resting his forehead against hers, just as he'd done after they'd made love. His whisper was a caress to her tumbling heart as it careened out of control toward the edge of a cliff she desperately wanted to avoid.

"I'm careful, Lace. I won't let anything happen. Rob wouldn't let anything happen to me."

She didn't want to think about it anymore. Sheila had been clear about what a part-time relationship did to a family. Then again, Rob and Sheila were working things out, so maybe there was hope. Lacy wondered if she could—or should—give up her job. She needed time to think, but her mind was running in circles.

"Don't worry, Lace. We'll figure this out together. I know how important your job is to you, and I know how much Fred respects your abilities. I don't want to jeopardize your happiness or your career. But honestly, I don't want to lose you, either. We'll figure it out." He kissed her forehead. "Let's go back to the cottage and fall asleep in each other's arms. No sex, no deep discussions. Let's just be close."

Lacy felt like they were trapped in a bubble of unanswered questions with a future that didn't seem attainable just outside. *If only we could find the answers and pop the bubble so we could grasp our future and hold on tight.*

Chapter Twenty-Four

DESPITE THE UNANSWERED questions that spun in her mind and her heart unraveling a little more with each passing minute, when they'd arrived back at the cottage, Lacy had fallen asleep in Dane's arms just as he'd suggested, and surprisingly, she'd slept right through the night.

Dane awoke in a full sweat. He shot straight up in bed, and Lacy followed.

"What's wrong?" she asked. She watched his eyes dart around the room.

"Just a bad dream. I'm sorry. I didn't mean to startle you," he said.

"Want to talk about it?" she asked.

He climbed from the bed and grabbed a towel from the bathroom. "It was my mom. She was right there with me, like she was in all the pictures at my dad's house. She was pushing me from behind." He washed his face and came back to the bedroom. "I haven't dreamed of her in years."

"Maybe you're really missing her right now because you were thinking about our future and having kids," Lacy said.

He smiled and touched her cheek. "Maybe."

"You'd better get ready. The alarm should go off in five

minutes. I want to get ready early, too. I'm going to stop by that toy store in town and pick up a few things for Katie and Charlie before I meet them." She touched his side as she walked into the bathroom. "I'm really looking forward to spending the day with them. I think it'll be fun. What's the plan after you're done? Do you want to call me?"

He wrapped his arms around her from behind and kissed the back of her neck. "Yeah, I want to call you. I always want to talk to my *friend*."

"Then I hope I'm the only *friend* you're *talking* with," Lacy teased.

"I was thinking that we might go to the concert at Nauset Beach tonight." He turned her in his arms and kissed her lips.

"That sounds like fun. Can we ask Rob and Sheila to come? Kids love the beach, and most kids like music. I bet they'd have a blast," she said. "Well, if they don't get worn-out at the fair."

"Man, I l…like you," he said.

"Careful now. No breaking our promise." The pact had become a joke, but Lacy felt that it was also a way for them to skirt around their real feelings, and while she was as keen as the next person when it came to jokes, in her heart she longed to hear him say those three words that tickled her tongue every time she was in his arms.

KATIE HELD LACY'S hand in one hand and tucked the stuffed bear Lacy had brought her under her other arm as they walked through the Barnstable County Fair. Every few steps, she did a little skip, sending her pigtails bouncing. Charlie walked beside Sheila, his lanky arms dangling by his sides and a brooding frown on his pink lips.

"I wanna ride the big roller coaster." Charlie pouted.

"You're a little too short. Remember? You have to be as tall as the wooden bear was," Sheila reminded him.

Charlie had been just a few inches shorter than the required height, and he hadn't let it go since. "How about the petting zoo?" Lacy asked.

"Animals are for babies," Charlie said. With his light skin and a spray of freckles across his nose, he reminded Lacy of Alfalfa from *The Little Rascals*. She'd had a difficult time finding an appropriate toy for him, as he was too old for stuffed animals and she wasn't sure what he liked, but he seemed to enjoy the Matchbox truck she'd bought him, which was clenched within his fist.

"Babies? I love animals and I'm not a baby," Lacy said.

"Charlie, be nice." Sheila wore a pair of navy blue shorts and a colorful tank top. Her long hair flowed freely down her back, and after reprimanding Charlie, she mouthed, *Sorry*, to Lacy.

Lacy mouthed back, *It's okay.*

"Animals! Animals!" Katie yelled.

"Sheila, why don't you take Katie in, and I'll hang out here with Charlie," Lacy offered.

"Animals are for babies, but I'm big enough to watch Katie." Charlie stuck his chin out at Sheila and reached for Katie's hand. "I'll take her in."

Sheila scanned the petting area, which was separated into an area for children only and an area for adults and children. "Great idea, Charlie. Why don't you take her into that one? I trust you, Charlie. You hold her hand and stay with her every second. I'll stand right here and watch. Katie, give me your bear."

They watched the kids go through the gate. Charlie held Katie's hand so tight that his arm looked rigid, and Katie stared up at him adoringly. Lacy leaned against the fence.

Sheila shook her head. "Am I a horrible mother for letting him take her in alone?"

"What? No. You're a good mother. Anyone can see that," Lacy assured her. "He needs to feel important, and letting him take her makes him feel that way."

"Even though I kind of tricked him and had him take her into the children-only area?"

"Look at them," Lacy said.

They watched the kids petting a baby goat. Katie giggled when the goat touched her with his nose, and Charlie stepped between the goat and Katie, then asked Katie if she was okay.

"They're happy, and he feels valued and grown-up. I'd say that's good parenting. Now, if you'd have wandered off to smoke a cigarette and drink a beer while they were in there, then you might qualify as a sucky mom."

Sheila sighed. "Thanks, Lacy. I'm just sidetracked, I guess."

"With all the stuff you and Rob have been dealing with, I think you wouldn't be human if you weren't knocked a little off-kilter."

"I guess." Sheila waved to the kids. "Did Rob tell you and Dane why I needed a break?"

Lacy shook her head, wondering exactly how they'd gotten back together so quickly.

"Because for fourteen years I've worried. Every time he leaves for a trip, I wonder what's going to happen to him. I don't worry about women or any of the other silliness that people worry about, but life and death, that's hanging over our heads every time my husband goes to work." Sheila wiped her eyes and looked at Lacy. "You don't worry about Dane?"

"Sure I do, but he's assured me that he's careful. He says that there's—"

"A better chance of getting hit by a car than bitten by a shark. I've heard it all a million times. For all these years, Rob has done what he loves doing with little regard for what it does to the people who love him," Sheila said.

"Sheila, Rob cares. Besides, you knew what he did when you married him, right?" Lacy asked.

"Yeah. Before Brave, he worked with another company. That one went under, and sometimes I wish Brave would do the same." She looked up at Lacy with sad eyes. "I know how awful that sounds. You know what Dane does. You know the risks. Is it stopping you from being with him?"

Lacy shook her head. "I'm not sure anything could keep me from him."

"That's the problem," Sheila said. "I'd do anything to be with Rob. He's my Superman. I still get butterflies when I see him, but now I worry about the kids needing him around more often. You're lucky. Dane's a lot younger than Rob. His reflexes are still fast. He's virile and focused. Lately, Rob's slowing down. He's getting tired. He's had a long career doing what he loves. I'd just like for him to do something else now. Something safer."

"He loves you and the kids, Sheila," Lacy said.

Sheila nodded. "He does. He adores us, and last night he told me he'd decided that I was right. I think we both needed time to clear our heads so we could see things more clearly. We realized that we couldn't live without each other, and Rob realized that it was time for a change. He's giving Dane a month's notice after the dive today."

"Really? Dane will be devastated," Lacy said.

"He will, and I feel bad, but it's time," Sheila said.

"See, the fact that he made that decision shows you that what you have is true love," Lacy said. *Neither of us is willing to give up anything. Does that mean we don't have true love?* She swallowed the thought. "I'm so glad you guys have worked it out."

Lacy hugged Sheila, silently pushing her concerns out of her head. Those were Sheila's worries, but they weren't Lacy's. Lacy hadn't spent nearly a year worried about if Dane was going to live through each day. She'd been too busy lying in wait, wanting to see him, longing to hear his voice—and working her butt off just to keep from worrying about the women it turned out he hadn't even been with.

Chapter Twenty-Five

DANE AND ROB donned their wet suits like second skins. Dane's head was clear as he prepared for one of his favorite dives—the free dive. Bubbles from regulators tended to spook sharks, but with free diving, there were no oxygen tanks. There were no bubbles. Dane and Rob had spent years honing their free diving abilities, until each of them could hold their breath for almost five minutes. Dane could hold his breath even longer, pushing five and a half on his best days. Today they were accompanied by three members of a local dive team, one to watch the boat and two for dive assistance.

"Hey, man, I was going to wait and talk to you after the dive, but I gotta tell you something," Rob said to Dane. His wet suit stretched tight across his thick barrel chest, and when he crossed his arms, the suit looked as if it were painted on his muscular biceps.

"Sure. Shoot." Dane sat on the deck and rested his arms on his knees.

"You know Sheila's been asking me to stop diving for the last two years," Rob began.

"Yeah, I know. You said you dealt with that already."

"Yeah, well." Rob ran his hand through his thick brown hair

and dropped his eyes. "The thing is, she's worried about the kids. She said Charlie's having a hard time, and she can't take all the worrying anymore every time I go to work. That's why she needed a break, Dane. She said it's too hard. She worries, and with the kids getting bigger and needing me around." He shrugged.

"What are you saying, Rob?"

"She only came back because I told her that I'd quit. I'm old, Dane. You know that," Rob said.

"Baloney. Taggers do it into their seventies. You're the one who told me that. You said you'd tag way past when you could get it up, and I know you're not having any trouble in that department, Rob." Dane looked away. He was well aware of Sheila's concerns and how they'd grown over the past two years, but he never would have guessed that Rob would quit. He figured he had at least another ten years with him.

"I've gone over it a hundred times. I can't see any other way. She left me, Dane. Up and left. Took my kids. You saw what that did to me. It sent me right over the edge. I can't afford to be in that place, and losing my family would do that to me. If she left for good, I'd be back on the bottle in no time." Rob held Dane's stare. "We've had a good run of it."

"Had a good—Rob, do you hear yourself? This isn't happening." Dane stood and paced. "Maybe you should have waited to tell me. How are we going to be placid down there with this crap hanging over us?"

"This *crap* is my life, Dane." Rob rose to his feet, planting his hands on his wide hips.

Dane looked at him and shook his head, then blew out a frustrated breath. "I'm sorry. I get it. I don't want you to lose your family. You know that. But, Rob, I don't want to lose you either. You're my partner, man. We're like two sides of a coin. We don't balance without each other." He swung his arm over Rob's shoulder. "This is really the only option?"

Dane felt as if his left leg had been ripped off, but if Rob were Rex, Treat, or any of his siblings, he'd support his decision to be with his family, and Rob was just as important to Dane as they were. He took a deep breath and blew it out slowly.

"So I guess this is our last dive mission together?" he asked.

Rob shrugged. "As I said, I can't see another way around it." He scrubbed his face with his hands. "Man, if there were any other way…"

Dane heard the defeat in his low voice. "It's okay, Rob. It sucks, but you're right. Family has to come first." His mind drifted to Lacy, and no matter how he turned it over in his mind, he knew that if they'd had a family and she said she'd leave, he'd probably do the same thing. "But does it have to be all or nothing?"

"Whaddaya mean?" Rob asked.

"I'll still need a guy to run the boat, someone to work the deck. No water work. No tagging, no diving. Would Sheila be okay with that?" Dane hoped Rob would take him up on the offer. Losing Rob altogether would be too much for Dane to handle. It would really feel like losing one of his siblings.

"Not sure," Rob said. "I can't see why not, but, Dane, you'd have to raise more funds. You'd have to hire another diver and train them. You probably can't absorb the extra expense."

Rob knew about Dane's trust fund, and he also knew how Dane felt about dipping into it. But for Rob, Dane didn't care if he had funding or not. He'd make it happen. "Dude, what does my dad always say?"

"Family knows no boundaries," Rob said with a smile.

"That's right. And you and Sheila are family. If Sheila's okay with it, then it's a done deal. And we'll work out a schedule where you're home most of every month. I need you around a little, too. Like a security blanket." Dane nudged his arm.

Rob pretended to punch Dane in the gut. "Sissy." He laughed. "Thanks, man."

"Hey, let's take another half an hour and chill before we dive," Dane suggested. With free diving, the diver needed to be in a calm mental state. They needed to be balanced. If either Dane or Rob was feeling agitated, he would jeopardize the dive.

"Good. I was just thinking the same thing," Rob said.

Thirty minutes later, Dane was breathing easier and Rob was joking with one of the other divers, which further eased Dane's mind. He took stock of his own emotions. He closed his eyes and took a deep breath, weighing his frustrations. Rob was doing what he had to do. He loved Rob, and the last thing he wanted was for him to end up on the bottle for good. *He's doing the right thing.* Dane opened his eyes feeling calm and confident.

He patted Rob on the back. "Are you going to be okay on this dive? You wanna sit out?"

"I'm good," Rob said. "Let's do this."

While the other two divers donned their gloves, boots, and wet suits and prepared their spear guns and goggles, Dane and Rob slipped into the murky water, knowing that after they descended, the other divers would remain at the water's surface, flapping their hands and kicking their feet to attract sharks, and if that didn't work, they'd throw a bit of chum in the water.

Dane and Rob kicked straight down, descending about forty feet, where they reached neutral buoyancy. The ocean stopped pushing them toward the surface and started pulling them toward the floor. With their arms by their sides, they sank effortlessly to the ocean floor. Rob swam away to Dane's right. They crossed their legs and waited on the sandy bottom. After only a minute, Dane saw the dark shadowy figure of a shark approaching. He ascended slowly, knowing Rob would be doing the same. The shark was twenty feet away, ten, and nearing quickly.

This sucker's about nine feet. Dane looked for Rob, and in the murky depths, he made out a figure a football field away to his right, rising parallel to him. They rose in sync with each other to a depth of roughly twenty-five feet. The shark torpedoed past Rob, and Dane saw Rob change directions, ascending at an angle toward the boat. A breath away from Dane, the shark shot up toward the surface. Dane followed in its wake through the murky water. The shark disappeared from view. *Two minutes.* Dane spotted the diver's feet kicking at the surface. He scanned the area for Rob, searching for the familiar blur of his powerful legs kicking, his streamlined body angling upward, but Rob was nowhere in sight. He turned to his left, then to his right, wishing the water were clearer. His line of sight was too murky. He squinted, trying to pull Rob's shape from the depths of the sea, when the shark burst through the darkness and sped past Dane. Dane shot toward the right, then spun around and searched again for Rob—and spotted him floating lifelessly, his arms out to his sides, his neck hanging limply forward. Fear shocked him into action. Dane swam faster than he ever had to Rob's side, his heart hammering against his chest, emergency procedures running through his mind. He grabbed ahold of Rob beneath his armpits and kicked for all he was worth toward the surface. *Damn it! Move. Move. Hang on, buddy! Hang on!* His lungs burned. His muscles were on fire despite the cold water as he kicked against the helpless weight of Rob's body. Every foot he ascended felt like a mile as he pushed his lungs past their limit and silently prayed for Rob's life to be spared. The other divers came into view. Dane couldn't think past the need to get Rob out of the water. The divers swept down a few feet from the surface. They grabbed Rob and pulled his lifeless body into the boat. Dane burst through the surface gasping for air. *Rob. Save Rob.* He pushed through the dizziness that threatened to steal his ability to think and hauled himself into the boat. Each breath burned deeper than the one before.

"What the hell happened?" He bent over Rob's mouth, listening for breathing sounds beyond his own hard pants. *No breath.* He fisted his hand and smashed it into the center of Rob's chest. Dane's body shook with fear. His lungs still burned, but he didn't notice or care. "Come on. Come on! Radio it in. Get to shore!" He felt for a pulse. *No pulse.* Dane administered another precordial thump to the center of Rob's chest. Rob's face was ashen, his lips tinged blue.

"He got hit in the head by the shark's tail," one of the guys yelled.

Dane's felt for a pulse. *No.* With tears streaming down his face, Dane channeled all of his fear and all of his muscle into a third precordial thump. "Come on, you bastard!" He grabbed Rob's wrist. "Faint pulse. Get a blanket." He bent over Rob's face and listened for breathing sounds. Someone covered Rob's legs with heavy blankets.

"He's not breathing," Dane yelled. He couldn't hear past the roar of the engine as they neared shore. He tilted Rob's head back and held his nose closed; then Dane covered Rob's mouth with his own and blew a desperate, heavy breath into his friend's lungs. He lowered his ear to Rob's mouth. "Come on. Come on," he said through gritted teeth. He covered Rob's mouth with his own again and breathed life into Rob's lungs again, then listened for Rob's breathing to kick in. "Come on, Rob." Again he tilted Rob's head back, plugged his nose, and covered his friend's mouth with his. He breathed air from his lungs into Rob's until he had no more air to breathe. Water dribbled from the corner of Rob's mouth, and relief swept through Dane. He bent over and listened again. Rob's shallow breathing was music to his ears. His pulse was thready. Dane yanked the blankets to Rob's rib cage; then he began chest compressions one second apart. *Sixteen, seventeen, eighteen…*When he hit thirty, he breathed for Rob again. He had to help the blood flow through his friend's body. His arms trembled and shook as he administered thirty more compressions, then breathed air into Rob's lungs.

Dane was still hunkered over Rob, counting compressions, when the rescue team climbed onto the boat. "Nineteen, twenty…"

"We got him from here," someone said.

Dane continued. "Twenty-nine, thirty." He bent over to breathe for Rob and a strong hand pulled him back. Dane twisted out of his grip. "I have to help him. His breathing's shallow. His pulse is weak."

Two strong men held Dane back as he twisted and fought to get to Rob. "Get the heck off me. I have to help him."

Rob was already on a stretcher. They were taking him to the ambulance.

"Dane!" a deep voice hollered.

Dane shook his head, jolting himself out of his state of shock.

"Come with us. We have to check you out, too," the man

said.

"I gotta get to Rob," Dane yelled, finally noticing the paramedic's uniform.

"I'm a paramedic, and I'm taking you to him. You did good. He's being taken care of."

With Dane in his grasp, the paramedic guided him into the ambulance.

Chapter Twenty-Six

LACY HELD KATIE against her chest as she, Sheila, and Charlie burst through the emergency room doors. Her body shook; her mind refused to process Treat's call. *Dane's in the hospital.* Treat was a major supporter of the hospital, and they'd called him right away. *Dane's okay, but Rob's on shaky ground. They had a diving accident. No blood, but Rob's unconscious.*

"My husband, Robert Mann, he was brought in. Diving accident," Sheila said through her tears to the woman behind the registration desk.

"And Dane Braden, they were together," Lacy said with Katie clinging to her. Katie had been crying since they'd received the call from Treat, and although Lacy was sure she didn't understand what was going on, she panicked in response to Sheila's and Lacy's reactions. They'd packed up the kids and sped to the hospital.

A tall, African American nurse came around the desk. "Mrs. Mann, please, come with me. Unfortunately, your son will have to wait here. Can your friend watch him?"

Sheila shot a helpless look toward Lacy. Her brown eyes were red and swollen, and her makeup ran in streaks down her cheeks. Charlie stood beside his mother, his face the same brooding mask it had been earlier in the day.

Lacy could hardly breathe. "Go. I've got them. Go," she said. *Dane. Please be okay.* She held her hand out to Charlie. "Come here, sweetie."

Charlie took her hand.

The woman behind the desk said, "Your name?"

Lacy contemplated lying. *Sister. Wife?* Finally, she spit out her name. "Lacy Snow," she said. "Is he okay?"

The woman scanned a clipboard. "Yes, there you are. He gave us your name. He's okay. He was in shock." The woman held up a finger toward Lacy, then said something to a male nurse behind her. "Mike can take you back to see him if you have someone with you to watch the kids."

"Thank you." *The kids. Darn it.* She felt her lips quivering and turned back toward the desk. "I don't have anyone to watch them."

The woman shook her head. "I'm sorry. We can't allow them in the back."

Lacy ran through possible solutions. She didn't know anyone in Chatham. Not anyone she could leave someone else's children with. She turned back to the woman behind the desk. "And the man he was with? How is he? Rob Mann?"

"I'm sorry, but we can only release information to family members or those who are on the release form," the woman said.

Lacy groaned. She bounced Katie, trying to calm her down while her own mind ran in circles. "Can you let Dane Braden know I'm here, but that I have Rob's kids and I can't come back with them? I hate him being alone. I need him to know I'm here."

"We can do that," she said.

"Thank you."

Torn between being relieved that Dane was okay and worry-ing about Rob, Lacy took the children to a small table in the corner of the room, where there were toys and coloring books strewn about. She set Katie on the chair beside her, and Charlie sat down with his arms crossed. Lacy looked back at the doors to the patient area, thinking about Rob. *Please let him be okay.* Katie clutched her bear and reached for a coloring book with her free hand.

"Did my dad get bitten by a shark?" Charlie asked.

"No, honey, no. He didn't get bitten by a shark." *But he could have been.*

"When can we see him?" he asked.

"I'm not sure, honey. They'll tell us when you can." Lacy wished Danica were there, or Kaylie, or someone who could help. She considered her options. *Mom? What if Sheila already called someone?*

"Ms. Snow?" Lacy spun around.

"Yes, I'm Lacy Snow."

The male nurse from earlier pulled her to the side and said quietly, "Mr. Braden has asked to be released, so you'll see him in just a few minutes. He asked me to let you know."

"Thank you. Thank you so much," she said. *Released. He really is okay.*

Lacy turned her attention back to the children.

"Lace?"

"Dane!" She spun around and flew into Dane's arms. "I was so worried. Are you okay? Treat didn't tell me much," she said.

Dane looked at the kids. "Hi, guys. I'm just going to talk to Lacy over here for a minute."

Lacy's stomach plunged. "What happened? Dane, what

happened to Rob?"

Dane's eyes filled with tears. He shook his head. "I...I shouldn't have let him dive."

"Dane, look at me. What happened?"

"We were free diving, and he got hit in the head. Hard. He was knocked unconscious."

"Unconscious? He was or he is unconscious?" Lacy looked at the emergency room doors again. *He's back there. Sheila's back there. Alone.*

"Was. He's breathing. He wasn't breathing. He didn't have a pulse. I helped him. He's breathing now, but he still hasn't regained consciousness," Dane explained.

She searched Dane's eyes. They were flat, like he was lost or dazed. "But you're okay?" She ran her hands up and down his arms.

He nodded. "Yeah."

"Sheila's alone. She needs someone. Dane, I have to go back there," Lacy said. "Please, can you get them to let me back there? She's gotta be so scared."

"I can. Treat's a big supporter of the hospital. They put two and two together when they signed me in and said they were calling him. I told him to call you. They'll let you go in the back with Sheila." He looked at the kids. "I'm sorry, Lace."

"Sorry? It sounds like you helped him. This isn't your fault," she said. "This is..." *A risk of your job.* She couldn't say it aloud. His job was a heck of a lot more dangerous than walking across the street. "Can you watch the kids? Are you okay enough to?"

"Yeah, I'm fine," he said. "I'll go talk to the nurse and have them bring you back."

Chapter Twenty-Seven

LACY COULDN'T REMEMBER the last time she'd been in a hospital room. She stood in the doorway of Rob's room. The antiseptic smell permeated her senses as she took in Rob, lying with his head back, a thick white tube down his throat and an EKG monitor strapped across his chest with wires running to a machine by his bedside. Another monitor was attached to his index finger, and an IV line snaked from his arm. Sheila sat on the opposite side of the bed, holding his hand, tears streaming down her cheeks. Lacy took a step inside the room, feeling sick to her stomach.

"Sheila," she whispered.

Sheila turned to face her. Her eyes were wet and puffy, and her slim, upturned nose was pink from crying. Her hair was a long, tangled mess. Her shirt had come untucked from her shorts and hung awkwardly from one side.

Lacy embraced her. "I'm so sorry," she said through her own tears.

"Where are the kids?" Sheila managed. She clutched a handful of tissues in her trembling hands.

"Dane's with them."

Sheila nodded. "He's okay?"

"Yeah, seems to be. What did they say about Rob?"

Fresh sobs ripped from her chest. "He…They said if he wakes up soon, then he'll have less of a chance of any deficits."

Deficits. He was going to quit today, and now he might have deficits. "If…? Do they think…?" Lacy wiped the tears that streamed down her cheeks.

"I don't know. They don't know. Dane thought a nine-foot shark whacked his head and knocked him unconscious. A freaking shark." Sheila covered her face. "This is why…" Sobs swallowed her voice.

A shark. This is real. This could happen to Dane. Or worse.

"What am I going to do? I can't live without Rob. The kids need him. What if he doesn't wake up?" Sheila stood and touched Rob's cheek. "He's my life."

Lacy reached for Sheila again.

Sheila didn't collapse in to her this time. She grabbed Lacy by the shoulders. Her dark eyes were filled with fear and venom. Her thin lips turned down at the edge in an angry frown. "Lacy, this could be you and Dane. This is what I was so afraid of."

No. I don't want to hear it. Please stop. Stopstopstop.

"Honey, I know you love him, but think about it. This is real, Lacy. Real."

"I'm sorry, Sheila. I'm so sorry," Lacy said, and they fell into each other's arms and held on tight. "What can I do? Who should I call? We can stay with the kids for as long as you need us to."

"I called my parents. They're on their way. I know Dane's going to feel guilty, and the doctor said he saved Rob's life. Please tell him thank you for me. Please tell him that I don't blame him. I know Dane, and he'll blame himself." Sheila took Rob's hand in hers again.

"I will."

"What did you tell the kids?" Sheila asked.

"Nothing. I didn't know what you wanted me to tell them. They're so sweet, and they are very worried. Do you want me to sit with Rob while you go see them?" Lacy asked.

"Should I? I don't want to leave him." Sheila looked from Rob to Lacy and back again.

Her eyes widened, and Lacy knew she wanted her to give her the answer. "I don't know. I'm not a mom, but I think they'd want to know you're okay and hear something about their dad."

"What if it upsets them more, and then I have to leave them again?" she asked.

"I wish I had the answers." Lacy reached for her arm, just to reassure her that she wasn't alone in all of this. "I can tell them whatever you want if you'd rather."

"No, I should do it. Will you stay with Rob? I want him to know someone's here with him." Sheila stood and moved toward the door. "I'll only be a few minutes."

"Of course."

As she sat alone in the room with Rob, the machine beeped in a constant eerie cadence—a gruesome reminder of Rob's condition. Lacy crossed to the other side of the bed and noticed the bandages covering the left side of his face. *A nine-foot shark whacked his head.* She reached for her thigh and wondered if his cheek looked the same beneath the bandage. A flash of pain ran through her leg as she remembered being grazed by the shark.

She thought of the pride she'd seen in his eyes when he looked at Charlie and the love she'd seen for Sheila and Katie. He had been so vital last night. Now his skin had lost its sheen. It looked pasty, like it had lost all of its elasticity. *How can that happen overnight?* Anger stirred deep in her belly. *A shark whacked his head.*

This was a choice. Nobody forced him to dive. He chose this lifestyle. Dane chose this lifestyle. *For all these years, Rob has done what he loves doing with little regard for what it does to the people who love him.* She could replace *Rob* with *Dane. With little regard for what it does to the people who love him.* Her hands began to shake. *Would you give up your career for me?* Why hadn't she seen his answer for what it was? *Come on, Lace.* He'd said it like she was asking a silly question. It wasn't a silly question. *And now. Now?* She looked at Rob and felt a thread of longing for the man he had been the day before.

Sheila returned to the room, and Lacy's whole body was shaking.

"I feel a little better having talked to the kids," Sheila said. "My parents should be here in half an hour. Did he move at all?"

Lacy barely registered her words. Tears tumbled down her cheeks. She felt sick to her stomach.

"Lacy?" Sheila said.

Lacy didn't respond. She couldn't. What if it had been Dane? What if it was Dane tomorrow or next year?

"Lacy? Honey, are you okay? Should I get the nurse?"

She felt Sheila's arm around her shoulder, she heard her voice, but she couldn't process the words she was saying.

"What are you going to do?" The words came out as a whisper, without thought, without inflection. Flat and dry.

"I'm going to stay right here until Rob wakes up. And if he doesn't wake up, I'm going to sit here some more. I can't lose him, Lacy. I have to believe he'll be okay." Sheila touched her arm. "Honey, are you okay?"

Lacy managed a nod.

"Dane said Rob told him he was quitting, and he'd offered Rob a job driving the boat and helping in other ways, not diving, not tagging. I think Dane's still in shock. He's having a really hard time."

Lacy shook her head.

"Lacy?"

"Huh?" she said.

Sheila looked at Rob, then back at Lacy. "Lacy, why don't you go be with Dane? He needs you."

Chapter Twenty-Eight

AFTER SHEILA'S PARENTS took the kids home with them to Connecticut and Sheila assured Dane and Lacy that she'd be okay staying with Rob, Lacy drove Dane back to the marina in silence. When they arrived at Treat's boat, Lacy followed Dane down to the cabin, clutching her keys and unable to think past the accident. She couldn't get the image of Rob out of her mind, and Sheila's words pummeled her mind over and over until she felt like they were coming from her own lips. *For all these years Rob has done what he loves doing with little regard for what it does to the people who love him.*

"Lacy, we should talk." Dane's eyes were full of sadness, but the rest of his face was emotionless. His mouth hung slightly open, and there were tension lines across his forehead. He looked as though he was still in shock.

Lacy was unable to concentrate or even think past the new worry that had taken over her mind.

He sank onto a cushioned bench. He didn't reach for her hand; he didn't pull her close. He didn't look into her eyes the way he always had. Dane folded his hands in his lap.

"My job is risky," he said.

"It is," she said robotically.

"When I held Rob's lifeless body in my arms..." Tears sprang from his eyes. "I was sure I'd lost him."

Seeing Dane cry tugged tears from her eyes, too.

Dane stared at the floor. "He might not wake up. Sheila and the kids might lose him tonight. Lacy, he quit before we dove. He was giving up diving, and now...now he might never wake up again."

"Yes." Lacy's mind was impotent. She couldn't form a coherent thought. She felt reality staring her in the face. Dane could have been the one who was hit. Their conversation came rushing back to her. *What if something happened to you? What if I gave up everything and, I don't know, you get eaten by a shark or something?* He'd answered her so easily, like the risks associated with his job weren't real. *Lacy, that's not going to happen.* She held on to the wall for stability.

"I can't do it to you, Lacy. I can't ask you to be with me knowing the reality of what could happen," Dane said. "I can't live knowing that you could end up in the same place that Sheila is right now." His voice was cold and hard.

"I know." Fresh tears sprang from her eyes. She clenched her keys so hard they cut into her skin.

Dane shook his head. "I promised not to fall in love with you." He raised cold eyes to her, and when he spoke, his words came out hot and mean. "I lied. I love you, Lacy. But I love you too much to let you be with me."

"I understand." Lacy couldn't feel her face. Her lips were numb.

"You should go. It's too hard to see you, knowing we shouldn't be together." Dane looked away then, his hands fisted by his sides, his teeth gritted. "Leave, Lace. Please leave. You deserve a life with a man who will come home every night in one piece. Alive. Please, just go."

Her legs were controlled by someone other than herself. They had to be. They were moving up the stairs. *No! Go back!* And then she was running. Running faster than she'd run in years. She was in the car, driving. She didn't remember any of the turns or stopping at red lights. *How did I get here?* She stood on the porch of the cottage. She unlocked the cottage door. *The cottage that Dane rented me.* She didn't remember turning on the bath or soaking until her fingers and toes had pruned. She didn't remember hearing the phone ring and ignoring it—multiple times.

When Lacy opened her eyes as the morning sun streamed through the curtains, she couldn't remember ever feeling so lost. She buried her head beneath the pillow and closed her eyes again. Maybe she could stay here forever, in this nowhere land, this gray state of half awake and half asleep. Maybe if she tried hard enough, she really could disappear. No, she couldn't do that. *Rob's unconscious. Sheila needs me.* She had to get to the hospital. She tried to move from the bed, but her body wouldn't respond to her command. When had she become so exhausted? *Dane. Dane will come. No matter what I need, he'll come for me.* She collapsed back against the mattress with the weight of a dead man. Dane wouldn't answer her pleas. Dane was gone. They were done. She closed her eyes and allowed herself to be whisked away into another day of blissful sleep.

DANE SHOT UP in bed. His eyes darted around the cabin, his pulse racing. *Stupid dream.* He looked at the empty space beside him, where Lacy should have been. The evening before came back in bits and pieces. *Rob. Oh no, Rob.* The next thought brought Lacy, and reality hit him like a brick in the face. He'd sent her away. He'd had to protect her. *I did the right thing.* His chest burned. *If I did the right thing, why do I feel like someone turned my body inside out and kicked me to the curb?* He wanted to stay in his cabin and never face the world again. He wanted to go someplace far away, where he could disappear and wallow in his despair.

He dragged himself from bed, went into the bathroom, and turned on the shower. He stepped under the warm spray and ran his hands through his hair, thinking of his call to the hospital last night. *No change.* Rob had been moved to the ICU, and he was being treated prophylactically for aspiration pneumonia.

The feel of Rob's weight in his arms was ingrained in his muscle memory. The feel of his friend's stilled chest beneath his hands came back to him, and the rush of fear that had torn through him returned. Dane fisted his hands, remembering how hard he'd thumped Rob's chest. His lungs burned as they had yesterday. He'd have climbed into Rob's body and pumped his heart by hand if he could have. He thought of Lacy running into his arms at the hospital and, later, walking off the boat and sprinting away. The images came at him all at once. Lacy, naked beneath him. Rob laughing on the deck of the boat. The damn shark whipping up toward the surface. Dane covered his face, trying to stop the flow of tears that burned as they left his eyes. He didn't recognize the rumbling in his chest. He didn't hear the desperate cries as they tore from his lungs, or feel the muscles in his legs tense when he dropped to his knees on the shower floor and buried his face in his hands. He didn't feel the terror that ripped through him at the thought of losing Rob and

Lacy. A piercing pain seared through his heart. *Finally.* A pain he recognized. The same gut-wrenching pain that had speared him the day his mother had died. He cried out again, this time with determination. The words that came were indiscernible, but they didn't matter. He had to let the incessant gnawing pain out of his body before it ate him alive.

Chapter Twenty-Nine

DANE'S PHONE HADN'T stopped ringing all morning, and as he pulled into the hospital parking lot, it chimed again. *Treat.* He couldn't deal with him right then. He couldn't deal with Blake, or Savannah, or Hugh, or Rex, or any of the others he'd received calls from. Every time the phone rang, he looked to see if it was Lacy—half wishing it was her, though he knew he wouldn't have answered it. *I did the right thing. She could be sitting by my bed in the hospital right now.* The thought sucked the life from him. His family would have to wait. He barely had the fortitude to do what he had to do and visit Rob.

He left the phone in the car and lumbered into the hospital, stopping just inside the doors to gather his wits about him. He scrubbed his face with his hands, then ran his hand through his hair, thinking about Katie and Charlie, now with their grandparents, probably petrified about their father's situation. *Please let Rob be okay. Take me. He has a family. Please. Take me.*

He made his way up to the ICU and stood outside Rob's room, taking one deep breath after another. *Hold it together.* The door felt too heavy, wrong, as he pushed through it and stepped inside. The sight of Rob's immobile body diminished beneath the sterile sheets, the tube still down his throat, and

Sheila asleep in a chair, her hand encircling his, was too much for Dane. Tears threatened again, and he struggled to hold them back, for Sheila's sake. His chest lurched with each constricted sob that he held hostage.

The door slipped closed behind him, and Sheila raised her head with a start, her hopeful eyes finding Rob before realizing the noise came from the other side of the room and shifting her gaze to Dane.

"Dane," she whispered.

He moved toward her, his arms open wide. She met him at the foot of the bed and collapsed against him, opening the flood gates for his tears.

"I'm so sorry, Sheila. I wish it had been me."

"I know you do," she said. "This wasn't your fault, Dane. It's a risk of the job. I know that. Rob knows that."

Tears slipped down his cheeks as he held her, strangled by guilt. "What...what are the doctors saying?" he managed. Sheila went back to her chair, and Dane squeezed Rob's other lifeless hand. His heart sank when Rob didn't respond. *It's real. This is real. Oh man. Rob.*

"They're hopeful. They said we wait." Sheila stood and touched Rob's cheek. "I can't lose him, Dane," she whispered. She kissed Rob's cheek. "Don't you leave me. Don't you leave Katie and Charlie."

A tear slipped down Dane's cheek. *Don't leave me.* "I did everything I could. The second I realized what happened, I got him out of the water. If only I'd been closer to him. If only I'd been the one at the rear of the shark."

"Stop," Sheila whispered.

"Sheila, I'd do anything to have had it be me. Rob has everything to live for. I've ruined your family. Your kids...They need their father."

"Stop," she repeated.

"He quit. I shouldn't have let him go down. He was probably distracted. I should have stopped him," Dane said.

"Stop, Dane. Please stop. You can't change what happened. You can't make it all better. All we can do is pray he gets well. And if not..." She turned away, her shoulders rounded forward, rocking with sobs.

Dane wanted to take Sheila's pain away. This had to be his fault. Maybe he'd been too distracted by Lacy lately to see what was going on around him. Maybe that's why he'd missed the warning signs that Rob was going through a difficult time. In an effort to take some of the burden and all of the blame for all that had happened between them lately, Dane said, "I ended it with Lacy."

She turned to face him, shaking her head.

"Maybe if I wasn't thinking about her all the time, I would have seen the trouble you and Rob were having."

Sheila sniffled through her tears. "No, Dane. Rob didn't want you to know. He didn't want to quit. Don't break up with Lacy because of that. None of this is your fault, and in your heart you know that."

He clenched his eyes shut against the tears that tumbled down his cheeks. He knew it was selfish to keep talking about himself, but he couldn't stop the confession from leaving his lips. "This is real. I can't do that to her. What if it happens to me in a year, or a month, or ten years?" He shook his head. "I can't do it. She deserves a normal life."

"Oh, Dane. Yes, it could happen to you, too."

For a moment everything in the room felt as though it stopped, except for that insufferable beeping from the machine.

Dane felt like he'd been thrown against a wall. *Yes, it could happen to you, too.*

"I'm so sorry," Sheila said. "She loves you."

Dane shook his head. *Stop thinking about Lacy. That's over. Focus on Sheila and Rob.* He wiped his eyes with the crook of his elbow.

"Tell me what you need and it's yours. Don't worry about finances. I've got you covered forever. Rob always knew I would if anything ever happened, but what can I help with? The kids? Anything?" He remembered from when his mother was sick and they didn't know which way she'd turn the next hour, or day, or week, that there were no words to heal the despair that buried itself in a person's soul while they waited for a loved one's body to decide its fate, but knowing Dane was there and willing to do whatever she needed might give her comfort.

She shook her head. "I just want Rob. He's my best friend, Dane. He's my life."

Dane leaned over and kissed Rob's forehead. He took his healthy cheek in his palm and whispered, "You can pull through this. You're the strongest man I know. Your run's not over yet. I love you, man."

"He knows you do," Sheila said.

I'm not so sure.

Chapter Thirty

STOP THAT INCESSANT banging! Lacy lay on the bed staring up at the ceiling. She'd been in that position for hours, thinking about Sheila and her children, worried about Rob. She wondered if Rob had had any final thoughts when he was whipped with the tail of the shark as it careered through the water, or if he went from excitement over seeing the stupid thing to nothing. Unconscious. And then her mind traveled back to Dane. *It always comes back to him.* She wondered for a moment if it was him banging on the door, but that thought disappeared with her next breath. She'd seen the finality in his eyes.

She curled up in a fetal position, praying that whoever was banging would go away. How could she move with a broken heart? The reality of the dangers of Dane's job were staring her in the face, and they'd apparently hit Dane like a bullet train. *He said what I'd been thinking but was too weak to admit. We're doing the right thing.* That didn't mean she didn't feel like she'd been run over by a Mack truck.

The banging stopped, and Lacy flipped over to her other side and stared at the curtains. How could the sun be out when Sheila was sitting in a hospital room wondering if her husband would live or die? *Oh, no. Rob could die.*

"Lacy, open the door!"

Kaylie? Lacy's body went rigid.

"Lacy! It's us. Please open the door. Lacy, are you okay?" Danica banged on the window again.

Lacy sat up, wanting to climb through the window and run into her sisters' arms, but she also wanted to wallow in her pain and sadness. She wanted to feel the pain of losing Dane, if only to help her believe it was true.

"Lacy, it's us," Kaylie said. "Please open the door. If you did something stupid like overdose, I'm going to kill you."

I almost wish you would.

"Kaylie!" Danica chided.

Lacy pushed herself from the bed and peered through the curtains at her sisters' worried faces. They were staring at each other, whispering something Lacy couldn't hear. They didn't notice her. She released the curtains, went out the front door, and listened to them arguing about calling the police. Lacy stepped off the porch and stumbled through the grass. Her legs felt like lead, and she grabbed hold of the side of the cottage to keep from falling over as she reached the side yard.

"Oh my goodness. Lacy, honey, are you okay?" Danica wrapped her arms around her and pulled her against her chest. "I was so worried."

"Why didn't you answer your phone?" Kaylie asked. "We've been calling since last night."

Lacy couldn't talk. She closed her eyes, hoping that somehow Danica's body would absorb her own and she would disappear.

"Come on. Let's go inside," Danica said.

Lacy felt her sisters guide her into the house and to the

couch.

"Lacy, you need to talk to me." Danica crouched before Lacy, staring into her eyes. "Look at me, Lace."

Lacy lifted her eyes.

"Good. You need to talk to me, honey. Max called and told us what happened. No one could reach you or Dane. We were worried sick. Please talk to me. Please, Lacy," Danica urged.

"Rob's unconscious," Lacy whispered. "Yesterday morning he was fine. Now he might die," she said.

"We know, honey," Danica said.

"Dane said he can't put me through what Sheila's going through." Lacy's voice was flat, emotionless, and that's how she felt, like someone had stolen her will to feel anything. She'd gone numb. She was the living dead.

Kaylie brushed Lacy's hair from her face. "Oh no. We didn't know that. Oh Lacy, I'm so sorry."

Lacy shook her head. "It's for the best. He could die doing what he does. Why go through that?" She shook her head again. "I just need to live my life, do my job, and move on."

"Oh, Lacy." Danica hugged her again. "What can we do?"

"Take me to see Sheila. She needs me," Lacy said.

"Can we clean you up first?" Kaylie asked.

Danica shot a look at her.

"What?" Kaylie asked. "If she weren't so upset, she wouldn't want to go to the hospital looking like she does. I'll help you get ready." She took Lacy's hand and pulled her to her feet. "Come on. We'll just fix your hair, put on a little makeup, clean clothes. It'll only take a minute."

Danica appeared in the bathroom doorway. "Your phone rang, and I found it behind the couch pillows. You have twenty-seven missed calls. Twenty are from us, three are from Max, and two are from a number without an ID. Two are from your boss. Do you want me to call your boss back?"

Kaylie had washed Lacy's face and fixed her hair. Now she was busy putting concealer on the bags under Lacy's puffy eyes. Lacy shrugged. *Dane didn't call.* His words flew back at her, causing a pain so great in the pit of her stomach that she moaned. *Please, just go.*

Danica crouched beside her again. "Lacy, what is it?"

She shook her head, tears streaking the newly applied concealer.

"Let me get that." Kaylie took a washcloth and wiped the makeup from her face. "You know what, Lace? You don't need makeup. Let's just get..." She looked at Danica, and Lacy watched as Danica shook her head, silently telling Kaylie to stop trying.

"Come here." Danica pulled Lacy to her feet and hugged her again. "We can do this, Lacy. Together we can make it through anything. You tell me what you need."

"Sheila. I need to see her," Lacy managed.

"Okay, then let's get you dressed and we'll go see her." Danica took her hand and led her into the bedroom.

Kaylie grabbed a pair of shorts and a T-shirt and helped Lacy dress.

Lacy followed the commands of her sisters—*Slip your feet into these sandals. Let's go out to the car.* The ride to the hospital was a blur of landscape. *Let's go inside. He's in the ICU.* The elevator hummed beneath her feet. The doors slid open.

Her sisters' hands found hers. They were warm and small. Safe. They were safe. The antiseptic smell of the ICU made Lacy's pulse race. The memory of Rob lying in bed with a tube in his mouth, things strapped to his chest and more tubes running from his arm stopped her cold.

"Lacy?" Danica squeezed her hand. "It's okay, honey. We can wait. When you're ready, you let me know."

Ready?

"I texted Max, and Treat arranged for them to let you into the ICU, so take your time. There's no pressure," Danica said.

"That's his room." Lacy clenched Danica's and Kaylie's hands, staring at the entrance to Rob's room, three doors away from where they stood. A nurse and two people in scrubs rushed past them and flew through Rob's door.

Kaylie and Danica exchanged a worried glance.

"Kaylie, why don't you take Lacy to sit down in the waiting room and I'll go talk to the nurse," Danica urged.

"Did he die? Oh, no. Did he *die?*" Lacy's voice rose. "Is he dead?"

Kaylie stared down the hall with wide eyes.

"Kaylie," Danica snapped. "Take her to the waiting room."

"No," Lacy said. She bolted toward Rob's room. "No. No. He can't die. I have to help Sheila. No." She ran toward the door with Danica and Kaylie on her heels, tears streaming down her cheeks, thoughts of Charlie's and Katie's sad faces whirling in her mind like a tornado.

Sheila and a nurse came out of the doorway as Lacy arrived.

"We'll know soon. Give the doctor space. He's very good. Let him do his thing," the nurse said.

Sheila noticed Lacy. "Lacy. Oh my—"

"Is he…" She couldn't say the word.

"He's awake. He woke up," Sheila shrieked. She hugged Lacy. "I was holding his hand and talking to him and I felt his fingers move. I thought it was just me hoping, but then I felt it again, and then his eyelids moved."

"He's a-alive?" Lacy asked.

"Alive and awake, Lacy." Sheila hugged her again. "The doctor's with him now. Thank goodness, he's awake," she cried.

THEY'D SPENT FORTY-FIVE minutes with Sheila, and during that time, Lacy's mind and body came back to her. The doctors said that Rob appeared not to have any mental deficits, but his breathing was shallow and he was still being treated prophylactically for aspiration pneumonia. He'd need to remain in the hospital and he'd need the breathing tube until his lungs recovered. He'd been mildly sedated when they'd left, but not before seeing him write a note to Sheila that read, *I'm so sorry.*

Danica, Kaylie, and Lacy had returned to the cottage, and Rob's note haunted her. *Was he sorry that he'd gone diving again? Sorry that he'd been hurt? Or sorry that he hadn't listened to Sheila when she'd first begun asking him to change careers?*

Kaylie was in the kitchen fixing lunch. *Food always helps my kids when they're upset,* she'd said, and Danica had been watching Lacy as if she were about to jump off a bridge.

"You didn't have to come here, but I'm glad you did," Lacy said.

"When Max called and told us what had happened, I was worried, but I knew you'd call if you needed us. But then, when we couldn't reach you and Max said no one could reach Dane, I started to worry," Danica said.

"Maybe Dane went back home." Lacy's voice was just above a whisper. It hurt to say his name, and knowing that he might have left the state brought another wave of sadness. She curled her feet beneath her on the couch. The couch where she'd tried to seduce Dane. *Stop it.* She swallowed against the lump in her throat.

"Blake called his father's house and he's not there," Danica said.

"No. I meant his home. He lives on a boat in Florida when he's not traveling," Lacy said.

Kaylie brought a plate with grilled cheese sandwiches into the living room and set it on the coffee table. "Comfort food," she said.

"Thanks, Kaylie," Lacy said.

"Lacy, I don't want to sound ignorant, but from what Danica shared with me, it sounded as if you and Dane were headed down lover's lane. Why would Rob's accident change that?" Kaylie picked up a sandwich and took a bite. "I swear grilled cheese really does help."

"I'm not sure anything will help this," Lacy said. "We were heading in that direction, or maybe we had already found the lane and run down it, but Rob's accident changed everything. After Danica and I talked—Oh wow, this hurts so bad." Tears fell from her eyes. "I love him so much that everything hurts. From my eyes to my stomach to my frigging feet. I ache all over. I miss him so much."

Danica pulled her close. "I'm sorry."

Lacy took a deep breath and continued. "We tried to figure out how our relationship could possibly work. He wanted me to travel with him." She smiled through her tears at the memory of his friendship proposal. Her smile faded as more recent memories invaded her mind. "Then Rob had his accident and I realized—he realized—we both realized that I could give up everything to be with him and something like this could happen. Or worse, he could get killed. Rob was lucky."

"But, Lacy, something could happen to anyone," Danica reminded her. "Look at Blake's partner. He died in a skiing accident. Something could happen walking across the street."

"I know, but still. I can't change my life to be with him, no matter how much I love him, knowing that I could end up losing him any day that he went to work. Sheila told me how hard it was to be married to Rob because of what they do. She worried every day. Then her kids began worrying. You know that every day you love someone you just love them more—and I love him so much already."

"I know you do," Kaylie said. "It's written all over your face, like a crack that says, *Fix me. Please get Dane to fix me.*"

"How can I go into a relationship knowing I'd be tortured every day with worry? It seems unhealthy at the least, and unfair, and…I don't know. Danica, don't you have any support for me here?" *Please tell me what to do.*

Danica sighed. "Lacy, honey, I can't tell you what to do. You have valid concerns, and you're right. You'll probably worry every day. Every job has risks. Granted his is riskier than most, but still. Women marry police officers and firefighters all the time."

"Seeing Sheila mourning her husband as he lay there in the hospital bed—"

"I know it was difficult, but he lived, Lacy. He's okay," Danica said.

"*This time,*" Lacy said. "I don't think I can do it." *And Dane doesn't want to.* "Especially now that I can't deny how unsafe his job really is." She touched her thigh. "He asked me to leave," she whispered.

"He…You were both in shock. I'm sure he didn't mean it," Danica said.

"Maybe you should go talk to him, Lace," Kaylie suggested.

"I can't. If I see him, I'll see Rob and then I'll see Sheila falling apart and wondering how she'll survive. And then the kids' little faces. You should have seen how scared they were when we arrived at the hospital," Lacy said.

"Everyone goes through scary trips to the hospital at some point," Danica said.

"And kids are resilient. His kids won't even remember this in two years. It'll be like a bad dream," Kaylie said.

"Maybe not, but Sheila will, and I know I will. If I see Dane, I'll beg him to take me back, and what happens if next time it's him in that hospital bed? What then?" She swiped at her tears. "You think I should give up my whole life for a guy I might lose because he's got some stupid idea about saving sharks?"

"Lacy, calm down," Danica said.

Kaylie shot her a look. "You don't tell a woman who's upset to calm down." She put her hand on Lacy's shoulder. "Honey, love comes with worries, no matter what job a person has. And it's scary and all consuming at times, but if you love him that much, isn't it worth it?"

Lacy couldn't think past her pain again. *Worth it?* How could anything be worth losing the person you love? She looked at her sisters, and for the first time since the accident, Lacy felt sure of one thing. "I want to go home."

Chapter Thirty-One

DANE FLEW THROUGH the ICU doors twenty minutes after receiving the message from Sheila. He shouldn't have turned off his phone, but his family's incessant calls were driving him mad. He'd turned the phone on for only a minute, to call the hospital, when his messages rolled through. Seven from his family and one from Sheila. He entered Rob's room out of breath and unprepared to see the tube still down his best friend's throat.

"I thought...?" Dane fumbled for words.

"He needs the tube until his lungs recover," Sheila said.

Rob lifted his sleepy eyes and met Dane's. Tears spilled down Dane's cheeks. He leaned over, and with one arm on each of Rob's thick shoulders, careful not to knock the tubes and wires that snaked Rob's body, Dane put his face against Rob's healthy cheek. He needed to feel Rob against him, and he wanted Rob to feel what was left of his strength and to draw from it whatever he needed.

"I missed..." Sobs swallowed Dane's voice. "You scared the crap out of me."

Rob pointed to a notebook in Sheila's hands. She handed it to him, and Rob fumbled to grip the pen, then dragged it across the paper slowly. His hand shook as he passed the pad to Dane.

Did they tag her?

Dane laughed and wiped a tear from his cheek. "You crazy moron. You scared the crap out of me. No, they didn't tag her. We were too busy saving your hide." Dane wiped his eyes. "I'm sorry, man. I shouldn't have let you go down. It was selfish and stupid."

Rob wrote something on the pad again and handed it back to Dane.

You couldn't have stopped me.

"I'm still younger than you. I could have stopped you," Dane said, but he knew that he couldn't have stopped Rob any more than Rob would have been able to stop him if the tables were turned. "None of it matters. I'm just glad you pulled through. I've got you covered. Anything you need. You know I'm here."

Rob nodded.

"Sheila," Dane began, but words evaded him.

She came around the bed and embraced him. "You had a good run," she whispered.

Their last dive together would haunt Dane forever. It was the defining moment that shaped his decision to move on alone.

"I backed out of this assignment and the next one. Now that Rob's doing better, I'm going to sail Treat's boat back to Wellfleet; then I'm taking off for a bit," Dane explained.

"Where will you go?" Sheila asked.

Dane shrugged. He'd sent Lacy away so he could continue his career without the possibility of her getting hurt, but knowing she was no longer a part of his life crushed his passion to continue and hindered his ability to function. "Florida to start, to get my boat. After that, I'm not sure."

Rob pulled his sleeve and pointed to the notebook. Dane handed it to him and Rob wrote, *Lacy?*

Dane ran his hand over his face, gathering the strength to say aloud the painful truth. He couldn't do it. Instead, he shook his head.

Rob wrote, *Because of me?*

"No, Rob. It's because of me." *It's my career choice. My risk. My selfish need to do what I want to do and my desire to protect her from getting hurt, no matter how much it hurts me.*

Chapter Thirty-Two

BACK AT WORLD Geographic, Lacy moved through her days like an automaton. Fred advised her of the hold that Dane had put on their assignment, and Lacy explained that if he requested that she run the program in the future, she respectfully declined. She kept in touch with Sheila and learned that Rob would be going home in a few days. The kids were elated, and Sheila was beyond thrilled, although worried about what Rob's career change might mean for the family. She didn't want him going back on the boat, but she knew he would never be happy working a typical land-based job. Lacy hadn't thought about Rob's love of the sea, much like she hadn't thought about Dane's love of his job in that way. Hearing Sheila talk about the sea as if it were Rob's lover made Lacy realize why Dane could never give up his chosen career. If the sea was Rob's lover, it was Dane's lifeblood.

She'd had a lot of time to think in the week since the accident, and once the ache of Rob's scare eased, the loss of Dane took over. She'd thrown herself back into work, and even now, as she tried to form a strategic plan for one client and a marketing concept for another, her mind waded back through that thick fog of pain to the memories of her and Dane together.

Dane hadn't called her and she hadn't reached out to him, although every night before bed she'd turned on Skype and set her cell phone by her bed, just in case. She longed to hear his voice, but each time she thought about calling him, she remembered Sheila standing at Rob's bedside, not knowing if he'd live or die. That was enough to keep her from punching in his speed dial number.

"Can I see you for a minute, Lacy?" Fred asked from her office doorway.

"Sure, of course. Come in."

Fred closed the door behind him and sat across from her desk.

"Lacy, were you there when Rob had his accident?" Fred asked.

"No. I wasn't on the boat with them, if that's what you're asking," she said.

He nodded. "And did you get really close to him while you were there?"

Lacy narrowed her eyes. "Rob? Not really close, but we became friends. We had dinner together. I spent time with his wife and children. Actually, yes, I guess I would say we were close."

"Do you need some time off? I know you said you didn't want any time off originally, but I've noticed your work hasn't been up to your usual high standard."

Lacy saw the worry in Fred's serious gaze and the way he leaned forward when he brought up her quality of work, like he was saying something even he didn't want to hear.

Yes. I'd like a lifetime off. I want to disappear and never have to think again. Or feel. Or be. "I'm sorry, Fred. I know my work hasn't been up to par, and I promise to do better, but I don't want time off. I need to keep my mind occupied."

"I'm worried about you, Lacy. Are you sure you don't want to go visit your sisters, or spend some time just relaxing? Tasha can handle covering for a few days," Fred said.

Before going to Chatham, the idea of Tasha covering for her just to take time off would have knocked her from her seat. Now, sitting with Fred and begging him to let her do a subpar job to keep her mind off of Dane seemed ridiculous. Maybe she should take time off. Heaven knows that every time she walked by Fred's office, she remembered finding Dane there. Maybe she should go visit Kaylie and the kids and immerse herself in them for a while. Or maybe she should take off work and stay home and wallow in her loneliness. Either way, having Fred look at her with pity wasn't the answer, even if it meant Tasha earning the promotion she had wanted so badly. *I don't care anymore.* The truth of her thought startled her.

She needed to clear the chaos from her mind. She glanced at the clock. "I really appreciate your concern, Fred. I'll think about it while I'm at lunch. Can we talk later this afternoon?" Lacy promised herself she wouldn't dwell on Dane while she was at lunch. She'd get a cold Diet Pepsi, a *People* magazine, and sit at the café down the street and just veg for a while.

"EVERYTHING SUCKS. THAT's just the way my life is right now." Lacy held the cell between her shoulder and ear as she pulled out of the office parking lot.

"I know it feels that way, Lace, but you're really very blessed when you look at the bigger picture," Danica said.

"Oh, I know. I have a great family, a good job that I might have just jeopardized, and I've got a nice place to live. I think I'm just tired and stressed. I'm going to grab a rag mag and chill for an hour. And I'm not going to think about Dane. Uh oh...hold on." Lacy slammed on her brakes and dropped the phone in her lap. "Jerk," she yelled at the car that cut her off. She looked down for a split second to retrieve her phone and stepped on the gas to cross the intersection. Lacy never saw the Honda Civic coming her way, and she never heard Danica's scream coming through the phone when the sound of metal against metal sent her car spinning and her phone flying through the air.

Chapter Thirty-Three

IT WAS A typical New England evening. Dane sat on the deck of Treat's bungalow, having decided not to return to Florida after all. He wanted to be able to visit Rob as he recovered and be there for Sheila. They were both doing much better. Rob was getting stronger by the day, and without the ventilator, he was able to speak freely, even if a tad gravelly. He and Sheila were looking forward to returning to their home in Florida, and they were grateful for Dane's generosity, as he covered Sheila's hotel stay and any medical bills that insurance didn't cover. He'd offered Rob a job with Brave on the boat or in the office—the choice was up to him—and for as much as his friend's life was coming together, Dane felt unglued within his own.

Every time he thought about going back to his boat, he thought of Lacy. He knew he'd see her in the cabin and feel her in bed beside him. He'd stayed in Treat's cottage to avoid being in the cabin of that boat because the memories were too fresh, his emotions too raw. He'd done the right thing. At least he thought he had. Who was he to ask her to live a life surrounded by risk and worry when she'd so willingly been overcoming her own fears? He loved her too much to allow that. As he watched the sun set over the bay, he knew that another reason he'd stayed in Massachusetts was that the act of physically leaving would finalize their breakup. As silly as it seemed, somehow being in the same state made him feel closer to her.

His cell phone rang. *Dad.* His family had been all over him for ignoring their calls after Rob's accident, but in the end they'd all understood his need to be alone. He picked up the phone.

"Hi, Dad."

"How are you doing, son?"

Hal's voice wrapped itself around Dane.

Lonely. Sad. Feeling like taking a step on a boat might hurt too much. "Not bad. How about you?"

"Fairly well. I was down at the barn this afternoon with Hope. She's doing well. Strong. Rex takes good care of her."

When his mother had first become ill, his father had bought her Hope, a mare, and his father treated Hope as though Dane's mother lived within her. Although that had always bothered Dane, he knew it brought his father comfort, and for that he was grateful.

"Good, Dad."

"Dane, what are you doing out at Treat's place? Why aren't you back home?" his father asked.

"Home?" His father never pressured any of his children to visit, and his question brought a string of worry to Dane. "Is something wrong?"

"Home, Dane. Your home. On your boat."

Dane sighed. "I'm headed that way, Dad. I just needed a little time to make sure Rob was okay." *And to make sure I was ready.*

"All right. What have you been doing for the past week?"

"Uh, you know, going out on the boat." The lie tasted like

acid on his tongue. "Trying to get past Rob's accident."

"Treat's boat?" his father asked.

Dane shook his head. He knew his father didn't believe him. All it would take is one call from Treat to the resort to know that he hadn't even sailed it back. He'd paid to have it returned.

"Dad."

"Something you want to tell me, son?"

Dane pictured his father sitting in his favorite leather recliner wearing a flannel shirt and a pair of Levi's, his face a mask of worry. "Not really," Dane said.

"What's your plan?" his father asked.

"I don't know, Dad. I guess I'll head back to Florida at some point and get back in the game. Right now I'm trying to remember what it all means," Dane admitted.

"What it all means? Like what it means to save sharks?"

He knew his father's inquisition could not be deterred. When Hal Braden set his sights on making a point, he made it. Dane wondered what today's point would be and decided he'd better cut to the chase and fess up now if he wanted to get to the point of it.

"Life, Dad. Work, relationships, death. I'm trying to figure out the point of it all." He closed his eyes and waited for his father's wisdom to enlighten him. When his father didn't answer, he said, "Dad?"

"Yeah, I'm here."

"You asked me a question, and I answered. Don't you have anything to say?"

"I was kind of waiting for you to tell me the answer. I never knew life, work, relationships, or death had a point," his father said.

Dane kicked his feet up on the railing. "Good, then I'm not alone in this quandary."

"Son, you're never alone in anything. You know that. Your brothers and sister are worried sick about you. Max had to practically tie up Treat to keep him from chasing after you these last few days. He said you shouldn't be alone, but your mother—" He took a deep breath. "I thought that you needed this time to think."

Hearing his father stop himself from mentioning what his dead mother thought made Dane smile. He and his siblings were used to the messages their father received from beyond their mother's grave. Dane didn't know if he believed in his father's supposed connection with his mother or not, but if she was what allowed him his privacy this past week, then he was thankful.

"Thanks, Dad. I think I need about a year, but since that's not reasonable, I'll take what I can get," Dane said.

"Rob's doing okay, I hear."

Dane could always trust that Braden grapevine to ensure news traveled swiftly. He knew the information about Lacy wouldn't be far behind.

"He is. He's going home soon."

"Glad to hear it. I've always liked Rob and Sheila," he said. "And Lacy Snow?"

Dane stood and paced. He knew the question was coming, but it still hit him like a punch to the gut.

"She's back at home. You know, work and all that."

"Uh-huh. Son, did you ever figure out what your heart wanted?"

"Yeah, I did, Dad, but sometimes that's not all that matters," Dane said.

"Oh, no? I wish you had been around to tell me that when I was a teenager and fought to be able to date your mother. You could have saved me weeks of headache, and come to think of it, a black eye, too."

Dane sat back down and leaned his elbows on his knees. "A black eye?"

"Sometimes love hurts, son. There's no two ways around it. But it was worth every painful second, and I'd do it all over again if I could have her back in my arms," his father said.

"I know you miss Mom."

"Every minute of every day, but that's because she was stolen from me. I'd never have sent her away. Like I said, I'd have done anything to be with her."

Dane sat back again and looked out at the waves rolling in against the shore. His father knew what he had done. *Thanks, Treat.* He might as well face it head-on.

"I did the right thing, Dad, and I think that's one reason I never allowed myself to get too close to anyone before. I never knew if I'd return after leaving. Think about it. Think about my job," Dane said.

"You told me it's safer than driving down the street and, son, if you tell me that, no matter how much bull I think it is, I'll accept it as true, because you wouldn't lie to your father."

Dane closed his eyes again, trying to escape the truth and knowing he couldn't. "Statistically, it is safer. But now…"

"Now you think otherwise?" his father asked.

"Now I see it from a different perspective. Seeing Rob's family hanging on a ledge while he teetered between life and death, that's perspective, Dad. I don't ever want to be the cause of that kind of pain."

"You're a smart man, Dane, and I've been the one hanging

on the ledge. Heck, I spent years hanging on the ledge," his father began.

Mom.

"You know, if I could have loved someone else, maybe I would have. If I could have had some notice...You know that's the thing that stinks the most. There's no advance notice to stuff like what happened to your mom or to Rob. It just happens. If we could have had notice and avoided it, that would have been great. Then I could have...I don't know...divorced her? Sheila could have run away from the pain of it? Right, son? Is that the answer?" Hal's voice rose as he spoke.

"That's not what I meant," Dane said.

"That's exactly what you meant. Why love someone if something might happen to you and you'll be the cause of their pain?"

Do you always have to point out the obvious? "I made my decision."

"I know you did. But is it one you can live with?" his father asked.

Dane didn't answer.

"Dane, we all come with an expiration date. We just don't know when our number's gonna come up. But I can tell you this, and you can bet your butt it's true. Loving your mother was the best darn thing that ever happened to me aside from you children. And maybe she's even better than each of you, because without her, you wouldn't be alive. And even though we had years of too many hospital stays and teetering on ledges, in those few years we had together, that woman filled my heart enough to hold me over for my whole life. Heck, she filled my heart until it overflowed. How do you think I found the strength to carry on and raise all of you nitwits?"

Dane smiled at the term. His father had called them that as kids when they did stupid things like trying to sled off of the barn roof. Tears pressed forth again. He was so lonely for Lacy, and so sad without her, he was beginning to get used to the brutal emotions that plagued him.

He mustered the courage to speak through the longing that ripped at his soul. "Remember when Mom died?" he asked.

"That's a time I'll never forget." His father's solemn voice coalesced with the memory of his mother's passing and the first few weeks of getting used to a house where when he yelled, *Mom*, no one would answer.

"It hurt so bad." Dane sobbed silently into the night, swiping at hot tears and wishing his father were there to wrap him in his strong arms, as he had so many years ago.

"I know, son," his father said softly. "You needed time alone then, too. Do you remember running away?"

"Yes," Dane whispered through his tears.

"That's always been your way. Climb into your shell until you think it's safe to come out. I'm sorry, Dane," his father said. "You know your mother would want me to push you one way or the other, but I'm not going to do that."

Dane ran his hand over his face, remembering the dream he'd had about his mother doing just that. Pushing him forward.

"I wish life were easier, and I wish love came with guarantees. But sometimes the only right answer is the one with the most risks. It's the one that scares the stuffing out of you but won't let you go."

"I love her so much, Dad. I've never loved anyone the way I love Lacy. She's always right there on my mind. I can feel her beside me when she's not there, and I can hear her voice in the middle of the night. Dad, am I losing my mind?"

"No, you're not losing your mind. You're in love, and love does strange things to a man. I think you have your answer," his father said.

"I feel like going home without her will kill me. I can't even leave the state," Dane admitted.

His father took a deep breath, and when he spoke, the strength had returned to his voice. "Luckily, the woman you love is still on this earth. You have a choice to make, son. Can your heart live without her?"

"There's no piece of me that can live without her," Dane admitted.

Chapter Thirty-Four

LACY SAT ON the edge of the hospital bed, a bandage on her left arm and her head thundering. Every part of her body felt as though it had been slammed against a brick wall, and all she could think about was how fast the accident had happened. *Just like Rob.* Lacy held the hospital phone against her ear.

"I called your insurance company and they're arranging for a rental car for you. The police report is being faxed and, Lacy, I wish I could be there with you. Are you sure you don't want me to fly there for a day or two?" Danica asked.

"Thanks for calling them, but there's no need for you to come here. I'm fine, just sore. That car came out of nowhere. I never saw it coming." *Just like the shark.*

"The cop said the driver ran a red light and that you were lucky your car spun out instead of rolling."

Lacy tried to concentrate on what Danica was saying, but her thoughts were trapped in a tunnel. *It happened so fast. I never saw it coming. Just like the shark.* Danica's words came back to her. *You'll see some kind of sign, and it will push you both in the right direction.* Dane's smile flashed before her. *Less risky than driving down the street.*

"I could have died," Lacy said.

"Yeah, I guess you could have," Danica said.

"Just like that, and then what?" Lacy scanned the empty room. "Then what?" She hopped off of the bed and grabbed her purse with her free hand. "If I had died, then what, Danica?"

"Lace, you're scaring me."

"I'll tell you what. I would have died feeling sad and lonely and without the one person I want to be with. Without the man I love," Lacy said. *Without Dane.*

The curtained enclosure opened, and a young nurse walked in. "I'm sorry, but can you please keep it down?"

"Do I need to sign out somewhere in order to leave?" Lacy asked.

The nurse checked her chart. "Yes, I think that's where your doctor went, to authorize your release."

"Great. Thank you."

"Lacy, do you want me to call you a cab?" Danica asked. "Why are you so mad? And why do you sound like you're rushing?"

"I need a cab but, Danica, I don't have my cell. Are you calling me from work?" she asked.

"Yeah."

"Good. Can you text Dane for me and ask him where he is?" *It could happen to anyone. Anytime. In any profession.*

"Sure, but I need his number. Why?" Danica asked.

Lacy gave her his cell number from memory, and Lacy realized that she'd memorized just about everything about Dane without even trying. She closed her eyes and recalled the scent of him. "You said the universe would give me a sign. I don't think a sign could be any clearer than this."

"Hold on. I just got his text."

Lacy's heartbeat sped up as she waited.

"He said he's still at the Cape. He's staying at Treat's cottage in Wellfleet," Danica said. "He wants to know why I asked. Should I tell him about your accident?"

"No. Don't tell him about the accident. Just make something up. Tell him that Blake's going to Florida, and you wondered if he was there so the two of them could get together for dinner." Lacy's eyes darted across the floor. "Everything in life has risks. I get that now, and I'm not going to change who I love because of them. I can't. I just can't." Lacy was talking to herself more than Danica. "I'm not sitting around feeling sorry for myself because Dane has a risky career. My accident proved his point ten times over. Geez, I have to get a phone. And make a plan."

"Lacy, what are you going to do?"

"What I should have done a week ago." Lacy blinked away tears.

Chapter Thirty-Five

AN HOUR AFTER talking to his father, Dane packed his bags and headed off the Cape. He'd been there long enough. He couldn't hide from his feelings forever. He'd put his career first for his entire adult life, and now it was time to put something else first. Or rather, someone else first.

He picked up his cell to call Lacy and then set it back down in the center console. He hadn't contacted her since the day he'd asked her to leave. *She probably won't take my call.* He considered asking Danica to step in, but he'd already pulled that favor once with the therapeutic advice, and he felt bad that he wasn't in Florida to meet Blake.

Once he was off the Cape and on the highway, he stopped at the first exit, grabbed a Diet Coke, and texted Lacy.

He got back on the highway, set his GPS, and continued driving.

NOTHING WAS GOING as Lacy had hoped. The cab took forever to arrive at the hospital, the employee at Sprint moved slower than molasses, and it had cost her a fortune for the cab to wait, although she was glad to have a replacement phone. Once she charged it, she'd put her plan into action. Thankfully, the employee at the car rental company moved quicker than the Sprint employee. By six o'clock, she was back at home and charging her new phone.

She picked out three outfits and tossed them into a back-pack, then headed into the bathroom to take a quick shower. She didn't want to waste time, but she couldn't make her big entrance with dried blood smeared on her arm. She stripped off her dirty clothes and glanced in the mirror. Her breath caught in her throat. Her hair looked like she'd been caught in a wind tunnel, all frizz and no curl. Her forehead was streaked with dirt and blood, and her chest and upper arms were already showing black-and-blue marks. Combine that with the bags under her eyes from a week of no sleep, and she would surely frighten small children. She'd been so frenzied to get her errands done and get to Dane that showering hadn't even crossed her mind.

Her cell phone buzzed like it was on steroids. *It's finally charged.* Lacy hurried to the bedside table and watched as messages came in one after another. She scrolled through the messages, grateful that the mediocre Sprint employee had been able to transfer her contacts from her broken phone. Danica, Fred, Danica, Kaylie, Danica, Danica, Kaylie, Kaylie, Fred, Dane, Danica, Danica, Dane, Dane. *Dane?* She scrolled back up and stared at his number. Her pulse raced as she read the messages.

I'm an idiot. Can we talk? I miss you. Lacy lowered herself to the bed. *He misses me. He misses me!*

Half an hour later, *Lace, I'm sorry. I haven't slept in a wk. Have you?*

Her lower lip trembled as she shook her head. She checked

the time the next text had arrived. Forty minutes after the last. *I'm not giving up on us. I know ur mad and hurt, but I love u more than sharks.*

Lacy laughed. She began texting back, *Sorry my phone broke. I miss u 2. I'm not ma—*

A knock at the door interrupted her text. She peered out the window and saw Dane's car parked on the street. Lacy reached up and touched her hair. She rushed to the mirror and tried to pull her hair back. Goose bumps rose on her arms. Fluttering started in her stomach and found its way to her chest. She carried the phone out of the bedroom, her hair, her pain, the accident forgotten, and she reached a trembling hand toward the doorknob. As she pulled it open, Dane's voice filtered in.

Dane stood before her with sorrow in his eyes, and behind that sorrow she saw hope and an immeasurable amount of love. "I'm here, Lace."

Hearing his voice after being without him for so long weakened her knees, and she fumbled for the doorknob for support.

"Me too. I'm right here, and I'm not going anywhere," she said. She couldn't believe he was there. The last week felt like a year, and just like that, she was thrown back to when they'd spoken every night, and the rush of excitement hadn't faded. If anything, it had grown stronger, as evident by her inability to stop her hands from shaking.

"I miss you." Dane took a step forward. "I'm so sorry, Lace, and I know you don't have to forgive me for sending you away, but I wasn't myself, babe. I was so lost with everything that happened to Rob and what Sheila was going through, and I couldn't imagine you in her place."

She wanted to fall into his arms, but she couldn't move. It was all she could do to speak. "I know. I shouldn't have left. I should have stood up for us, but I was in shock or something. I don't know." She took a deep breath. "Dane, I lied, too."

Dane's eyes filled with pain. He drew his eyebrows together and shook his head.

"I fell in love with you, too," she said.

He closed his eyes and smiled, and when he opened them, his eyes were damp. Dane opened his arms. His eyes never left hers as she walked forward and met his embrace. She breathed in the scent of him, and it felt like she'd come home. Her chest hurt as he held her, but she didn't dare move. She'd never move away from him again.

"I love you, Lace. I've made all kinds of mistakes, but that's all done." He leaned back and looked at her; then he cupped her cheeks in his palms. His eyes searched her face, as if he had only just seen her bruises. "Baby, what happened?" He kissed her forehead.

Her heart soared. "You love me?"

"More than I can express. Yes. I love you, every spec of you, from your kinky hair to the birthmark on the heel of your left foot," he said.

"You noticed?" she asked. *Gosh, I love you.*

"The first time you wore flip-flops. It's adorable."

"You love me." *He does; he really does.* "It was one thing to hear it when you were asking me to leave, but it's a whole other thing to hear it now," she said. "Tell me again."

He looked into her eyes, and before the words came out, she could feel his love surrounding her like a cloak. "Lacy Snow, I love you, now and always. I adore you."

"Oh, Dane. I love you, too," she said. She kissed him then, wincing when he held her too tightly.

"Tell me what happened," he said.

"A car ran into mine when I was leaving work this afternoon."

"Oh, baby. Why didn't you call me? Are you okay? Look at you. Let's get you inside." He guided her inside, his hand never leaving the small of her back. "I wish you would have called me. I hate thinking of you being scared and hurt without me there."

"I'm okay. Besides, it was at the hospital that I realized how much I wanted to be with you. I still can't believe you're here," she said. "I was going to shower and come to you. Oh no, the shower. I left it on." She hurried into her bedroom.

"I spent all those months wondering what it would feel like to be in your apartment. It feels right, Lace. It feels good," he said as he followed her into the bedroom.

"You really were coming to see me?" He held up the backpack.

Lacy came out of the bathroom wearing a robe. "Yes, I was really coming to see you." She draped her arms around his neck. "And I spent all those months wondering what it would feel like to have you in my bedroom, and you know what? It does feel right." She kissed him lightly. "I realized when that car hit me that you were right. I was just driving down the street and *wham*. It happened so fast. I didn't even have time to think, and then I saw it all so clearly."

Dane sat on the bed and pulled Lacy onto his lap. She ran her finger along the dark, sexy stubble that speckled his cheeks.

"It doesn't matter if we have a day, a week, or a year together, Dane. Whatever's possible, I want it. All of it. Every scary, risky second of it."

"Oh, Lace, so do I." He brought his lips to hers and kissed her gently. "I'm afraid I'll hurt you," he said.

"I'm okay, just sore. I still can't believe you're here. This last week has been like a nightmare."

"No more nightmares, Lace. Not ever."

"My eyes are open. I know the risks of being with you, and I know the way it feels not to be with you. I'll take the risks any day of the week," she said.

"I had two hours to think on the way over here, and I want you to know that I don't expect you to give up your job. I'll work my schedule around yours, and if you want us to be together every other week, then we'll make it happen. My job matters, Lace, but without you, nothing has much meaning."

"I've had a lot of time to think, too. I don't want visits every other week. After spending every day with you and then being yanked apart, I know how it would feel to be separated, and it's not a feeling I want to experience again," she said. "I want…"

"What are you asking?"

"I'm not asking, Dane. I'm offering. If the friendship proposal still stands, I would like to accept it," she said with a smile.

He searched her eyes, and she knew he was searching for surety.

"I'm certain, Dane. I want to be your friend-with-benefits." *I want to be so much more.*

He pulled her to him.

"Ouch, ouch, ouch."

"I'm sorry. Oh, Lace, you've just made me the happiest guy on earth. But I want more than friends-with-benefits. Can't you at least be my girlfriend?"

The sparkle in his eyes told her he was teasing. She kissed his lips. "I suppose I can do that."

"I almost forgot." He lifted Lacy up and set her on the bed beside him. "I'll be right back." Lacy listened as he crossed the floor and went out the front door, then returned a minute later and sat beside her.

"It occurred to me when we were in Wellfleet that you really are my shining light, Lacy. I love you and I wanted to give you something so you would always remember our first night together."

"Do you really think I'd ever forget our first night together?"

He handed her an eight-by-ten envelope. She withdrew a certificate from the International Star Registry, and as she read it, she ran her finger over the embossed gold star at the top.

Her eyes filled with tears. "You named a star after me?"

"The Lacy Star."

"This is the most romantic, thoughtful thing anyone has ever done for me. Oh, Dane, I love it." Lacy leaned over too quickly to kiss him again and winced.

Dane took her face in his hands and met her lips with his in a soft, tender kiss. "You need a warm bath and someone to love you until you feel better. I'll run the tub; you relax for a minute."

She watched him walk into the bathroom. *Into my bathroom.* She'd dreamed of him being in her apartment for so many months, and now that he was there, she realized she never could have dreamed how right it felt.

LACY RESTED HER head against Dane's chest. Bubbles surrounded them like clouds that had fallen to the bathtub from heaven. He closed his eyes, relishing in the weight of her against him, the feel of the silky skin of her legs against his.

"I could lie here all night," Lacy whispered.

"Mmm." He nuzzled against her neck. "I don't care where we lie as long as we're together."

"Thank you for coming here."

He gathered her hair and placed it over her other shoulder, then he kissed her glistening skin.

"Lace, I tried to do the right thing. I wanted to protect you, but I never wanted to be without you. This whole being-in-love thing is new to me, and I'll probably make mistakes, but there are two I'll never make. I'll never be unfaithful, and I'll never ask you to leave again." He cupped water in his hands and released it on her shoulders, watching it disappear into the bubbles.

"I know." She traced circles on his thigh. "I'm learning, too, about you and me and about us. I knew how close we had become after Nassau, but it was all one-step removed—always through electronics. Being here with you, spending those days together on the Cape, it's like you crept into my chest and sank into my heart. And when we were apart, I felt like you'd left this big, painful hole inside me. I can't imagine life without you."

Dane wrapped his arms around her waist and laid his head on her shoulder blade. "You'll never have to." He was careful not to hold her too tightly or move too suddenly. He worried about her pain from the accident, but every ounce of him wanted to be closer to her.

"Love my pain away," she whispered.

Could his heart get any fuller? He drew her face toward him and kissed her tenderly, but their kisses quickly turned fierce. She turned in his arms, as eager for more as he was. He felt the rapid *thump, thump, thump* of her heart against his chest, and drew back, but she pushed on, reclaiming his mouth in a demanding kiss.

He smiled into their kisses and said, "I'm trying to be gentle. I don't want to hurt you."

Her eyes glistened with desire. "You don't have to be gentle. Being close to you makes the hurt disappear."

Chapter Thirty-Six

Four weeks later...

DANE LAY BACK with his iPhone in his hand. The bed rocked with the gentle caress of the Atlantic Ocean. The sun-kissed skin between the open buttons of his dress shirt gleamed in the flickering light of the candle on the bedside table. He read the message on his screen. *Lacy wants to FaceTime.* The excitement of seeing Lacy hadn't dimmed one iota. If anything, the desire to see her grew with every call, every wink. He accepted the request and was met with her lust-filled blue eyes, her wayward curls framing her face. She'd never looked so pretty.

"There's my beautiful friend-with-benefits."

"Just one push of a button away," she teased. "I miss you."

"How much?" he asked.

Lacy looked behind her, then back into the phone. "I can't show you how much right now, but I think you can conjure up an image in your mind."

"Mmm. Yes, I think I can, of your naked body beneath—"

"Hush," she said, shooting a look behind her again. She sighed. "When are you coming?"

"You're not here. How can I?"

"You're such a pig," she teased. "Seriously, I've been waiting for you forever. Don't make me wait too much longer." She blew him a kiss, and Dane saw a male hand cover the spaghetti strap that rode her bare shoulder. "I gotta go." The screen went blank.

An ache of longing ran through his chest. Every minute away from Lacy felt like an eternity. He rose and looked at the framed certificate beside the bed from the International Star Registry. *The Lacy Star.* Dane hadn't even realized a person could name a star, but leave it to Treat, master of romance, to clue him in. *Oh, man. I love her, and I'm so lucky that she loves me.* Dane pushed the jealousy aside and went to the closet. Before reaching for his jacket, he ran his fingers over Lacy's clothes. They'd had to make a few changes to the closet setup to fit her clothing, and now Dane couldn't remember what the closet had looked like before she'd moved in. It was like she'd always been there, or maybe he'd just always been waiting for her to come into his life. He laid his jacket on the bed and went to brush his teeth. Seeing her toothbrush next to his still gave him a warm feeling.

He passed through the galley and reached out to touch the metal fish on the wall, remembering Lacy's sweet face when she'd said she could almost feel them breathing. The way that night had ended was something that at one time Dane had wished he could forget. He'd slowly come to realize that they'd made it through. *We made it through.* They'd gone back to Wellfleet and purchased the sculpture and all those tiny fleeing fish as a way to remember that no matter what they encountered, their love would pull them through.

Up on the deck, he spotted her with Rob and Sheila, each holding a glass of ice water. Dane was pleased that Rob had pulled himself together and fully recovered from his accident. He would be attending AA meetings for a long time to come, and Dane was proud of him. Lacy stood with a drink in one hand and tossed her head back. Her feminine laughter filled the night air. His father approached her from behind and laid his arm across her shoulder, as if she'd always been part of the family. Savannah and Hugh sidled up to him.

"I don't know how you convinced her to leave her job and move onto a boat," Savannah said.

"She didn't really *leave* her job. She's still working for World Geographic. She's just working remotely. The great thing is, Fred gave her the promotion she was after, so she calls the shots on which companies she works with," Dane explained.

Savannah had a drink in one hand and she put her other around Dane's waist. "I'm so jealous. All of my brothers are finding their soul mates, and I'm floating around wondering when my time will come."

"Hey, I'm not biting the couple bullet," Hugh said. He held his drink up in Lacy's direction. "She's a good egg, Dane, and boy, is she head over heels for you. It must be that shark hunting thing women love."

"I think that's the least of what she likes about me," Dane said. He took a sip of Savannah's drink. "Savannah, it's like Dad said to me. You'll know you've found the right person when your heart can't live without them."

"Well, my heart is thirsty, and New York feels like a desert of dry, egotistical men." Savannah retrieved her drink from Dane's hand. "Don't mind me. I just need a vacation or something."

"What about Connor Dean?" Hugh asked.

"Please." She rolled her eyes.

"If you'll excuse me, I know Rob and Sheila will start their renewal vows soon, and I want to have a minute with Lacy." Dane made a beeline for Lacy.

"That dress is truly sinful," Dane said, running his hand along the curve of her hip.

"Behave." She giggled. A flush rushed up her cheeks.

"Son, have you noticed that every time you get near your sweet gal, she gets all flustered?" his father teased.

Dane kissed Lacy's cheek. "I hope that never changes."

His father took his arm from Lacy's shoulder and raised his glass. "Before Rob and Sheila begin their ceremony, I just want to say that y'all have been a part of our lives for ten years—a good part of our lives and a tremendous part of Dane's—and I hope that will continue for years to come."

"Thank you, Hal," Rob said. "Actually"—he took Sheila's hand in his—"We've made a decision. We're going to accept Dane's offer, and I'll remain with Brave. I'll run the boat for Dane when he's closer to home, or gone for only a few days, and when he's out longer, I'll run the office. Brave has been too big a part of my life to leave it behind and, Dane, how could I leave the brother my mother could never give me?"

Dane lifted his glass. "And the run continues. Love you, bro." Then he whispered in Lacy's ear, "And our run has just begun."

Please enjoy a preview of the next
Sweet with Heat novel, PROMISE OF A NEW BEGINNING

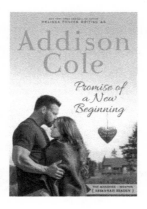

Chapter One

THE ENGINE OF the small bush plane echoed in Savannah Braden's ears as they flew past the edge of a colorful forest and began their rapid descent into the Colorado Mountains. September didn't get much prettier than the bursts of red, orange, yellow, and green foliage that were quickly coming into focus. The plane veered to the right and then cut left at a fast speed, shifting Savannah and the other five passengers in their seats. Savannah clung to the armrest and looked out the window as the dirt landing strip came into view. *The too-short landing strip.* She'd been flying her whole life, and never had she seen such a short landing strip. *Great. I'm going to die before I even get to clear my head.* She hadn't seen the pilot's face before takeoff, and now all she could make out was the back of his wavy brown hair, thick headphones over his ears, and a black T-shirt stretched tight over burly shoulders. She wondered what the man who was going to kill her looked like—and why the heck he thought he could land on a freaking Band-Aid–sized landing strip.

The couple in the seats across from her appeared far too calm in their hemp clothing and scuffed boots. They'd introduced themselves as Elizabeth and Lou Merriman, and they were traveling with their six-year-old son, Aiden. They seemed pleasant enough, but Savannah couldn't help staring at the reddish brown dreadlocks that hung past their shoulders, as if it weren't hair at all but thick, clumpy strands of the same prickly rope her father used back home on his ranch in Weston, Colorado.

"Do you mind?"

"Oh, sorry," Savannah said, pulling her clenched fingers from the armrest that separated her from the younger, sullen man next to her with his tuque pulled down low and his shoulders rounded forward. He hadn't said two words to her the whole flight, and she wondered if he was escaping civility and had sworn off the opposite sex, too.

Savannah's emotions were fried after finding her on-again off-again celebrity boyfriend, Connor Dean, in bed with another woman—again. Her eyes stung as she remembered the evening their relationship had come to a stormy end. *A final end.* On the recommendation of an article she'd read about how to reclaim one's life after a breakup, she'd taken Friday off from work to go on this stupid four-day survival retreat that the article touted as *The best way to regain your confidence and reprioritize your life!* The timing had been perfect. There was no way she was ever going back to Connor, and in order to accomplish that, she had to get out of Manhattan. Connor was just charming enough to make her forget that she deserved more than a guy who still acted like a high school jock, always looking for the next good lay.

The plane descended rapidly, and Savannah pulled her seat belt tighter across her hips and closed her eyes. She felt her stomach flip and twist as the engines rumbled in agony. Then the wheels of the plane made contact with the dirt and the brakes screeched, sending her forward, then slamming her back against the seat.

"Ugh!" Savannah's eyes flew open. Everyone looked at her: the granola couple and their young son, and of course attitude boy sitting next to her. Everyone except Josie, the young woman who sat across the aisle behind Elizabeth and Lou. She had her eyes clenched shut and was white-knuckling the armrest. *I should have sat next to her.*

"Sorry," Savannah said with a cringe.

Savannah looked out the window, and the landing strip was a good fifty feet behind them, but at least they were alive.

Maybe this was a mistake.

The engine silenced, and the other passengers stood and stretched. Elizabeth and Lou collected Aiden and smiled like they hadn't just seen their lives pass before their eyes. *What is wrong with them?*

Josie squealed, "We made it!"

The guy with the tuque shook his head, and Savannah prayed she wouldn't pass out from her racing heart.

The pilot craned his neck as he glanced back over his shoulder and removed his headphones. Savannah caught a quick glimpse of the most handsome, rugged face and piercing eyes she'd ever seen before he turned back around and she was left staring at the back of his thick head of hair again.

A thrill rushed through her.

Maybe this wasn't a mistake after all.

In the next breath, she realized he was the man she'd seen in the airport when she was racing to catch the plane and had fallen on her butt, sending her bags flying across the corridor. He'd been cold and standoffish—and far too handsome.

I'm screwed.

PILOT AND SURVIVAL guide Jack Remington sat in the cockpit of the small bush plane with a knot in his gut. He'd been so conflicted about where his life was headed that the last thing he needed was for his body to suddenly remember what a woman was. For two years, he hadn't looked at a single woman—had never felt a twinge of interest since his wife, Linda, died in a car accident. Then, today of all days, when he was running late and already pissed after having driven past the scene of her accident, he saw that gorgeous woman with auburn hair fall in the airport. He'd wanted to walk right by her, and when she rose to her feet, he just about did. But when he'd gotten close enough to really see her, he noticed a competitive streak in her eyes, and behind that determination, he'd seen something soft and lovely. He gritted his teeth. *I don't need soft and lovely.* He pushed the image of her away and allowed his anger to turn inward again. Once he felt the familiar fire in his chest, he opened the door.

The first thing he did when he stepped off the plane was

touch the earth. *His earth.* Jack considered every blade of grass, every tree, every bush, and every stream on this particular mountain to be his personal possession. Not in the legal sense, but in his heart. It was this land that had helped him to heal after Linda's death. Well, that was a lie. He hadn't yet healed. But at least he was capable of functioning again—sort of. He still couldn't sleep inside the chalet in Bedford, New York, that he and Linda had shared. He returned to the house only once or twice a month to make sure partying teenagers or vandals had not broken in. And on those nights, he slept on the back deck and showered in the outdoor shower. He'd spent most of the last two years in the safety and solitude of his rustic cabin—the cabin even his family didn't know about—set on two hundred acres in the Colorado mountains.

Last night, however, Jack had stayed at the chalet because of the early flight this morning, and before leaving the house, he'd sat out front with his motorcycle engine roaring beneath him, reminding him that he was still alive. When he'd reached the bottom of his steep driveway, instead of turning left as he always had, he looked right toward the site of Linda's accident. *Eighty-seven paces. Less than three seconds from our driveway.* Flashes of painful memories had attacked, and he'd gritted his teeth against the gnawing in his gut. *It should have been me.*

In one breath he wanted to leave behind the guilt and the anger of having lost her and move forward. He missed seeing his brothers, sister, and parents. He missed hearing their voices, sharing the details of their lives, and he even missed their loud family dinners. In the next breath he pushed the idea of finding a path back to them into the dark recesses of his mind and allowed the familiar anger and guilt to wrap its claws around him and seed in his mind, tightening each one of his powerful muscles, before he revved his engine and sped away. Jack didn't know the first thing about moving on, and no matter how much he might want to, he wasn't sure he ever would.

He turned and surveyed this weekend's group of yuppies-turned-survivalists with their nervous smiles and eyes that danced with possibilities. He'd been running survival training retreats as a means of remaining at least a little connected to civilization, and though Jack had plenty of money, the extra income made him feel like he was a productive member of society. He looked over his new students, silently mustering the energy to be civil and patient.

Lou and Elizabeth Merriman stood behind their young son, Aiden, each with one hand on his shoulder. *A granola family.* He knew from their registration form that they lived a green lifestyle, Elizabeth homeschooled little towheaded Aiden, and they were vegans. They were there to make an impression on their young son. He'd had enough granola families attend his survival camps to know that they all thought they had the answers to life and health, when the reality was that they had no answers at all. It wasn't the answers about life he was concerned with. Jack had yet to meet anyone who could give him the answers that really mattered—the answers about death and how to deal with it.

He shifted his gaze to their left. Pratt Smith, a brooding, brown-haired artist and Josie Bales, a dark-haired beauty who taught second grade for a living. Josie played with the ends of her hair. The two twentysomethings who were traveling separately—he, for kicks, and she, to find herself—were trying to pretend they weren't sizing each other up as potential hookups. *Great.* Jack didn't have anything against young couples getting together, but he sure wished they'd do it on their own time. His job was to bring them out into the woods, show them basic survival skills, and send them home feeling like they were Bear Grylls. The last thing he wanted to deal with was a couple sneaking into the woods seeking privacy and doing something stupid like getting lost or being eaten by a bear. And he didn't need the painful reminder of how good it felt to be in love shoved in his face every time he looked at them. Love had been off his plate since Linda died, and he wasn't looking for a second helping.

Now, where in the blazes was the woman who'd called and signed up three days ago? The pushy one who wouldn't take no for an answer when he'd said registration had already closed. He saw boots land on the ground on the other side of the plane. She was taking her own sweet time, and they had work to do. *She'd better not be a Manhattan prima donna.* He'd had enough of those whiny women to last a lifetime, and he never understood why they enrolled in the weekend courses anyway. He forced the thought away. The students paid for a guide, not a critic.

He planted his boot-clad feet in the dirt and opened his arms. "Welcome to survivor camp. You'll notice that there is no formal name for my program, and that's because emergencies don't come packaged neat and tidy with cute little names. We're preparing for survival. I've spoken to each of—"

"I'm sorry. The landing was a little nerve-rack—"

The woman from the airport made her way around the plane, cutting him off midsentence. As she flashed a broad smile at the others, he remembered her name. Savannah. *Savannah Braden.*

She glanced at Jack, and their eyes caught. Her smile faded; her green eyes narrowed. She was taller, curvier, and even more beautiful than he'd realized when he'd run into her at the airport.

Jack clenched his jaw. He cleared his throat and looked away, then continued.

"I'm Jack Remington, and I live on this land." His eyes drifted toward Savannah and he paused, then looked away and began again. "I served eight years as a Special Forces officer with the United States Army. I can get you in and out of here alive if you listen and work together. Let's keep the land clean and the attitudes friendly."

His eyes swept over Savannah in one quick breath—a breath that carried hope rather than the breath that had carried the pain of loss when he'd left his home earlier that morning. She was tall and slim with auburn hair and a killer body. *Too darn pretty.* It took all his focus not to stare, and out of his peripheral vision, he watched her brush dirt from her jeans. He allowed his eyes to follow her hands as they stroked her lean thighs, and when she glanced up, he dropped his eyes to the ground. *Cowgirl boots?* He shifted his gaze back to the rest of the group, silently chiding himself for looking at her in the first place. How on earth was he going to keep himself from looking at that gorgeous woman? *I must be losing my mind.*

"Let's get your bags. Then we're going to hike up the mountain to base camp. If you need to go to the bathroom, the forest is your toilet." He ran his eyes across the group, stopping short of Savannah to avoid getting lost in her again.

"Cool," Aiden said.

"I think so." Jack smiled at the wide-eyed boy. "I assume you all met on the plane? Got to know one another?"

"Yes, we introduced ourselves." Lou pushed a wayward dreadlock from his shoulder. "Well, most of us, anyway." He shot a look at Pratt.

Pratt stood with his hands in his jeans pockets, looking away from the group. *Great. Another prick.* Even as the words ran through his mind, he knew he shouldn't be too quick to judge. Some people would consider Jack a jerk, too, and they'd be right. Some broken men were jerks, and that's just the way it was. He made a mental note to try to talk to Pratt, but for now, he had to nip this crap in the bud.

He narrowed his gaze and spoke in his favorite cold voice—the one he usually reserved for beautiful women. He didn't have time for them any more than he had time for a kid with a bad attitude.

"See those woods behind me?" He turned sideways, as if clearing a path for Pratt's eyes to follow—which they didn't. "There are bears, snakes, poisonous plants, and all sorts of scary stuff out there. You may find yourself in need of someone's help, and if you're a di—unkind—to the group, no one's going to rescue you." He crossed his arms. "I suggest you introduce yourself."

Elizabeth and Lou exchanged a guarded glance. Then they each put a hand on Aiden's shoulder.

Jack hadn't caught his poor choice of words quickly enough. He knew he was being harsh, but bad attitudes caused accidents, and there was no room for accidents in his camp.

Pratt clenched his jaw and held Jack's stare. His tall, lanky body was no match for six-four, two-hundred-thirty-pound Jack Remington, but the hurt and anger in Pratt's eyes looked familiar, and Jack knew he wasn't contemplating anything physical. A spear of guilt ran through him. There was no turning back now. He'd taken a hard line, and backing down would leave him in a position of lesser authority.

Savannah touched Pratt's shoulder. She narrowed her beautiful hazel eyes and set them on Jack. Her smile remained on her lips, but behind the facade, he saw a challenge. His pulse sped up.

"Why don't we just call him John for now?" she suggested in a firm, nonnegotiable tone.

What the heck are you doing and why? As he pondered her motives, he couldn't help but notice the way her jeans clung to her lean legs and curved over her hips, then dipped in at the waist. And the blasted tank top she wore was now spotted with perspiration and clinging to her chest.

Look away. Look. Away.

His eyes would not listen to his mind, and he stared right back. "This is my show and I run it my way. He's part of the team or he's out," Jack said.

Savannah took a step forward and pulled her shoulders back. "What are you going to do? Fly us all back to the airport and return our money?"

He met the challenge in her eyes with his own heated stare. "Yes."

SAVANNAH'S CHEST CONSTRICTED, and a fist tightened in her stomach as jerky Jack Remington stared her down with his black-as-night eyes. He looked like Chris Hemsworth and acted like Alec Baldwin. A wild combination of sweet and bad boy that sent a flutter of sensual excitement through her. She was not going to look away. She'd gone up against meaner wolves than him in the courtroom. She crossed her arms and planted her legs like her brother Rex might do. She'd mastered the Braden stance for the courtroom and on the rare occasion of going head-to-head with some lowlife on the subway. She could do it just as well as her brothers, even if her legs were feeling a tad rubbery at the moment.

Remington didn't budge. His face was a stone mask of clenched muscles and strength. Savannah felt the worried gaze of the others upon her. She was just about to give in when Pratt stepped forward.

"Pratt, okay? I'm Pratt Smith. Twenty-eight, an artist, and I'm here to...heck...I don't know. Do something different for a few days. Now can we get on with it?" He looked away from the group.

Jack's stare had not wavered from Savannah's, and she knew that if she was the first to look away, just like in court, he'd win. She remained steadfast, though it was difficult not to allow her eyes to drift to the muscles that bulged in his arms.

Pratt picked up his backpack and headed for the woods. Jack grabbed Pratt's arm and held tight, finally disengaging from his eye lock with Savannah.

"No one hits that trail ahead of me," Jack said.

Savannah fumed. It was one thing to gain control of a situation and another to be a jerk all the time. Obviously, Pratt was going through something emotional. Why couldn't ice-hearted Jack see that? Jack wasn't her problem to fix, and by the sound of him, he needed a lot of fixing. *I'm here to fix myself. That's enough of a challenge.*

"We have safety instructions to go over, itineraries, and guidelines. Settle down, and let's get started." For the next hour, Jack explained the danger of the mountains—including everything from wild animals and poisonous plants to treacherous cliffs and harsh weather. "You will each carry your gear and your tents. If you can't carry them, you won't have them to use. If you don't like the food, then you'll drop a few pounds while you're here. Memorize the laws of three. A person can live only three minutes without air, three days without water, and three weeks without food. Got that?" He didn't wait for an answer. "Now, for the rules. Rule number one: Never put anything in your mouth without clearing it with me first. Rule number two..."

As he explained the guidelines, trail safety, trail hygiene, and other details Savannah was sure were important, she couldn't concentrate. She couldn't help but scrutinize their leader. He spoke with a deep, commanding voice—one that made her wonder what it might sound like in a dark bedroom. No matter who or what he looked at, whether it was one of the others in the group or a plant he was pointing out, his gaze was so intense that it made Savannah shiver. Attached to his belt was a long leather sheath with a black knife handle sticking out of the top. *Danger.* That's what came to mind when Savannah looked at Jack Remington. Even as she drank in every inch of his rock-hard body, he never shifted his eyes in her direction. In fact, he hadn't looked at her since the one quick inspection he'd given her when she'd first come around the plane. Savannah was used to men taking a second glance at her. At five nine, she was hard to miss, but to not even garner a second glance? That rubbed her in all the wrong ways.

"How far are we walking today?" she asked.

Jack answered while looking at Aiden. "Three miles, and the only one that's allowed to get tired is Aiden, and if he does, as we discussed"—Jack lifted his eyes to Lou and Lou nodded—"his mother or father will have to carry him." He put a large hand on Aiden's shoulder. "You hear that, buddy? If you get tired, your parents will have to carry you, and that's a hard job, getting up this mountain, so can you be strong?"

Aiden nodded.

Jack's cheeks lifted, and his smile brightened his eyes and softened his harsh edges. "Of course you can."

Maybe you do have a softer side.

He addressed Elizabeth and Lou. "There's no cell service up here. We talked about this, and you know the risks. It's your job to keep track of Aiden at all times, not mine or anyone else's. Got it?"

So much for the softer side. You really are a jerk.

Ten minutes later, they were making their way through the dense woods. Though they entered through what looked like a trail, the flattened landscape had faded fast, and Savannah had no idea how Jack could possibly know where they were headed. They were in the midst of two hundred thousand acres with no cell phone service with a guy who didn't know empathy from apathy. How on earth would she heal herself when being led by someone like him? She reminded herself that one of the main reasons she'd chosen this particular camp was that there would be no cellular service. If Connor couldn't reach her, he couldn't try to lure her back. *Whether Jack's a jerk or not, I'm going to succeed, and when I get home, I'll be stronger for it.*

She'd never been particularly lucky in love, and after watching four out of five of her brothers find their forever loves, she longed for more. If her brothers knew how Connor had treated her, they wouldn't care that she was a thirty-plus-year-old woman who could take care of herself. They would go after him without an ounce of hesitation—then they'd console her. It was after the consoling that worried her, when they'd look at her with pity in their eyes, not understanding how their bullheaded, smart-mouthed sister could ever allow a man to treat her that way. That was why she never told them. *It's complicated.* That had been her stance on her relationship with Connor.

Other attorneys had gone so far as to call her Bulldog Braden because she was relentless in the pursuit of right and wrong. *So why can't I be that relentless when it comes to my heart?* This trip was supposed to help her climb back into the armor she'd once worn and never allow herself to be treated that way again. She eyed Jack Remington as he pushed through thick branches and stomped over fallen trees. His muscles glistened against the afternoon sun. *So what if he's hot? He's probably a bigger jerk than Connor.* And if she read the shadows in his eyes correctly, he was also dangerous. *A bad combination for a girl on the rebound.* She thought about the article that had made this weekend sound like the perfect remedy for *women who had lost their edge.* Stupid article. There was no doubt that this trip was a mistake.

A big, giant mistake.

To continue reading, please buy PROMISE OF A NEW BEGINNING

Ready for more Sweet with Heat love stories?

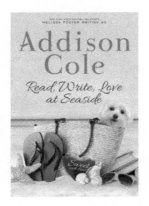

Dive into READ, WRITE, LOVE AT SEASIDE, the first book in the Sweet with Heat: Seaside Summers series, featuring a group of fun, flirty, and emotional friends who gather each summer at their Cape Cod cottages. They're sassy, flawed, and so fun, you'll be begging to enter their circle of friends!

Get your copy of READ, WRITE, LOVE AT SEASIDE

Fall in love with Reed and Grace in this fun and deeply emotional second-chance romance featuring the Montgomerys of Oak Falls.

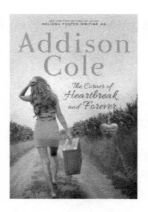

Leaving New York City and returning to her hometown to teach a screenplay writing class seems like just the break Grace Montgomery needs. Until her sisters wake her at four thirty in the morning to watch the hottest guys in town train wild horses and she realizes that escaping her sisters' drama-filled lives was a lot easier from hundreds of miles away. To make matters worse, she spots the one man she never wanted to see again—ruggedly handsome Reed Cross.

Reed was one of Michigan's leading historical preservation experts, but on the heels of catching his girlfriend in bed with his business partner, his uncle suffers a heart attack. Reed cuts all ties and returns home to Oak Falls to run his uncle's business. A chance encounter with Grace, his first love, brings back memories he's spent years trying to escape.

Grace is bound and determined not to fall under Reed's spell again—and Reed wants more than another taste of the woman he's never forgotten. When a midnight party brings them together, passion ignites and old wounds are opened. Grace sets down the ground rules for the next three weeks. No touching, no kissing, and if she has it her way, no breathing, because every breath he takes steals her ability to think. But Reed has other ideas...

More Books By Addison Cole

Sweet with Heat Big-Family Romance Collection

Sweet with Heat: Weston Bradens

A Love So Sweet
Our Sweet Destiny
Unraveling the Truth About Love
The Art of Loving Lacy
Promise of a New Beginning
And Then There Was Us

Sweet with Heat: Seaside Summers

Read, Write, Love at Seaside
Dreaming at Seaside
Hearts at Seaside
Sunsets at Seaside
Secrets at Seaside
Nights at Seaside
Embraced at Seaside
Seized by Love at Seaside
Lovers at Seaside
Whispers at Seaside

Sweet with Heat: Bayside Summers

Sweet Love at Bayside
Sweet Passions at Bayside
Sweet Heat at Bayside
Sweet Escape at Bayside

**Stand-Alone Women's Fiction Novels
by Melissa Foster** (Addison Cole's steamy alter ego)

Chasing Amanda (mystery/suspense)
Come Back to Me (mystery/suspense)
Have No Shame (historical fiction/romance)
Megan's Way (literary fiction)
Traces of Kara (psychological thriller)
Where Petals Fall (suspense)

Acknowledgments

It takes a community to raise a book, and I'd like to thank my readers for believing in me and the many bloggers who have been there every step of the way to encourage me and spread the word about my books in the reading community.

Special thanks goes to Charles "Bud" Dougherty, for sharing his knowledge of boating with me. All errors and creative liberties are mine and not a reflection on Bud. Bud, thank you for being so generous with your time. Denise Collier, you are always willing to reach out and help, not just me but many others as well. Thank you for sharing your diving experience with me. I learned a lot about doing something that I would never be brave enough to try. Keri Nola, your guidance with the psychological side of Lacy's fears was tremendously helpful. Thank you.

Kristen Weber and Penina Lopez, I swear you are made of patience and the keenest sets of eyes around. Thank you for steering me in the right direction and helping my work shine. Lynn Mullan, Juliette Hill, Elaini Caruso, and Justinn Harrison, you are my last sets of eyes on my manuscripts, and I'm sure my readers appreciate you as much as I do. Thank you for your time and attention to detail.

To my hunky hero husband, Les, and my children, as always, your patience and continued understanding of my crazy work schedule and weird conversations with people who exist only in my head is greatly appreciated. I love that you hash out plots and story lines with me when I know you'd rather be watching *Dr. Who*. Thank you each for being who you are. I love you.

Meet Addison

Addison Cole is the sweet alter ego of *New York Times* and *USA Today* bestselling and award-winning author Melissa Foster. She enjoys writing humorous and deeply emotional contemporary romance without explicit sex scenes or harsh language. Addison spends her summers on Cape Cod, where she dreams up wonderful love stories in her house overlooking Cape Cod Bay.

Visit Addison on her website or chat with her on social media. Addison enjoys discussing her books with book clubs and reader groups and welcomes an invitation to your event.

Addison's books are available in paperback, digital, and audio formats.

www.AddisonCole.com
www.facebook.com/AddisonColeAuthor